Offended Sensibilities

Offended
Sensibilities

Alisa Ganieva

TRANSLATED BY CAROL APOLLONIO

DEEP VELLUM PUBLISHING

DALLAS, TEXAS

Deep Vellum Publishing
3000 Commerce St., Dallas, Texas 75226
deepvellum.org · @deepvellum

Deep Vellum is a 501c3 nonprofit literary arts organization
founded in 2013 with the mission to bring
the world into conversation through literature.

Support for this publication has been provided in part by the Mikhail Prokhorov Fund's Transcript Program to support the translation of Russian literature.

 transcript

LIBRARY OF CONGRESS CATALOGING-IN-PUBLICATION DATA

Names: Ganieva, Alisa, 1985- author. | Flath, Carol A. (Carol Apollonio), translator.
Title: Offended sensibilities / Alisa Ganieva ; translated by Carol Apollonio.
Other titles: Oskorblennye chuvstva. English
Description: First US edition. | Dallas, Texas : Deep Vellum, 2022.
Identifiers: LCCN 2022029006 | ISBN 9781646052233 (trade paperback) | ISBN 9781646052493 (ebook)
Subjects: LCGFT: Political fiction. | Novels.
Classification: LCC PG3491.94.A554 O7513 2022 | DDC 891.73/5--dc23/eng/20220622
LC record available at https://lccn.loc.gov/2022029006

ISBN (TPB) 978-1-64605-223-3
ISBN (Ebook) 978-1-64605-249-3

Cover design by Emily Mahon

Interior layout and typesetting by KGT

PRINTED IN CANADA

It's indisputable that we no longer have that reverential and awed attitude toward denunciation that existed before.

—Aleksander Zinoviev, *Homo Sovieticus*

Eagle-eyed, observant.

—Fedor Sologub, *The Petty Demon*

CHAPTER 1

A MAN WAS RUNNING, LURCHING AWKWARDLY in the drizzling rain. "Drunk," thought Nikolai, braking at the red light, "look at him staggering." Dusk had drawn a veil over the streetlights, which flickered uncertainly on their aluminum posts. The mercury in the bulbs must be running low. Ivan the Terrible, Nikolai suddenly recalled, was poisoned by a mercury salve he used to treat his syphilis. He rubbed his feet with it. Or maybe someone else did?

> *Down by the river,*
> *On the other shore,*
> *Marusenka washed her feet so white.*
> *Where were you all night,*
> *Who were you with,*
> *Mar . . .*

A great hand slapped palm-down against the wet driver's-side window. Nikolai lowered the glass. Same guy. Expensive jacket, gold ring on his finger. He looked upset, but still, a man of substance. Tipsy, maybe, but not a complete boozer.

The man nervously wiped the rain off his face. "Give me a ride, brother!" he pleaded in an unexpectedly low bass voice.

"Do I look like a taxi driver?" snorted Nikolai, offended.

"Please, friend, I really need a ride! I'll pay!"

"Was something not clear? I'm not your personal chauffeur!"

The light turned green, and the cars behind them blared their horns. But the strange man collapsed against the car heavily, like a sea lion, and Nikolai couldn't budge.

"Hey, bug off!" he yelled, but the stranger reached in and waved a bulging wallet under his nose. The wallet smelled of fresh calfskin. The man started tossing handfuls of five-hundred-ruble bills into the car. The banknotes rained down on Nikolai's shoulders and his potbelly and scattered on the floor under the seat. The cars behind them kept honking angrily.

"What the hell is your problem?" grumbled the bewildered Nikolai. He hesitated, then unlocked the back door. The man, panting heavily, clambered in and collapsed onto the back seat. The door slammed, and the car heaved forward with a groan.

Nikolai adjusted the rearview mirror, provoking a gentle clatter from the string of beads hanging there.

Beads in your hand; broads in your head ... flashed through Nikolai's mind, unbidden. The passenger's reflection stared anxiously out the rain-spattered window.

"Where are you headed?" Nikolai asked sternly.

The man started. "What about you?"

"To Central Street."

"Me, too. But can you go the long way around?"

"What, are you running away from someone?"

The man didn't answer, just continued panting, taking short, rapid breaths. Strange—he didn't smell of alcohol. Nikolai focused on the wet road ahead and let his mind wander. He had read somewhere that at any given minute seven percent of the world's population was drunk. What does that add up to? Nikolai furrowed his brow and tried to do the math. Fifty million? If this wheezing guy really was soused, he ought to reek of alcohol. Maybe the herbal sachet that his wife had hung at the windshield had muffled out the smell. Essential oils. She'd sewn it herself. The seam was uneven.

His wife said that since they'd bought the car used, it was tainted with the energy of its former owners. They needed to perform a ritual cleansing. You light a candle using a paper banknote—as little as a hundred rubles (the amount is not the point; the main thing is to be sure that it burns completely)—and hold it over the hood, shouting, "Paid for success!" Walk clockwise around the car, making twelve complete circuits, then extinguish the flame, toss the stub into a vacant lot, and you're good to go.

Nikolai breathed in the lavender aroma through his nostrils.

"Did you know?" he addressed the passenger, politely now. "A colleague told me recently that ants communicate through smell; have you heard that?"

"What? Huh?" The man stirred in the back seat.

"Ants, I'm telling you. They have pheromones. If an ant dies, the pheromones remain on his body, and the whole ant clan spends a week just hanging out with him, shooting the breeze, can you picture it? Until the biochemistry wears off. They think he's still alive. It works the other way around, too. If you sprinkle a living ant with the smell of carrion, it's as though he's already decomposing, and that's the end for him. They haul him off to the ant cemetery." Nikolai chuckled. "Poor little bastard, he resists, tries to scurry back to the ant-hill, but they just grab him again and drag him back to be buried. How about that? Can you imagine?"

The passenger nodded; he seemed to be following. But he kept wheezing, and his hand convulsively clutched at the chest of his stylish jacket.

"I didn't know that ants had cemeteries."

"They could even have their own ant wheelbarrows; it wouldn't surprise me a bit," chortled Nikolai. He was in a good mood now; he'd managed to pick up a passenger just like that, without even trying. "Why didn't you just call an Uber?"

The man darkened.

"Uber-Buber . . . so people can keep track of my comings and goings? No, I've had enough of that."

"Who's following you?"

But the rider clammed up again.

"Everyone is afraid of something," mused Nikolai aloud. "Some are afraid they'll leave their phone at home. My daughter is like that. There's even a name for it, I've forgotten, something-phobia. People are afraid of microbes. Of getting old. Moles, airplanes, gold, blindness. Getting cancer, stepping in dog shit. Getting married. Falling in love. Farting in public. Being onstage in front of a crowd. Doctors, their mother-in-law, their reflection in the mirror. Lice, radiation,

AIDS, terrorists. To go to sleep and never wake up. A hair in their food. Clowns, computers, drafts. Bad breath. Empty rooms. Tunnels, heights, water, money, medicines. The evil eye . . ."

"What do you do for a living?" the passenger interjected.

"I work for a construction company. What about you?"

"A construction company? Which one?"

"You, too?" Nikolai again adjusted the mirror, trying to get a look at the man's face.

But instead of answering the man peered out again into the rainy darkness.

"Where are we?"

"Just like you asked. We're about to get on the bypass, and from there we'll go to Central Street."

The man seemed calmer. He turned from the window and confided, "About things people are afraid of . . . I have gotten scared of my telephone recently. Eyes everywhere, you know what I mean?"

It seemed Nikolai did know. A clouding of the reason. Persecution mania. That thing, what do they call it, paranoid schizophrenia. It had been creeping gradually into town and now everyone was in its grip. Nikolai's friends had taken to sitting on their cell phones during conversations, tucking them under their warm butt cheeks; they covered their webcams with insulation tape; they tiptoed onto the Internet, using anonymizers.

Nikolai recalled some funny old propaganda posters:

On the phone, be quiet and wise.
Blabbermouths attract the spies.

The enemy is vicious, mean, and hard.
Never let down your guard.

His mother-in-law had come running from the clinic, all in a lather. It had come to light that some patients' test samples—urine and feces—had been sent to a commercial medical lab. And from there they had supposedly gone straight to foreign agents to be used in some kind of monstrous sabotage plot. What it was exactly, no one could explain coherently, but government officials had already gone over the entire lab with a fine-toothed comb. And the whole thing had started when an alert citizen had conveyed a single piece of information to the right people.

Where people are alerted
Nothing can be subverted.

Nikolai replayed in his head his mother-in-law's alarmed, birdlike gestures. He was a long way from retirement. And this was no joking matter—buckwheat kasha and black bread. He recalled a joke Stepan, one of his coworkers in General Contracting, had told him the day before:

"Information. What's your question?"

"Hello, dear, can you give me the phone number of where they pay the pensions?"

"I'm sorry, we don't give out international numbers."

Nikolai had guffawed and the office hag Belyaeva had shot him a nasty look. Like, just what are you trying to say?

Nikolai had lucked into his job; he'd gotten it through a friend. Procurement. They handled large orders from the mayor's office and the government administration. Recently they'd completed an ice arena for the big sports festival. Cameras flashed; red ribbons fluttered in the breeze; lush speeches flowed like rivers. Then one of the arena's walls started leaking—the joints hadn't been sealed properly. All the big shots blamed it on the subcontractor. Stepan joked, "We should have done it like the Chinese when they built their Great Wall. Mixed boiled rice in with the cement."

Nikolai didn't like rice, but word on the street was that some of the metal roof tiles had been spotted on the new roof of the boss's country house. Marina Semyonova was the general director. Young blood, meticulously groomed hands. Nikolai had seen her in the flesh just once, at the New Year's bash. But her portrait hung in the lobby. The work of the trendy artist Ernest Pogodin, in oil. Sable fur coat, a sassy squint. Light brushwork, lacquer coating, and scumble. A gargantuan gold frame. Discounts for the artist's regular clients.

The car lurched along the black, pitted road, its wheels bouncing across gaping potholes and sloshing through puddles. Nikolai cursed. Last year's asphalt; they'd paved during a snowstorm, mixing the asphalt in with the mud in a mad rush to complete it by the deadline and put it down on paper as done. And now behold: gullies and a sea of mud.

"How much longer?" the passenger asked hoarsely.

"You're the one who sent me on a wild goose chase, now all of a sudden it's 'how much longer?' We're almost there," Nikolai shot back across his shoulder.

The rain started pouring down, thick and greedy, whipping the car roof insolently, like a man's palms slapping his woman's fleshy sides. The windshield wipers drummed out an insistent tachycardic rhythm. The wooden residential barracks on either side had disappeared, and they were now driving past a solid concrete wall—that classic Soviet "PO-2" type: concrete slabs with a pattern of convex rhombuses. It was impossible to read the graffiti in the darkness, but Nikolai remembered a couple of the largest inscriptions, which had been there for years. A sprawling advertisement: "Toastmaster, Accordionist" with a phone number and a slanting, half-effaced exclamation: "Russia for sad people!"

"All right, here's where we turn; it's right around the corner. How are you back there?" Nikolai called to the passenger, who was slumped over on the seat; he seemed to be drifting off and just wheezed indistinctly.

"That's all I need, for him to blow chunks back there," thought Nikolai. The road surface under the wheels had become downright crumbly, and the car roared, churning a puddle into filthy froth.

"We're skidding!" yelled Nikolai, slamming the brake down as far as it would go. Again and again. The tire scraped against the jagged edge of the asphalt, and the vehicle's bulky nose lurched upward; the car shuddered and groaned but could not take hold, and slid back down into the watery mess. Not enough power, just barely. Now if the passenger would just get out for a second . . .

Nikolai turned around. The man was half lying on the seat, slumped against the side door, out cold by the looks of it.

"Hey, man!" Nikolai called him. "We're stuck! Get out!"

Silence. No reaction.

"Macaroni-baloney-rigatoni . . ." muttered Nikolai through his teeth. He pulled up the collar of his raincoat and started climbing out carefully, into the seething, sopping unknown.

His leg plunged immediately into cold water up to the knee. Nikolai cursed even louder and began to carefully make his way around the submerged trunk of the car, trying to step in the shallower places. "This bozo in the back is completely wasted; he won't lift a finger. But I can't do it myself, someone will have to pull over and give me a push," thought Nikolai, hunching over and shivering from the cold. Of course there was no one at all on the road, just one ugly eighteen-wheeler that thundered by, drenching him with a great gray wave.

When he reached the opposite-side back door, Nikolai rapped his knuckles a couple of times on the window glass, but his traveling companion didn't move a muscle. His nose pressed against the window, forming a shapeless white blob.

"Come on," bleated Nikolai. He jerked on the handle and flung the door open.

The man tumbled out of the car and crumpled limply to the ground at Nikolai's feet. His forehead knocked against the curved edge of a curb that jutted out of the puddle; his arms were crushed in an unnatural position under the weight of his torso. His feet in their elegant polished leather ankle boots were submerged in the black water. The man did not stir.

"Hey, listen!" gulping convulsively, Nikolai yelled in a shrill voice that was not his own. "You playing some kind of game with me?"

He squatted down and shook the man by the shoulder. His body was completely inert. Down his forehead ran a thin bloody line that the rain diluted and rinsed off. One motionless eye fixed a frozen stare on the road, on which raindrops danced. The second eye looked downward. Nikolai's teeth chattered shallowly. He placed his fingertips on the man's Adam's apple and slid them down one side to the soft hollow of his neck. He waited. No pulse. It dawned on him that his cell phone must have a flashlight. The main thing was not to attract attention from cars passing by. Though there weren't any cars on the road in any case. It was the weekend, an out-of-the-way part of town. No lights. Not a living soul.

He turned on the flashlight and directed a beam of light into the man's eye, the one looking upward. No reaction. In spite of the cold, drops of sweat trickled down Nikolai's chest. He had to do something. Call the police? Of course they would immediately suspect him of murder. No way. Rummage around in the man's jacket, find a passport, a cell phone? The man ought to have a wallet, with credit cards in it . . . No, don't leave any fingerprints.

Run—that's all he could do! Nikolai grabbed the man by the collar of his leather jacket and tugged him upward onto the thing that could, with some imagination, be called a side-walk, and over to the wall. The wet jacket, which had become completely slick and almost liquid, like tar, slithered out of his clenched hands. His heart thumped in its bony cage. "Faster, faster!" Nikolai repeated to himself. After releasing the corpse, he slapped his raincoat pockets—to make sure that everything was in place, that he hadn't dropped anything in the puddle. He rushed back to the driver's side. Jumped in, closed the door, gripped the wheel, exhaled. And set the car in motion.

For some reason he thought about the bills that the doomed man had tossed into the car. He imagined them soaked through, under his seat, under his dripping raincoat. "Why, why did I let this wacko into my car?" the thought cycled through Nikolai's mind over and over like a song on a street organ. He drove out onto a well-lit street and sped off, not knowing where, through the pouring rain. His unfortunate traveling companion, now sprawled dead on the ground, had sunk his claws deep into his consciousness. At this very moment the man's body lay at the concrete wall facedown, nostrils in the mud. Newly departed. Even if by chance he had still been alive before, by now he was dead as a doornail. The back of his neck was elevated, his wet leather collar hiked up. Nikolai contemplated the fact that dead people can move even after death. Electrochemistry. The muscles contract. The extremities twitch. The fingers curl up. The head jerks madly under pressure from internal gases as they bloat the body. The vocal cords groan suddenly at a puff of air passing through them . . . Maybe this guy, too, had curled in on himself like a cat or reared up like a wheel.

Somewhere in the glove compartment his telephone pealed. Slow, like church bells—his wife, wondering where he was. Nikolai should have been home long ago after visiting his old school buddy. The buddy had invited Nikolai to visit him in his single-family home, one of many that had been cropping up in town recently. He wanted to order a tension ceiling for his living room at a wholesale price, using his connections.

"Friendship-brand power saw," Nikolai suddenly recalled, and was horrified at his idiotic train of thought, but this idiocy had firmly rooted itself in his consciousness. Friendship: a single-cylinder carburetor engine. Four horsepower. Got its name in 1954 to commemorate the tricentennial

of the union between Ukraine and Russia. Hetman rule and
Russian tsardom. Fifty-four, so now, six decades later . . . First
the restoration of friendship, and then the restoration of historical justice, and then . . . restoration of damp drywall . . .
Damn it all! What's going on in my head?" Nikolai groaned
aloud.

The ringing persisted. No, he couldn't talk with anyone now. "Which bell starts the melody?" he asked himself.
The small one or the big one? If it's the small one, that means
it's for a funeral. That seems right. But maybe not? Nikolai
strained his ears, as though his entire future depended on the
order of the bells' ringing. But the melody broke off suddenly.

He passed the chipped walls of the former Pioneer Palace
and realized that he'd already passed it multiple times, that
he'd been circling the same block over and over, driving
repeatedly through the same intersections. What if some surveillance camera noticed him? Though most likely the flood-
ing had knocked them out of service. Nikolai pulled over onto
the shoulder, turned off the engine, and stared blankly at the
drops streaking down the windshield. His mother was allergic to rain. During downpours her eyes turned red, her voice
became hoarse, and she broke out in hives. She was afraid of
rain; she'd close and lock the windows, retreat into the most
distant interior room. She was scared . . . The man had said
that he was scared.

Nikolai went over and over in his memory the moment
the stranger had tumbled out of the car. Slammed his forehead against the curb. The curb. Vibro-pressed side stone.
Nikolai's hand convulsively detached from the top of the
steering wheel and hit the horn. Drenched human silhouettes

flitting past along the sidewalk stopped to see where the honking was coming from, then ducked into a building, folding up their umbrellas. A coffee shop.

Within a few minutes Nikolai was sitting inside, too. His voice detached from his will, and he heard it cheerfully greet the waitress and order a cup of coffee.

"Don't forget the milk."

"We're out of milk," answered the waitress. "May I recommend an Americano?"

Nikolai nodded. The waitress was young, probably his daughter's age. Hair in a single braid. A maroon-colored apron. Slightly pigeon-toed. She vanished behind some tables where a group of young people sat huddled over their coffee, chattering merrily. The café was crowded. In one corner, some guys were yukking it up. Their mouths gaped, baring glistening gold crowns. Nikolai for some reason recalled one of his wife's friends, who'd contracted hepatitis in one of the local dental clinics. Colgate toothpaste. Literal translation from the Spanish: "Go hang yourself. Go . . ."

Nikolai clutched his throbbing head, unable to rid himself of the random nonsense whirling around in it. Think of anything, anything but the vacant, moist gaze of the man sprawled facedown out there under the rain, in the darkness. Nikolai felt his pants, which were soaked through. A little longer and he'd catch cold, freeze. Another pointless question flashed through his mind: Why does hot water freeze more quickly than cold water? If the temperature drops below freezing tonight, and the puddles freeze over, what will happen to his deceased companion? By now he must be completely submerged.

The waitress clinked a coffee cup down on Nikolai's table. Black inside, with a white rim. She turned and went over to the laughing guys, who had summoned her. The loudest one, flashing his gold crowns, tells her some joke; it makes her uncomfortable, and she fiddles with her braid. Above them on a flat screen attached to the wall, the local news is playing on mute, flashing one image after another. An inspection of damaged electrical wires; an old woman in a flannelette robe, gesturing with brown hands, complains about the lights being out. In the studio, the interviewer, a woman with impeccably smooth hair, opens and closes her mouth incoherently.

Nikolai took a sip of coffee and frowned—bitter. Looked up at the screen again. A close-up of some government official with a cityscape in the background. A face, familiar but not memorable, an oval-shaped figure, a swanky jacket, dashingly unzipped . . .

No! It can't be! Nikolai was transfixed. He stared at the speaker's face. How could he have failed to recognize him? There, before him on the screen, his recent passenger looked straight out at Nikolai, making some kind of official statement. Could it be true? Nikolai closed his eyes tight and then opened them again, wide. Yes, it was the guy. The one now sprawled out on the cold, wet roadside. No doubt whatsoever. Nikolai took a huge swig of coffee, burning his throat, spit it out hastily onto his saucer, and rounded his lips to take in great gulps of air. The man on the screen kept moving his chin energetically: Andrei Ivanovich Lyamzin—none other than the regional minister of economic development. Now deceased, though as yet no one, except Nikolai, had the slightest idea.

A wave of nausea came over him; he had to get to the toilet immediately. He stood up and strode rapidly to the men's room, controlling his steps as best he could.

CHAPTER 2

"**WAIT, YOU MEAN NOTHING WAS STOLEN?**" Anechka, the secretary, couldn't believe it.

Stepan nodded. "Officially there's no comment, but the reporter from the *Siren*, what's his name, Katushkin, writes that the deceased man's wallet and telephone were found intact. Though the circuit board was soaked through."

"Anything Katushkin says has to be cut down by half. When the normal news has something to report, we'll know the truth," Belyaeva cut him off and started noisily reloading the stapler.

Nikolai sat dejectedly in the corner of the Procurement Department sharpening his pencil. All morning his coworkers had been discussing the nightmarish news, crafting different scenarios out of the facts that had come to light. The management team had rushed upstairs for an urgent meeting. Minister Lyamzin's sudden death threatened to derail the company's big construction projects. The news feed was ablaze. The internet had gone wild.

"Strange, him being there alone in that out-of-the-way place," said Anechka for the nth time.

"Strange they found him at all," Stepan added. "The water company never goes out that far. They haven't even bothered to fix the huge puddle on the central square—it's been there for three years now. And here suddenly they spring into action, drive around town to inspect the rain damage. Hear me, Kolya? They decided to do their job. And if they hadn't, the minister would still be lying out there by the side of the road. The dogs would have eaten him already."

Nikolai grunted indistinctly. Belyaeva clicked the stapler in a fury. Everyone in the department knew that she had alopecia. Patchy hair loss. Belyaeva took great care to cover the bald spot with a chignon. An ad was posted in the elevator of Nikolai's building. "Chignons and wigs, we'll pay good money for your hair." Yesterday at breakfast his daughter had talked about how in the old days, people in the royal courts had worn black wigs in the morning, brown ones during the afternoon, and white ones for evening. A principle of contrast. Yesterday at breakfast—before everything fell apart . . . Tiny wooden skirts with red hemlines emerged from the sharpener blade; the pencil lead gave off a muted gleam.

"How long had he been lying there?" asked Anechka.

"Come on, Anechka, we read the news together. No more than twelve hours. That's all they've said so far," responded Stepan, pacing the room. "Hey, Kolya, what do you think, did he just up and die or did someone off him?"

"Could have just died," mumbled Nikolai.

"Have you heard the joke?" Stepan chuckled and, as always, without waiting for an answer, went on:

"A banana and a cigarette got into an argument over whose death was worse. The banana says, 'My death is horrible. They flay off my skin and eat me alive.' And the cigarette says: 'That's nothing. They set my head on fire, and then suck air in through my ass to keep the fire going.'"

Stepan brayed hoarsely. Anechka blushed. Belyaeva pursed her lips in disapproval and clattered her desk drawers open and shut.

"How about this one?" Stepan ignored her. He was on a roll. He continued to pace back and forth across the office. "So a black dot appears on the ceiling in this guy's apartment, and the next day he keels over and dies of a heart attack. Then the same thing happens in a different apartment; the man living there notices a black dot on the ceiling. And next day he keels over and dies of a heart attack, too. So then the black dot turns up in Ivanov's apartment . . ."

"I'm so sick of your jokes," Anechka sighed loudly.

"Like I was saying," Stepan raised his voice. "The guy phones House Management. 'Hello,' he says, 'There's a black dot on my ceiling. Can you come repair it? OK. And how much will it cost?' The person on the line says something. 'How much?' repeats Ivanov, and, bam, drops dead of a heart attack."

Stepan snorted again.

"When you die, Stepan, I'm going to laugh, too," Belyaeva snapped, then stood up and stalked out of the room. A bustle of activity could be heard in the hall outside the office. Male voices boomed, and women's heels clicked briskly by. Anechka darted over to the door, stepped out, then poked her head back in, announced in a horrified whisper: "Semyonova is here!" and vanished again.

"Well if the general director is here, that means something is going on," concluded Stepan and sat down next to Nikolai. Nikolai had finished sharpening the pencil and now was just staring blankly, blinking his eyes at the desk calendar on the table in front of him. The days of the month were below, and above, under the inscription, "Loyal sons of Russia," against a background of golden cupolas, bogatyrs on horseback galloped into the sunset.

Stepan looked at Nikolai, sighed, and asked in a barely audible voice:

"You know that our Semyonova was called in for questioning?"

Nikolai started:

"What for?"

"What do you mean, 'what for'? Lyamzin was her main squeeze. What, you didn't know that?"

Vague rumors and hints were always flying around, but for whatever reason, during the course of that whole long sleepless night, they hadn't crossed Nikolai's mind even once.

"So?" he stared at Stepan.

"So, yesterday she was supposedly expecting a visit from him. Lyamzin let his chauffeur go and started off in a cab. And even got to her building, apparently. But he didn't go up. Never made it to her apartment, or so Semyonova claims. Could be bullshitting, though. Maybe she's rushed over here to burn documents."

"What documents?"

"Kolya, don't be a moron," Stepan began to hold forth, tumbling over the words. "Think, why have we gotten the biggest contracts? Lyamzin rejected all the proposals from outsiders, he came up with all kinds of reasons. The time-lines, he'd go, are wrong, or the formatting is crooked. And meanwhile we're in high clover: the ice arena, the new clinic, the train station renovation, which we sat on for three years, siphoning off the funds. All that—ours, plus, you recall, the bridge . . ."

"Course I do. Suddenly it turned out the land didn't belong to the city. They had to buy it from some shady office."

"Correct. And whose office would that be?" Stepan winked knowingly.

"Damned if I know."

"Semyonova's! But it was listed under her sister's husband's name. So she cashed in twice at the city's expense. They had to fork over both for the land and for the contract. And Lyamzin did his part. Course he didn't neglect himself in the process. Took home a little kickback."

"How did he manage all this time without getting caught?" Nikolai shook himself out of his stupor.

"To judge by appearances, he didn't. Lyamzin had been walking a tightrope. Today the manager told me about some rumors that had been going around. Lyamzin had been plagued with anonymous letters to the effect that we're onto you, we'll spill the beans, inform the governor. That kind of thing. He was in a state of constant terror."

"Meaning, the guy who was going to rat him out went and killed him?" blurted Nikolai.

Stepan shushed him, waved his hand:

"It's just rumors, no point in spreading them around."

Sounds were again heard in the corridor—urgent voices, the thumping of footsteps. Stepan got up, cracked the door, peeked out, shrugged, and darted back to his desk. He fiddled with the mouse, searching for updates. Nikolai also looked at his screen, the town's forum page. They were discussing the minister's murder. But his eyes drifted; he couldn't concentrate. Gaudy, pulsing ads on the side of the screen competed for his attention: "Age-related fat cannot withstand an easily available, cheap . . ."; "If you're sixty-five and want to look forty-three, every night, ten minutes before bed, get in the habit of . . ." Photos flashed on all sides: love handles, pink warts, female breasts enhanced from an A to a C cup.

"Styopa, I'm guessing it's break time. I promised to have lunch with my daughter," Nikolai said finally, turning away from the screen. "I'll be back in an hour."

"Go for it," responded Stepan, without looking up.

Nikolai threw on his coat and went outside. It was windy, chilly, damp. Occasionally a random raindrop hit him in the face. The sky seemed to have come apart at the seams, shredding into gray tatters. Nikolai recalled the distracted look in Lyamzin's eyes. So someone really had been following him. It was not paranoia, but the exact opposite. Or might "the exact opposite" be a different diagnosis? Pronia, it's called. When you believe that people are plotting not to destroy you, but to save you. Nikolai recalled a story he'd heard once about a music teacher from Croatia, who had survived a train accident, an airplane crash, and three car wrecks. Twice he'd been in a fire, and one time he'd nearly drowned in icy water. He'd fallen off a cliff once but had managed to catch on to a tree growing on the side. Invisible salvation.

Nikolai's path was blocked by a one-legged young man in a military uniform, with a pair of old wooden crutches. The crutches' ribbed rubber tips were rooted firmly in the wet mud, and a St. George ribbon bow was attached to the chest pocket of his tunic. His sun-darkened forehead was a mass of wrinkles.

"Spare a cigarette for a Donbas veteran?" the one-legged man asked politely.

"I don't smoke," answered Nikolai, and he passed the man on the right and proceeded onward, heading for his car.

"Hey, smart-ass, listen here," the veteran tapped his crutches after him. "While you were warming your butt on the home front, your humble servant here was defending our common motherland, you follow me?"

"I do," Nikolai answered respectfully, digging in his pocket for his keys.

"It's for Russians just like you I lost my leg."

"I didn't ask you to," answered Nikolai.

"Give me some money for a prosthesis, my good man. For medicine, how about it? The bureaucrats tossed us veterans out in the trash! Humped us and dumped us. How about a couple thousand, how about it?" The beggar's voice suddenly turned gentle, ingratiating.

Nikolai got in his car without a word. The veteran yelled louder and louder, working himself up, and then released a string of curses:

"You're no better than the Fascists, you fucking shithole. You prick, I know your license plate number; I'm not the only one here, there's a whole lot of us! We'll scratch that fine hood of yours, you faggot . . ."

The motor revved up, temporarily drowning out the man's words. Nikolai turned the car slowly. The aggrieved veteran continued his rant: "Fascist! Fascist!" and the car began to ease out of the courtyard, which was flooded with deep puddles after yesterday's downpour. The one-legged man's reflection quivered in the rearview mirror. "Another ten years," thought Nikolai, "and they'll be able to grow human limbs artificially, for anyone who can afford it." All you'll need will be some corpse's leg. A carcass. Mix in muscle cells from the new host, put the thing in an incubator, hook up some oxygen . . . Would it have been possible to bring Lyamzin back to life? Cardiopulmonary resuscitation. Nikolai hadn't even tried. The guy might have still been alive. How can you tell? Declaring a death—Federal Law 66 . . .

After his sleepless night his brain was working at half power. At home his wife had asked him where he'd gotten so soaked. He'd lied, said the car wouldn't start, and he'd had to push it from behind. Using momentum. Momentum is mass multiplied by velocity. Seems right. The velocity of ejaculation is twenty-two meters a second . . . Nikolai looked at the wobbling arrow of the speedometer, then above it at the front windshield, and suddenly noticed a folded piece of paper pressed under the windshield wiper. He braked, hopped out of the car, stuck his fingers under the wiper, and pulled out a thick piece of printer paper, black toner ink. Big horizontal letters: "Murderer!" Just one word. Nikolai stiffened. Who did this? He glanced stealthily around. No one at the courtyard entrance: just a boy with a school backpack being dragged along by his exhausted-looking mom, and some guy trudging morosely down the sidewalk with a package. Could it have been the veteran?

Nikolai was rattled. He got back in the car and floored it. His hands trembled on the wheel and a heavy darkness filled his head. Thoughts began to form. Suppose it had been the one-legged guy who stuck the note on the windshield; but if so, who had hired him? Had someone hired him, or had he done it on his own? And why, oh why, hadn't Nikolai given him any money? He could have forked over a handful of change, would it have been so hard? And if wasn't the cripple, then who? The main thing was, he was being followed.

The note quivered on the passenger-side seat. "Murderer!" Nikolai tried to figure out how to identify the author. Used to be, you could trace a printed text back to the original press. Could you identify a printer from the ink? And if so, could he do it himself, bypassing forensic investigators? The thought of forensic specialists completely threw Nikolai for a loop. What if the ink had been colored? He had heard that color printers code their unique signature onto each piece of paper. Tiny, barely visible yellow dots.

A trolleybus stopped in front of him. Blurry faces of passengers wobbled in the dingy rear window. The driver in an orange vest got out and climbed up the ladder in the back to reattach the trolley poles, which had become disconnected. Trolleybus . . . The ones in Murmansk were the farthest north in the world, but where was the longest trolley line? Crimea? The driver finished fussing with the wires and descended briskly. The driver—driving force, driven, driver . . . In French, it's *chauffeur*. A chauffeur is a stoker, like on the railroad; his sister had told him. Why stoker? Must be because the earliest vehicles were fueled by coal, and the fire had to be stoked. The train was invented before the automobile . . . The trolleybus started off slowly, and for some reason Nikolai stayed behind it, didn't try to pass.

He wanted to throw away the accursed note. But how? Toss it out the window? He reached over to the passenger seat with his right hand, unfolded the paper and glanced at it out of the corner of his eye. "Murderer!" With an exclamation mark, to boot. Maybe someone from the office? Belyaeva had been in such a snit, she'd run off somewhere. Nikolai pictured her leaning over the hood, shoving the note under the windshield wiper. But how could she have known? No, it's insane, a hallucination. He was dreaming. Nikolai grabbed the paper, crushed it viciously and hurled it out through the open window, to be run over in the street. And immediately felt a loud, insistent rumbling in his stomach. He was in no condition to stop, take a breath, stop in a restaurant for a bite; his fingers refused to stop trembling. "Who did it, who?" Nikolai muttered, but automatically now, dully, like some machine in a factory, like a machine gun. Rat-a-tat . . . the same thing, over and over.

At some point he realized that he was following the route from yesterday. He passed the crossroads where Lyamzin had jumped into the car. Right there was the new, high-end apartment building, and, sure enough, that's where Semyonova lived, whom the minister had supposedly been shagging. And now he was driving toward the bypass, splashing through those same brown puddles. His stomach growled again. He felt an uncontrollable craving for a bowl of hot cabbage soup—shchi. "I'll just have a look, see what's there . . ." thought Nikolai, not knowing consciously what it was that he was expecting to see on that ill-fated roadside. Not Lyamzin's corpse, surely. But together with Lyamzin, the image of a bowl of steaming hot shchi forced its way into his head. Shchi and kasha, this is Russia. Where there's shchi, there, too, are we. His wife's shchi was pretty good, but his was better. The main thing is to make sure the cabbage is nice and sour. And add more meat. Pork ribs. They say the Neanderthals also made soup. They boiled bouillon in a leather bag, but only for sick people and people who had lost their teeth.

Nikolai bit his thick lip. There it was—the fence with the rhombuses. Torn posters. A photo of the woman who served as the local deputy, with the caption: "A woman is all heart, even her head"; an announcement in big letters: "Pork for Sale," illustrated for some reason with a picture of Winnie-the-Pooh. He thought of ribs again. Goods to the good, to the bad a broken rib. And finally the spot. Where he'd left his passenger last night. Several nondescript-looking men in civilian clothing stood there, shifting from one foot to the other and focusing intently on something; one of them was holding something, looked like a tape measure. Who were they? Detectives? Several cars were parked at the ditch, no inscriptions or flashers. Must keep moving . . .

Nikolai suddenly felt that one of the men was looking straight at him. He hastily averted his gaze and looked straight ahead at the road. He recalled that a good way to lower stress was to perform alternative breathing: first with the chest, then with the stomach. But only his stomach would breathe. It bulged and spilled out over his belt. Nikolai weighed eighty-nine kilos, he needed to lose weight. "You'll slim down in prison," sniggered his inner voice. Again the wheels of free association launched into motion. Elvis Presley used to sleep for days on end, anything to keep himself from eating. Sleep to keep from eating—not eat to keep from sleeping . . . Lyamzin had also been on the heavy side. But now he was asleep, sleeping an eternal sleep. There'd been this eight-year-old boy, a murderer who had bludgeoned a little girl in some exotic country, and explained that he'd put her to sleep. Worn-out toys sleep; books sleep . . .

Nikolai felt his eyes mist over. Was he really about to start bawling? Mix the tears of married women with rosewater, and you get an elixir with medicinal properties. Balsam for your wounds . . . Stepan had once had a paper cut in his eye, and he'd had to wear a special lens to keep the cornea from spreading out to the sides. Should he tell Stepan? No, he wouldn't understand, he'd blab.

He pressed on, forgetting his hunger, forgetting he had to go back to work. If fear does have a smell, then could people sense his fear? Should he turn himself in? Just tell everything, the way it had happened? After all, he hadn't killed Lyamzin, just given him a lift.

His phone vibrated. Nikolai picked it up. His wife started in:

"Kolyus, it's an outrage! They promised that they would get the lights on in the morning, so where's the light already? And there's no water either! Can you imagine it? Kol, can you hear me?"

"I hear you," Nikolai answered in a hollow voice.

"So can you do something about it? I called House Management and they're rude, like, half the town is without electricity, it's because of all the rain. Why feed me bullshit? They told me themselves they'd be done by noon. Their, what do you call it, emergency repair work. By noon! And it's now . . . look at the clock!"

"Well it's true, my little sunshine, half the town is without light," Nikolai made a stab at calming her down, but his heart wasn't in it.

"Where are you?" his wife sounded alarmed.

"On my way to lunch. A quick bite. Did you hear about the minister? He was found dead!"

"Lyamzin? Of course! What are they saying in the office? Does your boss know what happened? The diva, Semyonova."

"What about Semyonova?"

"About how she was supposedly his mistress. You told me yourself."

"Me? I'd forgotten . . ." Nikolai muttered weakly.

"I bet it was his wife. Did it in revenge. Got sick and tired of putting up with his cheating. Strangled him and tossed him out under the fence," suggested his wife, half joking, half serious. "You haven't forgotten, you'll stop by the store and get groceries on your way home? I gave you a list."

"Bone-in meat?"

"Yes, don't forget. And three bags of pearl barley. It's on sale. Twenty percent off. All right, Kolyus, don't forget!"

Nikolai nodded, as though his wife could see him. By the time he said goodbye, he had regained control of his voice. He had decided to turn himself in. He would go in this minute, would even skip lunch, so as not to chicken out. He sped up, in keeping with his mood. The damp streets flew past, together with their pedestrians: orange-helmeted electrical repair workers, mournfully calling out to one another, and the wires that had come down in the rain, and the Armenian, or was it Assyrian, shoe-shine shops. Nikolai passed a whole row of Stalin-era apartment buildings with mildewed balconies, then the Dawn, "Zarya," movie theater, with its row of posters and the new outdoor screen it had installed on the front that wasn't working yet, then the children's sports club, still standing from the nineties, where years ago he'd broken his nose. Rhino kyphosis, it was called. They would take a dramatic photo: a suspect with a ruler in the background. He had earned his hump nose, his Roman profile. Mug shot.

So be it. Better to be honest now than later, when all hell broke loose. Need to get a lawyer. Concern for his daughter stirred in him like a ferret in its den. She would develop a complex, would be ashamed of her father, worry about what her classmates would say. Maybe it would be best to talk with his family first? No, his wife would make a scene. And she'd just made a simple request: pick up some pearl barley . . .

Nikolai could taste the rassolnik, the pickled meat soup, on his tongue, with pearl barley in beef bouillon. Add a spoonful of sour cream . . .

The car gave a great heave and in its metal belly the front axle groaned loudly and snapped in two. It had plunged into a pothole.

"Oh futhermucker!" hissed Nikolai, for some reason keeping his foot on the gas. But the car was wedged in and just snarled and spewed clouds of smoke. Nikolai saw a curious passerby running over to help, but at that exact second there came a terrible roar and from the left something huge and relentless bore down and slammed into him. Time stretched and trickled out slowly and inexorably, drop by drop. "An eighteen-wheeler!" Nikolai thought within that last half second. "No way!" But at that moment something burst in his ears, screeched, and Nikolai was crushed to death.

CHAPTER 3

PANTING HEAVILY, KAPUSTIN YANKED UP HER skirt and slid his fat fingers clumsily along her lacy elastic garter. Marina Semyonova predicted it all with depressing certainty: the loathsome hand would proceed up her thigh; she would have to pull back and smack Kapustin on the shoulder; he would press harder, squeeze up against her, would get mad, and ultimately things would spill over into open conflict. And she had no desire to get into a fight with the regional chief prosecutor.

"You're so uptight!" murmured Kapustin hoarsely into Semyonova's flushed ear. He seized her by the thick hair on the back of her head and plunged his meaty tongue between Marina's frightened, tightly clenched lips.

"Why not?" Semyonova thought for a split second, but the prosecutor's tongue was so nasty, cold and thick, and his grip on her head so painful, that she emitted a throttled groan and abruptly, with unexpected fury, gave her oppressor a mighty shove.

"So that's how it is," muttered the aggrieved Kapustin,

releasing his prey and sputtering like an elephant after a dip in the watering hole. "With Andrei Ivanovich it was yes, with me it's no."

"I loved him." Even as she said it, Marina Semyonova knew how stupid it sounded.

Kapustin perked up. He chortled:

"How could you help loving him, Marina Anatolyevna? The late minister handed you your entire business on a gold platter. You were living off the fat of the land—forgive the metaphor."

He perched on the edge of the desk, directly under the crest with its great golden double-headed eagle, and stared straight into Marina's eyes, then let his gaze wander down to her half-open silk top, which revealed her rosy collarbones. At a loss for words, she picked up a massive pen from the table, the one that she had been using to write her testimony, fiddled with it in her sweaty palms, and put it back down on the desk. Only then did she respond:

"Well, as you can see, I had no reason to wish for Andrei Ivanovich's death. And the surveillance film from the security cameras proves it: he didn't come up to my apartment."

"No one is accusing you of anything like that!" Kapustin reassured her, beaming. "On the contrary, I sympathize with you. Who is going to protect you now if the police come sniffing around? Who, so to speak, will make sure the contracts keep on rolling in?"

"We'll land on our feet," Marina sniffed.

"Of course you will," Kapustin readily agreed. "Along with everything else, you have this other, what's it called, this Wildflower Aesthetic Cosmetology Clinic. Not to mention the real estate—lucrative rental contracts with three different offices. Plus a restaurant. You see, I'm keeping track of your business successes."

Semyonova slammed her fist down on the desk.

"So you're counting my money, too?"

Her nose broadened from rage, her cheeks, tender and resilient after their hyaluronate injections, quivered with suppressed sobs. She realized that she had miscalculated, that she should have kissed Kapustin, and made him think she wanted to, that now he would not forgive her squeamishness. But as if to give her another chance he advanced again, and his entire fat, panting face came right next to hers, and his stubby paw tentatively, lasciviously began to creep along her back, on the place that Lyamzin had particularly savored, calling Marina "Venus Callipyge."

"My little one," Kapustin slobbered into Marina's neck. "We'll go halfsies. Fifty percent of the proceeds, case closed."

"Closed?" Semyonova couldn't believe it.

"You'll just be a minor witness. It's very simple. Our unfortunate Andrei Ivanovich suffered a sudden rupture of the aorta."

When she replayed the conversation later with her confidant, Peter Ilyushenko, Semyonova couldn't sit still. She would spring up from the settee and pace nervously around her sumptuous living room, then return to her place, only to leap up again moments later. Ilyushenko, by contrast, was beyond relaxed; he was not sitting, but rather sprawling in a leather easy chair with his legs stretched out in front of him, in his black silk cassock. This cassock irritated the real parish priests, who considered Ilyushenko a half-wit moron and a fake; they held him in contempt for his tendency to run off at the mouth; they complained that he hadn't even graduated from seminary, how dare he wear a cassock? For his part, Ilyushenko preferred to introduce himself as an ecumenist, and over a glass of neat whiskey he'd get into disputes about filioque. He'd say the formula is utterly vapid and senseless, and it would be good to dispense with it once and for all and in doing so reconcile the divided churches. Marina lent him money and kept him with her instead of girlfriends, whom she'd lost track of during her student days.

"Rupture of the aorta?" Ilyushenko mused, dispatching a chocolate truffle with nut filling. "What I read was temporal trauma."

"And?"

"You said that you'd quarreled the night before."

"Petya, are you trying to say that I lured Andrei off into some Timbuktu somewhere and knocked his head against a curb? Are you completely off your rocker?"

Semyonova stood up again, rubbing her well-tended palms together anxiously. She suddenly recalled Lyamzin's hairless white back with the coffee-colored birthmark above his waist. The wandering pupils of his eyes, his face, distorted in moments of intimacy. His lavish gifts, inevitably accompanied by a note. Lena, his administrative assistant, delivered them; she was a pale, long-haired girl with limpid eyelashes and misshapen pupils that looked as though they were leaking.

Semyonova and Lyamzin had met some ten years ago, when he was still in the business world; he'd been a wheeler and dealer, a member of all kinds of high-level commissions and councils. Marina had been running down Central

Street in a white cotton T-shirt, in a bumptious, sassy flock of young activists. The girls' T-shirts were wet, and their hands gripped the necks of glistening sweet seltzer water bottles from the local bottling plant. "Spend your rubly rubles on our bubbly bubbles," crowed the ads. The activists' nipples jiggled in time with their steps, the green seltzer bubbled down their naked necks, trickled under their collars, and splashed and hissed to the laughter and shouts of the spectators. The Festival of Russian Food Production: celebrating the country's prosperity.

Lyamzin was the proprietor of that little factory. He hadn't yet been named minister. Under his flat nose he chuckled benevolently at the crowd, and his brows swept grandly upward. He contemplated Marina with treacly indulgence, as a kind of lovely domesticated creature. He seized the moment and extended his business card as she jogged past; she caught it matter-of-factly in her ungroomed fingers and ran on. A couple of days later they met in a restaurant. He ordered neck of mutton, and she had marinated salmon with red caviar. They washed it down with mature Tuscan wine, and the evening ended in the wee hours of the morning, in a room in one of the city's new hotels. Lyamzin lay drenched in sweat in a tangle of sheets trying to catch his breath. "Marechka, Marechka," his drained lips whispered. He was vanquished, crushed by the wave of happiness that had flooded over him. For her part, Marina bounced naked around the hotel room, looked out the window, darted to the trifold vanity mirror, unable to contain her jubilation. She seemed to sense that this man, so rich and important, was now attached to her apron strings, a part of her now, henceforth, and forever.

"I'm not saying that you hit him," continued Ilyushenko, crunching on a hazelnut. "Maybe you got into a fight, say, he got upset, and it all ended in this sordid mess."

"We had a quarrel the day before he died. Just one day before. And it wasn't me that upset him. What sent him over the edge was those damned anonymous notes."

They'd quarreled about a baby. Marina had gotten it into her head that she wanted to have a child, but Lyamzin was afraid to cross that line. Of course his wife knew about his long-term mistress and her cushy life, but a baby would be the black card that would bring everything crashing down. And that wasn't all: Marina wanted to get married, too. Lyamzin stalled, made excuses about his son, who was studying abroad, and his wife, to whom he owed everything he had, and he bought Marina a series of fancy new trinkets. Over the ten years they'd been together Marina had grown into a glamorous lady who rubbed shoulders with the mayor and the high and mighty of the town, who patronized actors and singers, was interviewed by fashion magazines about the latest trends, owned a cosmetics salon, and flitted off to Bali to be photographed in a bathing suit. With time she'd begun to lose her patience with Lyamzin, but she missed him terribly at night, and would sob into her pillow, and then would run off to the salon for collagen injections to remove the traces of insomnia.

Semyonova went over to the bronze-framed oval mirror, cast a disapproving glance over at Ilyushenko, who was making a mess with the chocolate crumbs, and took a few moments to admire her reflection. A face firm as a peach. Long mink brows. Almond-shaped eyelids. A sultry look.

"What was the squabble about?" Ilyushenko munched noisily. "He wouldn't let you have a baby?"

"He wouldn't even let me have a cat, he's allergic. I mean, was." Semyonova sighed.

"Cats are not mentioned even once in the Bible," Ilyushenko stated, out of the blue. "Dogs occur fourteen times. But cats—not a single mention."

"Not even once?" Semyonova again perched on the settee and was now fiddling with the hem of her ornate dressing gown, the one with fantastical needlework that Lyamzin had brought her from China. Red—the color of aristocrats; if commoners wore red they had their heads cut off . . .

Ilyushenko continued to munch his chocolate, gazing upward at the ceiling, with its six-winged seraphim fluttering among cumulus clouds, painted to order. And then he asked suddenly:

"Tell me, Marina, what did you need all that moolah for?"

Semyonova didn't know what he was talking about. "What?"

"Dough, bread, clams, lucre . . . All those shady deals, construction tenders. Lyamzin bought you these digs, built you a villa in the country; why did you need to have a construction company of your own, real estate? Covetousness, maybe?"

"Here you go with your religious mumbo jumbo! When I sent you on a cruise, all expenses paid, off you went without the slightest complaint. And came back with a fresh tan. What's gotten you riled up all of a sudden?"

"First of all, it was not a vacation," Ilyushenko objected, tucking his legs up under him. "It was an academic conference on theology. Questions concerning the church, society, and the state—"

"And?" Semyonova interjected.

"Secondly, I'm not about to fall on my sword over morality, I'm no prude. Not like that spiritual adviser of yours."

"Not mine, Andrei Ivanovich's."

"Doesn't matter whose. I'm not trying to teach you; I'm just curious about the psychology of it. Tell me why."

"What do you mean, 'why'?" Semyonova shrugged and got up again. "I'm not twenty-five anymore, you know this yourself. My cells are starting to get old; my skin is drying out . . ."

"You're saying you need money for Botox?" Ilyushenko interrupted. "But not that much! Let's talk rationally."

"I am talking rationally!" Semyonova snorted. He was getting on her nerves. "Do you have any idea how much laser depilation costs these days? For one round you can drop a hundred thousand, and even then you've got hairs sprouting where they shouldn't."

"All right, all right," Ilyushenko frowned.

"What about massages?" Semyonova went on, incensed. "LPG face-lifts? Laser blood irradiation? Cryotherapy? What about plasma? Fillers? And that's just for starters. Do you know how much a pair of good boots costs? A Burberry bag? Do you? A Dior dress?"

Semyonova clutched her head and paced the room. The front of her robe flapped open as she walked, exposing her impossibly white thighs.

"Calm down, Marisha." Ilyushenko stood up and, tracing elaborate, indeterminate patterns in the air with his hands, he coaxed her to sit back down. "You are all worked up. I'm not blaming you for anything. It is not cheap for a beautiful woman to take care of herself properly. But we're talking about millions here. No wonder Kapustin is choking on his own drool. He's built up quite an appetite."

"So what do you want, Petya?" Semyonova asked wearily, leaning her head on the curved back of the settee. Her anger had ebbed, and she was in a conciliatory mood. She recalled the time Lyamzin had taken her in this exact spot. He had come back from some meeting at the governor's, buoyant as a rubber ball and brimming with desire. He'd been publicly praised and cited as an example for others to follow. He'd mastered the task of managing state property and had arranged a process for substituting Russian goods for imports. And he'd revitalized the local Horizon plant, an industrial enterprise that produced polishing lathes.

Right there in the doorway, without even taking off his shoes, he tore off his belt, then dragged Semyonova into the living room (they'd tripped on a corner of the wool rug and knocked over a porcelain vase), pressed her down on the settee, flipped her over, as he put it, bottoms up, hitched up her dress, slapped her on her magnificent buttocks, imprinting them with fine red welts, and then entered her urgently and thrust furiously until he was completely spent. The pattern on the upholstery—little green flower buds, sinuous blossoming branches—had writhed madly before her eyes; her backside had stung like fire. When had that been? A month, just one month ago.

Ilyushenko sat next to Semyonova and began to explain, in measured tones, without haste:

"Here's what I'm talking about. You were in cahoots. Your lover sent tenders your way; you got first crack at them, while they were still fresh. You didn't miss a single one. From a deontological point of view it's wrong, it's criminal, in fact. But from a utilitarian point of view you're absolutely right. And Andrei Ivanovich is right, too. And every government official who takes a bribe is above reproach. And anyone who offers a bribe is also completely free of guilt. Consequentialism—"

"Zip it, Petya," Semyonova interrupted.

"Marisha, just listen. I'm trying to explain it to you. You don't feel at all guilty for, say, having a three-story villa, whereas a philosophy professor is crammed into a two-room hovel in a concrete Khrushchev-era jungle, nothing in the fridge but one measly carrot. You didn't even graduate, and you're living the life."

"I have a degree!"

"You mean the one the university just handed you? Like, 'thank you for the indoor swimming pool your company installed for the rector'? All you could manage was three and a half years."

"Petya, time to conclude," Semyonova requested, not the slightest bit angry.

"I am trying! You feel no guilt. Quite the contrary, you're happy. And Andrei Ivanovich—God rest his soul—was happy. And the rector is happy, and your workers in the construction company, and your sister and her husband, and your mama out in the sticks, all of them are utterly and completely happy. And speaking from a utilitarian point of view, if things are going well for you, then that means you are right, too. The end justifies the means."

"And?"

"And it turns out that the means are such that everything has supposedly been stolen right and left and supposedly there's all this injustice. But ultimately the result is pleasure and utility. You have your islands and your massages; your employees have their work and all the construction materials free for the taking; Andrei Ivanovich (during his life) had you. A real beauty. And the more he invested in you, the more he valued you. Returns on his investment . . ."

"You're going around in circles, Petya," commented Semyonova, chewing thoughtfully on the ends of her chestnut locks.

"All I'm trying to do is to show you, Marisha, that everything you did was logical. Everything. Like in the prisoner's dilemma. Imagine that you've been bitten by some crazy fly, and you've decided to give up all corrupt activities. Just try to imagine it."

"Nothing would change." Semyonova answered, with conviction.

"Precisely! Someone else would fill the empty space. And she would not let her chance slip away. So what is the result? No one benefits from violating the rules. But if millions of people in the country were to agree all at once not to give or take bribes, not to siphon off funds from the budget, not to try to set up their family and friends, then, yes, in that case, we'd have the rule of law. But so long as even one person is taking their cut, then it's to everyone else's benefit to do the same, do you see?"

"Now you're really off to the races, Petya," Semyonova waved dismissively. "Really, it's so boring, such platitudes!"

She got up, went over to the grand piano that Lyamzin had bought her for her thirtieth birthday, and tried to play a sad tune that had been haunting her. "The Doll's Funeral," must be. But the keys refused to obey, and after a few wrong notes, she banged down the lid.

"Tchaikovsky?" Ilyushenko asked, reaching for another truffle. "Did you know that he died from drinking untreated water? Could that be what finished Andrei Ivanovich off?"

Semyonova did not answer. She was looking at the curtains where she had been standing on the night of Lyamzin's death. She had been waiting for her lover to come up from the courtyard. And looking out the window, with the fierce rain battering against it. Recently Lyamzin had been spending more and more of his days off with his wife, blaming a heavy workload. That had set her off. What could he possibly have to do one-on-one with that massive, blubbery, unfeminine Ella Sergeyevna of his? A school principal, no less! Shepherdess of the next generation. Meanwhile, Marina Semyonova, under a flock of six-winged seraphim, was waiting for him, Andrei Ivanovich, in a new lace corset with detachable garters that she'd bought in a boutique. Droplets of perfume on her neck, her bosom, her wrists. Springy curls flowing down to her shoulders. And all of this—all of her—had to just sit and suffer, waiting for him to come.

"I've heard," said Semyonova at last, "that classical music lovers are not as prone to commit acts of betrayal as rock music fans."

"So," asked Ilyushenko, "admit it to me, as your confessor, did you ever cheat on him? On Andrei Ivanovich."

"You lecher," smiled Semyonova. "Only a sex-obsessed libertine would want to know something like that. I'm going to go put on some tea."

She went out to the kitchen, which was decorated with colorfully patterned ceramic tiles, like those on traditional stoves, that she had had custom-made. She ran some water into the electric teakettle and pressed the button. The teakettle's blue light-emitting diode lit up.

Had she cheated on him or not? Could you count that one time with one of her employees, Stepan? It was at a New Year's Eve party, and she'd been drunk. She'd felt so alone. Lyamzin and his wife had jetted off abroad to see their son, and she'd been left behind in town—no man, no warmth. She couldn't recall what it was that had attracted her to Stepan. It may have been the swashbuckling, slightly vulgar toasts he had raised over refreshments, which had harmonized nicely with his broad shoulders and sexy peasant name.

Semyonova herself had led him into her office. Drunk, they stumbled on the stairs, and he laughed and grabbed her by the rump. They left the lights off. They slammed the door and tumbled down onto the oak desk with its scratchy cloth cover. He lowered his trousers, and in intoxicated delight buried his nose in her generous breasts, freed from her blouse. She felt hot and languid, and wanted Stepan inside her immediately, but when the thrusts began, and his disheveled forelock jerked in the air over her face, and his tongue started to trace figure eights in the air, expressing interminable male ecstasy, her desire abandoned her. All she felt was an unpleasant pressure and rhythmic poking movement inside, and a conga line of completely irrelevant thoughts whirled in her head—about a button that had come off, about whether she should close her eyes for a sultrier look, so that Stepan wouldn't be able to tell that she wasn't experiencing the slightest bliss, that all she felt was this clumsy writhing of bodies, and a light queasiness, and the sounds of cars honking outside the windows.

A couple of weeks later she'd stopped in at the company to look at cost estimates, and Stepan lingered conspicuously in the corridor, hoping to catch her eye. "He might spill the beans to Andrei," thought Semyonova, and summoned him into her office.

"Marina," began Stepan with a suggestive smile, stroking the table's cloth cover—the very table on which he had experienced his ecstasy of love.

"Marina Anatolyevna," Semyonova corrected him sternly, with no excess verbiage, and handed him an envelope. "Here, Stepan, is a small bonus. Go take your wife and kids on a little vacation. You've earned it. As a member of the Department, uh . . ."

"The Procurement Department," Stepan completed her sentence, turning serious and respectful. But he did take the envelope, and retreated deferentially, as befitted an employee quitting the office of a someone very high up the ladder.

The Procurement Department . . . That was where that poor guy had worked, the one who had had the accident the other day. Trauma inconsistent with life. Fatal. Negligence in street maintenance . . . The teapot came to a boil, its little light started flashing. Ilyushenko went into the kitchen to help Semyonova get china cups from the cupboard. His little metal cross bounced and tapped against his cassock.

"Well, so, Marisha, how did things work out with Kapustin? The chief prosecutor."

"I got him to agree to thirty percent of the profit."

"That's all?"

"Plus I let him have my stocks in the seltzer water plant. A majority share. Andrei transferred them to me when he was appointed as minister. He couldn't very well leave all of them to his hag."

She recalled Kapustin's quivering chin. His quivering chin with its bristles and his predatory, but at the same time pleading, gaze as he looked down at her. He watched what Marina was doing with him down below, and a vein pulsed under the skin of his temple like a mountain stream. In Marina's hands Kapustin was small and fat like a mushroom stalk, and momentarily she felt a hot splash on her palate, the prosecutor convulsed and lurched limply backward, away from her. She got a paper napkin out of her Burberry bag and wiped her mouth so that her lips wouldn't dry out, so that Kapustin's seed would not form a crust there.

CHAPTER 4

ELLA SERGEYEVNA DREAMED THAT SHE HAD lost her boots. They were suede, black with high tops, kitten heels. "Lyalyusik!" Andrei Ivanovich called from behind the door, "Hurry up, we'll be late!" But Ella Sergeyevna's big feet in their nylons stomped on the parquet floor and she slammed the doors of the rattan wardrobe open and shut. The boots were nowhere to be found.

Then Ella Sergeyevna was in the little courtyard, and Andrei Ivanovich was standing there in his unzipped leather jacket, beckoning to her with his short, well-proportioned hands. "Hurry up, Lyalyusik!" he repeated impatiently, and she hurried toward her husband, stepping in her unshod feet on the cold tiles. Whether she reached him or whether she changed her mind and went back into the house, Ella Sergeyevna would never know, because at that exact moment there came a piercing ring—someone was at the gate. She gave a great shudder and woke up. "What? Who's there?" The questions hammered in her head. She freed her ponderous, varicose-veined legs from under the silk coverlet and looked up at Andrei Ivanovich. He beamed down at her from his silver-framed portrait with a smile tinged with contrition. Next to her on the bedside table lay the dark prayer book with its brocade bookmark tucked inside. Her spiritual adviser had instructed her to read a little each morning and evening, and with particular assiduity during the first forty days of mourning. "Thou art the comfort for those who mourn, intercession for the widowed and orphaned . . ."

After the process of identifying the body, and a series of terrible but necessary procedures, the thing that had once been Andrei Ivanovich was brought home from the morgue. Ella Sergeyevna had worried that the authorities would not release the body in time and they would not be able to have the funeral on the third day. She had nightmares featuring medical examiners clinking their big rib-cutting shears. But the forensic experts completed their investigation and issued their conclusion in good time: sudden cessation of the heart. Of course the strange circumstances of the minister's death and the discovery of his body lying out in the middle of nowhere under pouring rain had given rise to a flurry of rumors and gossip. Ella Sergeyevna had been summoned by the investigators and questioned about her family circumstances. She had released a flood of tears, had cursed Marina Semyonova. For nearly ten years that she-devil had sucked the man's blood. He had been distraught, his conscience had been gnawing at him. Anonymous ill-wishers had been harassing him with mysterious messages. Yes, he had been to the cardiologist. The doctors had forbidden fried and cured foods, pork fat, and salted fish. But Andrei Ivanovich had ignored their advice; he was stubborn by nature. Ella Sergeyevna's astrologer had often told her: "Aries, once they've dug their horns into the earth, nothing can get them to budge." But she had not foreseen his death. Violent death—that's the eighth house; a natural death—that's the eleventh. Venus opposite Saturn . . .

Ella Sergeyevna felt for the bathroom light switch. Her face was puffy and bare, so vulnerable without her thick principal's eyeliner, without the blush on her cheeks, without the string of pearls ringing the puffy flesh of her neck. She recalled Andrei Ivanovich's powdered face in the luxurious palisander coffin with its double lid. While the pallbearers were carrying it out, they bumped it against the doorjamb. Natalya Petrovna, his deputy at the ministry, had crossed herself and whimpered, seeing it as a bad omen. The governor had not come to the viewing; he was traveling on official business. The mourners had exchanged rumors, whispering discreetly. Someone had quietly uttered the word "payola"; another added, "blackmail," a third person—"depression." Ella Sergeyevna was not listening. She gazed at the thin, mute back of her son, who'd flown in from abroad. He had stayed less than two days; he had not shed a single tear and had left immediately to get back to school. Andrei Ivanovich had tucked away significant sums in trust funds abroad; no one could touch the money there, or initiate any legal claims to it.

Ella Sergeyevna strained her ears. The bell did not repeat. Maybe she'd dreamed it? Usually the housekeeper Tanya answered the door, but she had the day off today. After the wake, when she was clearing dishes from the dining room, Tanya had dropped and shattered a porcelain cup. It was in a set that Ella Sergeyevna's mother had given her as a wedding present, one that had been extremely rare during the lean Soviet years. When she saw the shards Ella Sergeyevna had a meltdown and called the housekeeper an idiot. Tanya, who was a woman of few words, just hung her head, and the knuckles of her dry, clumsy hands turned white. "I'll have to let her go in any case," thought Ella Sergeyevna now, rolling up a wet towel and lightly tapping her chin with it from below, to combat sagging.

She had been feeling a kind of vague unease around Tanya recently. It had intensified at the time of Andrei Ivanovich's death and begun to solidify and flap its wings inside her like a moth trapped in a jar. It had started with the picture that hung over the round oaken table in the living room—a large full-length portrait of the master of the house. The artist Ernest Pogodin had decided to paint Lyamzin in a general's uniform, with gold epaulets and with a blurry gold cross on his chest, as though foretelling some future official honors, honors which, alas, would never materialize. At one point Ella Sergeyevna had brought in some art specialists to clean the canvas, which had gotten dusty. When they were taking the painting down from the wall, she heard a clicking sound, and a black rectangular domino with one white dot on each half slipped out from the cavity behind the frame and bounced across the parquet. Ella Sergeyevna felt a sudden stitch in her side. The unexpected discovery had to be some kind of plant, an evil spell. But who could have slipped the domino behind the picture? Some guest? No, they never left their guests alone in the room. The sullen housekeeper, then. No one else could have done it. When Andrei Ivanovich had been found dead, Ella Sergeyevna had immediately recalled the duplicitous Tanya and her domino. Could it have been a voodoo spell that had worked?

The bell rang again—demanding, intrusive. Ella Sergeyevna tossed the wet towel into the sink and rushed to get the brightly colored floral robe her husband had brought back from China; she needed to have something on over her nightgown, which was flapping against her ankles. The preceding day stirred and lurched in her memory. It had been exhausting. Ella Sergeyevna had gone to work at the school for the first time since the tragedy. Her colleagues lined up to offer their condolences, one after the other. At first it had been sweet and soothing and sad to hear their words about her irreparable loss, their wishes for eternal memory, their shock when they'd heard the terrible news, their assurances that they shared her dark widow's sorrow . . . The teachers crowded around; mothers joined in, and after lunch there were so many people in her office it was impossible to move. The ladies from the Education Administration tiptoed in. Andrei Ivanovich's assistant, Lenochka, came and brought her late boss's watch, which he had left on his desk. A group of first-graders was ushered in, bearing bouquets of carnations—even numbers in each one, for mourning. What can you do with them? You can't just put them in a vase; it would bring on the unclean spirit.

The air reeked of the abyss, and a dark, trembling haze filled Ella Sergeyevna's heart, a vague terror that chilled her blood. Without Andrei Ivanovich, her protector in a high place, she was vulnerable, insignificant, and beset by a throng of gloating, carnivorous underlings. Out of the blue, the vice principal for moral-ideological education handed her a printout of a cheap exposé by the fraudster Katushkin, noting that he ought to be hauled to court for swill like this. The journalist hinted at heaps of gold socked away in Lyamzin's coffers, referred cattily to "the minister's captivating partner in crime," Marina Semyonova, and made a humorous crack about the governor's failure to pay his respects at the viewing. He added that the minister's thievery had already become public knowledge, and that it was only a matter of time before it blew up into a huge scandal. The anonymous notes that had been tormenting Lyamzin, he wrote, were riddled with lurid disclosures of the minister's adultery and abuses of power. Kapustin the prosecutor really had something to sink his teeth into. And the time was ripe to go after the widow, too. The wretch Katushkin capped the whole thing off with dark hints at shady dealings in Ella Sergeyevna's school.

Instead of flying into a rage, instead of hurling the filthy pages in the trash, she froze, giving way to the glob of terror that had formed inside her. What if they were to come after her? What if they were at this very moment checking Ella Sergeyevna's records and could prove that she'd been filling in social studies grades for the graduating class, grades for lessons which had never taken place? Or that for years she had schemed with the chief bookkeeper, a fat old biddy in an Orenburg down shawl, to document salary payments to nonexistent teachers? Not only did these ghostly pedagogues get their salary from the bursar every month, they were also showered with prizes for excellence in the classroom. And Ella Sergeyevna had hired a cloakroom attendant, actually a poor relative of hers, whose salary was paid every month, though she had only ever shown up for work one time. Ella Sergeyevna gulped down a mouthful of cold saliva and decided to fire the entire team of poltergeists in one fell swoop, citing some kind of violation.

The vice principals bustled around, their dyed hair spilling out of their plastic barrettes like cats' tails puffed up in terror. Ella Sergeyevna felt that they were also apprehensive about the uncertainty relating to recent events, that they would turn on her without hesitation at the first rooster's crow. But no, they couldn't; everyone, every last one of them was tainted. They all took their share. The diplomas were locked in a fireproof safe and were issued only to those who paid a secret fee. If you don't feel like paying your beloved alma mater, you can do without the diploma. "Donations for the computer lab . . ." she recalled. The money—sticky, crumpled bills—was brought to her in thick envelopes with the students' names listed on the front, along with how much each one gave. The computer lab door remained padlocked shut, but a flat-screen monitor appeared on the wall of Ella Sergeyevna's office. At a single wave of its mistress's hand, it would turn in different directions, like some living creature flashing its rectangular, liquid-crystal snout.

The teachers, though, they were a different story. At any moment they could attack, seize her in a death grip. She had kept them on slaves' rations for years. Regional holidays, inspections, elections, interscholastic Olympiads and conferences—at every occasion they were asked to cough up their overtime. And all the certificates of merit, letters of thanks, and awards went straight to Ella Sergeyevna. One time the language and literature teacher had sent up a complaint to the higher authorities, but, with some help from the late Lyamzin, his wife had come out smelling like a rose. As for the language and literature teacher, the bitch had plunged to the depths of hell. And after that not a single soul had the temerity to raise a hand against the school principal.

She slipped her hands into the sleek sleeves of her robe, and her three-part reflection in the vanity mirror shuddered and divided into six. Andrei Ivanovich's neckties swayed on their metal hanger. It was designed to look like a fish skeleton; instead of a head, there was a hook that curved around like a question mark. Her son had said that the stripes on American neckties go from the upper right corner to the lower left; but that British ties are the opposite. What if they go crisscross? You'd get a lattice pattern . . . She should give the neckties to Andrei Ivanovich's chauffeurs. He let his driver go that evening, Ella Sergeyevna recalled for the hundredth time. But why? . . . With fresh clarity, she suddenly realized that her husband was gone forever, for all eternity, and, forgetting the blaring doorbell, she sank down on the edge of her bed, which was still tousled from the night.

Damn that Semyonova. Ella Sergeyevna had suspected something early on, at the very beginning, when the geyser of his ill-fated passion had swept him away from her. He'd stopped coming to her at night with his tender, warm conjugal caress. Blaming his heavy workload, he would turn his head away and lapse into a cold, distant, snoring sleep. Wounded by his indifference, Ella Sergeyevna had tried a whole arsenal of secret elixirs: Spanish fly, horse stimulants, Arctic krill extract and fish liver tincture, ginseng infusion and wild pepper. A few drops in his evening cup of tea. But instead of flaring up in a paroxysm of desire and throwing himself on her like a rutting elk with a thickened neck and bloodshot eyes, Andrei Ivanovich turned green and locked himself in the toilet, where a violent fit of retching put an end to this misguided strategy.

Then he started going to official banquets and ribbon-cutting ceremonies without his wife. And Ella Sergeyevna pictured her there, the little slut, circulating among the guests decked out in their fancy clothes, scheming to sink her claws into Lyamzin's property. Loathing was eating Ella Sergeyevna alive; she didn't know who disgusted her more, Semyonova or her husband. She feared he'd leave her to a humiliating, lonely old age. But the years flowed by, and Andrei Ivanovich kept coming home to his family. At first he made little effort to conceal his knavish, blissful smile; later his lips would be clenched tight, and he would be irritated, out of sorts.

His assistant, the insufferable Lenochka, had whispered to Ella Sergeyevna at one point, during an anniversary celebration of the seltzer water plant, that she felt sorry for Andrei Ivanovich. That he had promised Marina Semyonova that he would get divorced as soon as his son grew up and went abroad to school. And here their son had grown up and had gotten into an elite college abroad, and nothing had changed. And now, supposedly, Semyonova was tormenting Lyamzin, nagging at him constantly, eating his brains out. Lenochka, fool that she was, had assumed that Ella Sergeyevna would gloat over his predicament and share her moment of gleeful triumph. But the wife only flew into a rage and glared at her. How dare this pathetic little nobody think she could share confidences with her, a former deputy of the regional assembly, a school principal, and a government minister's wife. She was to leave the premises immediately, the insolent, snot-nosed runt. Ella

Sergeyevna had had enough of these upstarts, these pathetic social climbers. Driven her up the wall, they had, these bedbugs, cockroaches, maggots! Just try to sink your meat hooks into Andrei Ivanovich!

Andrei Ivanovich was a fine one himself. God knows how many companies he'd signed over to his insatiable side bitch. How many millions he'd squandered on gifts for her. "They're not my millions anyway," Lyamzin had told her once, "they belong to the government." This was the first time they had discussed Marina Semyonova openly. The clock on the dresser ticked, twitching its gilded hands. It was after 2:00 AM, and Lyamzin couldn't sleep. His soft cheeks had broken out in cold drops of perspiration. He told his wife about the anonymous messages. About the threats, which had come from some unfamiliar email addresses. He had complained about the extortion attempt to Kapustin, the prosecutor, but Kapustin had jokingly tried to blame her, his wife. Had suggested that it was Ella Sergeyevna's way of getting him to come back into the fold. Lyamzin, on the verge of tears, had assured his spouse, "But I have not left you and I will not leave you"; he stroked her big fingers, bare, without the diamond rings, which she had taken off for the night. Toward the end his nerves had gone off the deep end. "Of course you won't leave, you jackass," thought Ella Sergeyevna to herself, "but only because the governor has announced a family values campaign. Just try to get divorced; before you know it, they'll kick you out of all your cushy jobs. And there will be no more cows for you to milk." So their little social unit remained intact and untouched.

The bell jingled even more insistently, it droned on and on like a dentist's drill. Ella Sergeyevna now detected a kind of distant, faint mechanical humming. "Are they actually going to cut it open?" Lyamzin's widow thought in terror. She leapt up from the bed and, bumping against the corners of the heavy mahogany furniture along the way, staggered downstairs into the yard. A note! She'd received one yesterday, ominous-looking printed letters on a thick piece of paper, which had been folded in fourths. "Guests are coming, hag!" She had found it in her office at the end of the day, after everyone had left. It was lying in the untidy pile of documents on her desk. She hadn't taken it seriously. She'd completely forgotten about it! But the note had taken roost in her brain like a dark blob; it haunted her sleep. The note that Ella Sergeyevna had tried not to think about. "Guests are coming . . ." And sure enough, here they were at her gate: uninvited guests. The videophone in the hall was on the blink; all it showed was a pattern of zig-zag stripes across the screen.

The oak stairs sagged under her heavy, bearlike steps. A turn, another turn. Her palm thwacked into the sparkly light blue bamboo-patterned wallpaper. Now the somber living room, with its curtains drawn. Andrei Ivanovich squinted down disapprovingly from Ernest Pogodin's painting; his general's epaulets had gone completely dull.

"Oh dammit!" cursed Ella Sergeyevna, bumping against a Renaissance stool, a gift from the minister of culture.

The thought of the note gave her no peace. "The students, Devil's spawn," she thought. "Who else?" The kids had gotten completely out of control. Recently she'd called in the upperclassmen, one by one, in turn. Tongue-lashed them, really let them have it. The little idiots had gotten into the habit of going to street gatherings, to take potshots at those on the seats of power and bad-mouth the authorities. Student agitators had gathered filth from the internet and spread it far and wide like a maggot-borne plague. Polluting the undeveloped minds of the young. The parents of the ringleaders had hemmed and hawed and bleated, had promised to take their offspring in hand, but Ella Sergeyevna had planted her hands on her hips and had boomed, her voice reverberating against the walls:

"Do you have any idea how serious this is? Your child is being used! It's a violation of the law! I will be forced to inform the Security Service—he will be put on a watch list and he won't get into college! This is a stain that will be with him for his entire life!"

The wayward youth just got bolder; brainwashed by their ringleaders, they ignored the warning. And that wasn't all. They turned up the heat on the principal and went on the attack, along the lines of, "you promised us a computer class by September, and the door is still locked, even now." And they pushed back in response to all her bans on attending "disgusting" street gatherings, yammering on and on about the Constitution. One shockingly mouthy tenth-grade girl went so far as to declare that the only ones trying to play mind games with her were the teachers themselves and especially the principal, who, she said, had plastered the school hallways with sycophantic hosannas to the governor and quotes from the top government authorities. Vile, insufferable little sneak. Very likely she'd been the one who'd planted the note.

"You are puppets!" cried Ella Sergeyevna at the time, bursting into the classroom with her generals—the class supervisor and the vice principal for moral-ideological education—all three of them in a lather. "Revolution? Blood? Is that what you want? You want it to be like in Ukraine? Good-for-nothings, dropouts, knuckleheads, all of you! You know nothing whatsoever of the world. If you'd had to live like we did during the nineties, you would have had your fill of filth and squalor. You'd be eating out of our hands now!"

But the upperclassmen were stuffed to the gills with reptilian provocations from the scrap heap of the internet; stoked with wreckers' propaganda, they yammered on and on about thievery, about injustice, about their parents' kopecks.

"And why are we living on kopecks? Tell us!" squawked the class supervisor. "Go ahead, tell us! Demonstrate your knowledge! We have an economic blockade going on, a blockade, hear me? Europe has got us by the throat; America is gnashing its fangs at us. And why is that, go ahead, tell us!"

"Because we violated . . ." Voices chimed out from different sides of the room.

"Because we're strong!" roared the vice principal. "Because they fear us!"

Locks of hair had escaped from her barrette, and her voice rasped like a worn-out mechanical coffee grinder. Ella Sergeyevna knew that the vice principal, a spinster, had begun a love affair with the janitor, a young brown-eyed man who had a wife and three children back in Central Asia. She kept him for horizontal pleasures, like a tiger, feeding him with the students' loose change. But Ella Sergeyevna craved love, too, her fleshy thighs had not yet withered; they still had some passion in them. But Lyamzin would just curl up under the covers and only rarely, with no evident interest, would respond to his wife's insistent overtures. It would happen just before dawn. Her strong hand would feel around and find the tip of his little beast, just waking up and lifting its head. And then the minister would yield and, half asleep, only vaguely aware of what was going on, with his eyes still stuck shut, would roll over onto his wife's ready, open body. But now Lyamzin didn't even exist. His study was empty. His gun collection had gone cold. Meanwhile, outside, the bell continued its malicious, merciless ringing.

Ella Sergeyevna began to unclick the bolts. The last thing was to run across the rose-colored tiles of the courtyard and unlock the gate. Voices could be heard outside. But her head still swarmed with the faces of the people from the night before. Who had done it? . . . But of course: the bouquet from Marina Semyonovna! The she-viper had sent a courier with a bouquet of flowers—forty burgundy-colored roses, lilies, and funereal greenery. A peace offering. Of course she could have told them to leave the note as well. What low cunning, what scheming! Ella had done the right thing when she'd ordered the janitor to throw the basket in the trash. She'd imagined them smelling not of roses, but of bug killer, of poison, of putrefaction. The janitor, of course, must have gone out and sold them on the street corner. What did the sex-crazed vice principal see in him, anyway? Dark-skinned neck, small face. Not his skin, not his looks, that was for sure.

Maybe these people had come to bring her another wreath, or basket, or some other token of sympathy. She suddenly realized that she was not dressed in mourning, that her chest was abloom with gaudy yellow Chinese flowers. "They'll think that I'm not grieving . . ." They say that the Scythians would cut off their ears and run arrows through their left hands as a sign of sorrow for the dead. Women in ancient Greece scratched up their faces with their finger-nails and shaved off their hair. Widowed Australian aborigines burned their bosoms with hot coals. European noblewomen lay in bed for six weeks after their husbands' deaths; they did not go to the theater, and they wrote letters only on black-bordered paper. Russian widows wore black for their whole life, buried themselves alive in convents. Hindu women immolated themselves on pyres; in Indonesia, widows chopped off their fingers . . .

Ella Sergeyevna still had all her fingers. They pressed on the lock button. She opened the gate and recoiled. Five men in civilian clothes broke noisily into the courtyard, and the smallest of them, a little guy with a mustache, introduced himself as a detective and waved an official court document and a search warrant in her face. Ella Sergeyevna gasped audibly and for some reason clutched at her earlobes, whose piercing holes gaped open. "But why?" she exhaled, "Why?" But her usual authoritative voice faltered and fell silent. "Because," answered the detective, smiling under his mustache. And strode into the house as though he owned it.

CHAPTER 5

THREE OF THE MEN, OFFICIALS FROM the secret police, had already spent several hours on the first floor, clicking their heels on the parquet; the others were witnesses; they tagged along behind, gawking at the Lyamzins' swanky décor.

"What's this bird of yours?" asked the detective, poking the pad of his fat finger at a Sèvres porcelain peacock in the living room.

"It's the Firebird—no orifices, though," answered the widow from her place in the leather armchair, where she huddled, sulking under the black woolen shawl she had grabbed off the hanger.

"Don't worry, we're not going to probe up its butt," guffawed one of the three officials. The stoop-shouldered witnesses snickered. They had felt self-conscious when they'd first come into the foyer, and had removed their shoes with some embarrassment; now Ella Sergeyevna scanned their loose, threadbare socks with disdain. "They must have dragooned these rubberneckers from the next district over," she thought, huddling in her chair. "Some new losers moved in there, these must be their gatekeepers."

She couldn't figure out for the life of her what the investigators were after. Her initial, suffocating terror at the possibility that they might come across some doctored school documents, and that she'd have to come up with a plausible explanation for the phantom teachers, had abated. Now she just felt cold and depressed. They rifled through the short-legged bookcase. The books—which no one ever read anyway—tumbled out every which way, and their spines thumped on the floor like nuts falling off a tree, and their pages rustled emptily.

"Tell me, if Sopakhin is the culprit, why are you wasting your time on me?" Ella Sergeyevna asked the detective yet again.

Sopakhin was the history teacher. He had worked at the school for fifteen years. He had not been a risk-taker, didn't cause trouble, didn't whine for raises; he took the students on field trips into nature, coached them to victory in interscholastic competitions. And now it turns out Sopakhin was a criminal; he had falsified history. Her veins swelled with indignation—how dare they rouse her, the inconsolable widow of Andrei Ivanovich Lyamzin, out of bed because of some measly teacher! The mustached detective was courteous; he leaned over her armchair and spoke in a solicitous tone, though with a clear focus on the matter at hand, enunciating clearly:

"Once again, Ella Sergeyevna, I regret that we have come to you so soon after your devastating loss. But this is an urgent matter. Your teacher is under arrest. And, I repeat, you and he seem to have been in cahoots. This is your signature, is it not?"

With exaggerated gallantry he plopped a bound sheaf of pages onto her lap. A detailed methodological plan for Russian History Week. Two coauthors—herself and Sopakhin. Her signature sprawled at the bottom of each page, the great jaunty Ls spread out like drunken accordion players, the curvy ripples of the flourishes.

"Sopakhin wrote the whole thing," Ella Sergeyevna said, with meticulous fidelity to the truth.

"With the two of you splitting the stipend?" smiled the detective.

That son of a bitch Sopakhin, how could he have foisted that swill on her? Though she was a fine one herself; she hadn't read the damn thing, had let it slip through. The widow scratched the bridge of her sweaty nose, going over in her mind the fateful program. Everything seemed to have been done properly. For the regular civil-defense session they had organized competitions: "New Martyrs of our Region" and "The Battle of Stalingrad." The program also included a patriotic song competition: "Our Motherland Calls." "Artillerymen, Stalin has issued the call, artillerymen, our Fatherland calls us all," sang the sixth- and seventh-grade classes. "Let there be peace in all the land, but if the commander in chief summons us to the last battle, Uncle Vova, with you we stand!" the eighth and ninth grades took up the chorus. "Nothing is forgotten!" shouted posters on the walls. "Rise, o mighty country!" urged the slogans. The ladies in the Education Administration had showered Ella Sergeyevna with praise. So where was the leak?

The detective, without turning off his smile, settled down comfortably at the round dinner table, directly under the portrait of the late Lyamzin, and stretched his long legs out before him:

"Let's try again, Ella Sergeyevna. Here we have a transcript of a video recording of the assembly. One of the parents provided the recording to us at our request."

Ella Sergeyevna squinted, recalling the event, recalled looking down over the throng of moms and dads fidgeting awkwardly in their auditorium seats. They held up their their smartphones, pointing them like sunflowers on the stalks of their hands toward the stage, where a restless herd of snot-nosed offspring stood arrayed in military forage caps with five-pointed red stars. She recalled the harvest dance of the wheat ears, the wall newspaper exhibit, the competition of speeches about the Victory. Where, in what dark little corner of this jubilant celebration, had the perfidy taken root?

"Well let's take the tenth-graders' staging of the Fascist attack on the USSR." The detective spoke deliberately, enunciating each syllable clearly. "What words can your Sopakhin be heard uttering backstage, off camera?"

"What words?" Ella Sergeyevna lurched forward anxiously.

"'After the signing of the criminal Molotov-Ribbentrop Pact and the secret protocol on the partition of Europe . . . ' 'Criminal,' do you understand?"

Ella Sergeyevna did not understand. She blinked dully. A bit of fluff quivered in the corner of her matted eyelashes.

"The point was," she said finally, "that the pact was a mistake."

"What do you mean, 'a mistake'?" The detective turned

serious. "You are a historian yourself, and you're saying the same thing! Same as Sopakhin, you're in cahoots with him!"

"I'm not in cahoots," objected Ella Sergeyevna, with alarm.

"That pact returned the Baltic States and Bessarabia to the fold. Territories that had been occupied by Poland. As for the secret protocol, there were no plans to partition Europe. We wanted to defend Poland; Poland didn't want to cooperate, and that's the long and short of it," lectured the detective. His two sidekicks in the meantime opened and closed the doors of the carved wooden buffet with its stash of forty-year-old Dalmore whisky in fancy bottles with silver reindeer head labels. The witnesses' unprepossessing faces burned with curiosity at the sight of the expensive spirits. "Are you following me?"

"Yes of course," nodded Ella Sergeyevna. "But I would still like to call my lawyer."

"We would seem to have settled this point at the outset," frowned the detective. "No phone calls during a search. There is a nonbinding right to have a lawyer present, but only when a formal request has been submitted. And there was no formal request."

"But I heard—" began Ella Sergeyevna, reinjecting her school principal's notes of authority into her voice.

"You may have heard many things, only one of which is relevant at the moment," interrupted the detective, tapping his fingernails on the table. "The most outrageous criminal activity is going on in your school, and you have been asleep on the watch, if not worse . . . Out of respect for your loss, for the moment we are simply going to issue you a warning. A preventative warning. And I would advise you, Mrs. Lyamzina, to meet us halfway."

He rubbed the tips of his shoes together. Patches of bright sunlight glistened on them, flowing into each other like fresh egg yolks. The crisp printed pages of Sopakhin's dossier crinkled in the detective's coarse fingers. Outside the window the day ripened and filled with light, and Andrei Ivanovich's widow had a sudden irresistible craving for fried ham. Greasy, drenched in fat and sprinkled with shredded cheese, served on warm wheat bread with mustard and a gar-lic-tomato paste. So what if it goes straight to the doughy flesh on her hips, if it makes the cellulite pocks darken and dig deeper into her ample derriere, if it stirs up the sugar in her blood and forms great globs of cholesterol? To hell with it all.

"I'm a distinguished, award-winning teacher," declared Ella Sergeyevna. "I have been a regional assembly deputy. I will make sure that Sopakhin learns his lesson."

"We will take care of that ourselves," smirked the detective, "our current task is to clarify your role in this criminal affair."

"Criminal?" asked Lyamzina. It was as though a thick wall had risen up between his words and her comprehension.

"Article 354, Paragraph 1, Part 2," clarified one of the detective's colleagues, who was measuring the drawing room with the compass of his thin legs. "Spreading knowingly false information to the general public about the activity of the USSR during the years of the Second World War. Abuse of one's official position. The fine is a slap on the wrist: the amount of the criminal's salary for a period of three years."

"Or incarceration for a term of up to five years of hard labor," the detective flashed a merry smile, "with deprivation of the right to work in a specific sector for a term of up to three years, in this particular case, in the educational sector. And, as it turns out, you are a criminal accomplice."

"Who, me?" Ella Sergeyevna squawked. "I never . . . I always . . ."

She tried to stand up, but the armchair gripped her tight in its deep, soft leather womb. A gnat had gotten lodged in her ear and launched into a thin, monotonous whine. The air around her thickened like bathhouse steam, smearing the room with watery spots, and the contours and edges of objects blurred. One of the three officers came over to her and raised a glass of water to her nose. A silver glass, for champagne, taken from the sideboard. What business do they have poking around in the china, what do they think they're going to find there? Ella Sergeyevna took a few big gulps and ran her tongue over her numb, ashamed lips, which felt like they belonged to someone else.

"All because of the pact?" she gasped.

The detective's shoes were now tucked under the chair and nestled there like baby animal cubs in their forest den.

"Why would you think it's just about the pact?" the detective was offended. "Your pupils spent half the show playing Germans freezing in the cold. To judge from your staging, during the war there were ten of ours for every two Germans. And the frost, blizzard, snowstorm, it went on through the whole performance! Styrofoam or whatever it was you had up there. White confetti?"

Ella Sergeyevna had completely lost her bearings. She sat

in silence, waiting for the man, who had settled in comfortably at her table, to explain everything.

"Don't bat your eyes at me, madam!" the detective abandoned his composure and boiled up like a teapot. "Your point being that it was the frost and blizzards that defeated the Germans?"

"No," Ella Sergeyevna made sure to deny it explicitly, dolefully folding the ends of her woolen shawl over her chin.

"It's a distortion of history, can't you see that?" continued the detective, angry now. His hand danced on the table's glossy surface, bending and knocking the knuckles and then rising onto the fingertips, like a Cossack performing the kazachok. "These children have been entrusted into your care; they are the next generation, our future. What are you and your underling Sopakhin teaching them? That it was not the great Soviet people, not the army, not our brilliant field marshals who defeated the Fascists? That it was a mere fluke, a stroke of luck with the elements? Winter, frosts—that's how it was?"

"That's not at all what we meant!" shouted Ella Sergeyevna, getting her second wind.

" 'Not what we meant.' Our expert analysis came to the opposite conclusion."

"What expert analysis?" gasped Lyamzina, but one of the sidekicks was already handing the detective a soft folder, bound with string. After a brief struggle with the strings, the detective briskly extracted an imposing-looking document dense with printed lines and waved it before the stunned Ella Sergeyevna's eyes.

"This one!" proclaimed his small mustached mouth. "By the way, the signatories include a professor at the institute. In a different league from these Sopakhins of yours. Here's his conclusion: 'In 1941 the frosts indeed set in early, in October, but this only made things easier for the Fascist tanks, which were now able to speed across open fields. Before the end of summer, General Zhukov mounted a brilliant counterattack at Yelnya, which forced the Germans to stay on the Eastern Front and wait there for the winter frosts.' Now, hm . . . OK . . . OK here it is: 'The collapse of the Wehrmacht was brought about not by the Russian winter, but by the heroism of the Russian soldier, the wisdom of those in command, and the incompetent planning of Hitler's generals, who had neglected to equip their soldiers with winter clothing and equipment. By teaching the students the opposite, the school staff crudely violated historical truth and desecrated the sacrifices of millions of their own people . . . ' "

At this point the detective fell silent, carefully returned the document to its folder, and cast a triumphant look around the room. His two colleagues radiated smugness. The two identical-looking witnesses, whom Ella couldn't tell apart, had begun to lose their concentration and were fidgeting and scratching themselves. One of the three officers kept a tight grip on her phone. They'd also set out her gray, dejected-looking laptop on the chaise longue in plain view, so they could spirit it away into the unknown. It was new, not yet cluttered with gigabits; the widow used it four times a week to talk with her faraway son.

"So Sopakhin did some foolish things; I don't dispute that. I never liked him anyway," said Ella Sergeyevna. All the leather folds of the armchair under her whined piteously. "But look at me! Me! I have the best statistics in the region. In all the elections I have the best turnout, the best percentages, everything, take your pick. All the other principals are kicked out after the elections because they can't get the parents to the polls. But me, I've been in my position for fifteen years! I've won awards—"

"We know, we know" the detective cut her off. "It will all be taken into account. But tell us about this teacher of yours. How could you have loosed this predator among the children? You are fully aware of how worked-up the students are, running wild on the internet, listening to loudmouth subversives and reactionaries from Moscow. And here this teacher, this pillar of strength and beacon of light, tasked with drawing them upward out of the swamp, turns out to be stooging for a gang of traitors. And he's not some lowly hireling; no, he's an official with a salary; at one end he feeds on government rations, while at the other, he shits on . . ."

"Shits on the Motherland!" one of the two sidekicks helpfully completed the sentence.

"Nail on the head! There's no other way to put it," the man with the mustache wiggled his brows.

Ella Sergeyevna looked at those brows, bushy and disheveled, with long, gray hairs mixed in every which way, and suddenly realized what a fool she'd been. How could she have opened her gate to these villains, how could she have let these strangers into her home? In her bedroom, diamonds gleamed in an unlocked safe, and the antique pinfire cartridge revolver which hung on the wall of Andrei Ivanovich's study was worth more than a fancy apartment in town. What was actually printed there on the detective's ID? Ditz that she was, and half asleep, she hadn't bothered to take a good look at it. What if the whole thing was a setup to get her to let them come in so they could steal everything? Five against one. They'd taken her mobile phone. And she had no way to protect herself; the security guard at the booth outside the house had asked for leave after Andrei Ivanovich's funeral, and he hadn't offered a substitute. Ella Sergeyevna had let down her guard and now she was vulnerable. And to top it off, this was the housekeeper Tanya's day off.

She again recalled the domino that had been slipped behind her husband's portrait. And the note. Had she, the housekeeper, been the one who'd planted it on her desk? "Guests are coming," the anonymous author of the note had predicted, which meant he knew about the search that was about to happen, which meant that he'd been rubbing his sweaty hands together, anticipating Lyamzina's helplessness. Tanya had said that her first cousin once removed was an officer with a rank of major. Could she have . . . ?

The detective again rummaged around in his papers, and his cronies scattered to the corners like startled bugs. The hands on the clock on the wall over the buffet had stopped yesterday at three thirty; Ella Sergeyevna had lost track of time and didn't know how many hours the unwelcome visitors had been prowling from room to room, or what they were trying to find. The three of them themselves didn't seem to have a clear understanding of what they were looking for; their hands just idly picked through everything that they came across.

The mustached man shook a paper folder, and the pages fanned apart, slid around like layers of a Napoleon pastry. Ella Sergeyevna licked her lips and fell into a reverie. She dreamed of being left alone with a big plate of food. Her belly moaned and whimpered like a pathetic street dog. But the mustached detective kept yammering on about the damned Russian History Week.

"So, the fact that you've got ten Soviet soldiers against one Fritz in your performance, that is unacceptable. Do you agree?"

"What?" asked Ella Sergeyevna.

"Just give me your answer!"

"I will answer only with my lawyer present," retorted the widow grimly, as though through a toothache.

The detective exchanged glances with his colleagues and puffed out his chest:

"So that's how things are, 'only with my lawyer present,'" he snorted. Well, you and your lawyer have your work cut out for you if you want to come up with a satisfactory explanation for this outrage."

"The might of the Soviet soldier," Ella Sergeyevna began, "is in our numbers. Tanks advance in a diamond formation. Truth is on our side. That's the point. What we teach. About our superiority."

"Oh, 'our superiority,' so that's it!" The detective scoffed, drawing out the words. "Though everything would seem to look quite different. What it looks like is that we, the Russians, purely and simply blocked the enemy with piles of our dead bodies. Not sparing our soldiers' flesh. Yes, yes, that's it, those same despicable lies that our enemies are spreading. And you, comrade pedagogues, scooped it up hook, line, and sinker. Ella Sergeyevna, I am seriously concerned for your students' welfare. How do they now view the history of their own Motherland after these seditious, forgive me, Russian History Weeks? Where are they to find a source of pride for their forefathers, for their country? That's how it starts, with something like this, and before you know it they're twerking on the brink of eternal hellfire."

A childish feeling of resentment stirred deep inside Ella Sergeyevna.

"I beg your pardon?" she whispered. "Why pick on me? What do you want from me? Tighten the screws on that fool Sopakhin. As for me, I'm a distinguished . . . Who put you up to this?"

"What do you mean? No one put us up to this," exclaimed the mustached man, moving closer and even stretching out his hands to her like a demigod in a Renaissance fresco. "I'm simply appealing to your civic conscience. Ten against one—believe me, it's a myth, slander. Tell me, how many souls did we lose in the Great Patriotic War?"

"I'm tired," answered Ella Sergeyevna. "And I'm not a student taking an exam."

"Yes, but still," the mustached man squinted and nodded to the witnesses. "Gentlemen, can you answer the question? How many, in your opinion, irreparable losses did the Soviet Union bear in the Great Patriotic War?"

The witnesses smiled self-consciously.

"Twenty million?" asked one of them, tapping his heel on the parquet.

"Bingo!" the mustached man shook his index finger triumphantly. "Did you hear that? Behold your students! Some will say twenty, others thirty, still others forty. They believe

anti-Soviet propaganda, do you understand? But it's utter bal-
derdash! Lunacy!"

He sprang to this feet and began pacing the room. Andrei
Ivanovich looked down from his portrait and observed the
man's trajectories. The peacock also contemplated the scene
from above, his beak gaping open in amazement. Next to him
a colorful porcelain owl kept its silence.

"Let us not be idiots. To speak openly of such gigantic numbers goes beyond simple ignorance. It's criminal,
dear friends," pontificated the detective. The offending witness blinked guiltily, fluttering his eyelashes, flip, flap. "The
actual number is different, you poor ignoramuses, it's different! Eight million and change! And that includes deaths from
wounds, illness, accidents, and executions, plus missing in
action! That's your total."

He ran out of steam and slumped exhausted onto the
chaise longue next to the confiscated laptop. It bounced up
lightly like a startled dog. Ella Sergeyevna took a great gulp
of hot saliva. She spooled the corner of her shawl onto her fist
and asked in a feeble, resigned voice:

"Tell me the truth, who ratted on me?"

"Not 'ratted,' just alerted us; we've been getting complaints for a long time," answered one of the threesome.
"Anonymous complaints.

"Of course, in accordance with Federal Law
59—'Communications from Citizens'—we do not take anonymous messages into account. But this was an exceptional case.
We were informed that you not only condone the falsification
of history in your school, but also . . ." the detective broke off,

betraying some discomfort. ". . . but also have been planning a murder."

The living room fell silent. A ray of sunshine groped restlessly at the windows, trying to feel its way into the house.

CHAPTER 6

LENOCHKA RADIATES TORSION FIELDS, and these fields spiral to the right. So it's always nice to spend time with Lenochka. At a speed of 828,000 kilometers per hour Lenochka spins around the center of our galaxy. The ether of creation generates in her. Spirals and whirlwinds burst into bloom in the keyholes of her pupils. "Coloboma of the iris," is what the doctors call it. "Cat eye," they add lyrically. Sunlight blinds Lenochka, the world blurs in her eyes. She wears dark contact lenses and smoke-colored sunglasses. Her chestnut locks cascade below her shoulder blades. Lenochka used to wish she was a redhead, but her late boss Andrei Ivanovich had once said, while in a state of intoxication, "All redheads are prostitutes." She took it seriously and gave up the idea of dying her hair.

In the summer Lenochka goes out walking without her underwear. With each step the terrestrial, feminine forces of Earth rise up and are absorbed into her being through the lower chakras. The Svadhisthana chakra opens in the area of the womb, where an ardent passion blazes up. The Anahata chakra throbs at her heart, and her chest fills with reverent love. The Vishuddha chakra pulses rapturously in Lenochka's throat, radiating inspiration.

She had been with a man once, but it was brief and fleeting. She couldn't keep him. She needs to hone her skills. Every day Lenochka follows the instructions of local masters or itinerant teachers. They mentor her in her development. "Release your request into the Universe, and the Universe will answer you," she notes down in her tablet, trying to catch every word. Single women in half-buttoned blouses, lips brimming with honey and light breathing, throng the studios. They greedily absorb words of advice from coaches in the art of catching a man. The clientesses' skirts are short and daring, their stretch stocking-boots rise above their knees.

"Exercises for your most intimate muscles, five minutes every morning and evening," writes Lenochka. "Letters to your inner goddess, daily." "Make him fall in love with you by causing him pain. Touch your hair, exposing your bare neck to the man. Make two compliments within the first five minutes. Determine his type: visual, kinesthetic, or audial. Keep a list and record your profit after each gift." Her efficient fingers jot everything down. Endless the list, high the stakes, intimidating the homework. "I am a fool," Lena declares to male strangers she meets on the street. As she speaks, following her coach's instructions, she thinks about her nipples. She is losing her inhibitions. Her biochemistry is changing. Men think she's crazy, but when they look at her they smile; their eyes go moist, their shoulders relax. The tips of their rough shoes point in her direction, their thumbs are hooked under their belt—body language that signals interest. Lenochka enters little plus marks into her tablet. It's working; her personality is developing.

Late in the evening, after work, Lenochka runs into a rented locker room on the seventh floor of a half-dead research institute and there, in sweatpants and a scarf with little bells, practices belly dancing. Her knees jab the air in Egyptian style, her meager butt cheeks gyrate, her shoulders undulate, her hips trace figure eights around her equator.

"Your whole foot!" shouts the dance teacher, her seductive layer of fat swaying, her belly wobbling, "Knees soft! I said, knees soft! The only thing moving is your hips. Now, ready, go, twist! Forward, back, forward, back! Keep your vertical axis!"

And Lenochka's hips obediently move forward and backward, and her feet stand on tiptoe, and her little breasts jiggle invisibly in their sports bra.

After Andrei Ivanovich's death everything collapsed. She no longer smiled at men she passed in the hallways at the ministry, calibrating the display of her teeth. Expose only the upper row, not, under any circumstances, the lower. The upper row is youth; the lower—old age. She cried. Not just cried, but whimpered loudly where she sat at her workplace in Lyamzin's reception area. At first Lenochka had tried to hold it in, but her organizers and gadgets kept reminding her, with malicious glee, "14:00: AI meeting at the governor's." And ultimately the tears would gush forth. There would be no meeting. AI was dead.

Tolya, her colleague at the ministry, skinny and long-legged like a grasshopper, poked his head in the door and couldn't hold back a smirk.

"Lost your boss," he jeered. "Lena, get a handle on yourself!"

But Lena took it hard. Her throat emitted a strident rattling sound, like the blades of a pair of rusty shears. The details of the late minister's schedule filled her messengers, attachments, and electronic calendars for a whole month after his death. Working group meetings, discussions on improving labor efficiency, an assembly of agrarians. A visit to farms in his jurisdiction, a report on policy for reducing inflation . . . Other kinds of notes, too: make a reservation at the restaurant in the new business tower, table for two (duh, date night with Marina Semyonova). Have a bouquet of flowers sent to the Wildflower Aesthetic Clinic. Marina Semyonova again. It was a whole ritual: red chrysanthemums—torrid, sultry love. Gone now, all of it, Lenochka's whole existence crumbled into dust, nothingness.

The ministry throbbed with activity. Andrei Ivanovich's deputy, Natalya Petrovna, had been appointed acting minister. She immediately swelled upward and outward: she grew a few inches taller and her imposing bosom jutted forward. The minister's office—purged of his things, from the wristwatch he had left on the desk to the photo of his son in its pinewood frame—parted its somber loins before Natalya Petrovna and lay naked before her like a patient before surgery. Soon they would put it to sleep and cut it open lengthwise and crosswise, would extract everything that didn't belong, then stretch the tissues and nodules back in place, splice the veins, refresh and relaunch the organism, and sew up the raw edges of the wound with vicryl sutures.

Rumors spread through the halls like a plague, leaping from body to body, from lips to ears like some kind of virulent pink herpes. Natalya Petrovna's joy was painful to behold. With unseemly briskness she ordered Lyamzin's polished metal nameplate removed from the office door. A new one was installed with Natalya Petrovna's name gleaming against a mirrored yellow background, which blurrily reflected the faces of people walking by. "She was gunning for him," Tolya whispered to Lenochka, and she peered suspiciously out at the acting minister's vast bust as it sailed past down the corridor.

This morning they were expecting the priest. He would bless the office. The new occupant's guardian angel would take its place in her workspace. And Natalya Petrovna would be protected from Andrei Ivanovich's sad fate. No one would harass her with abusive anonymous letters. No one would torment her until her heart gave out. No one would toss her into a puddle to choke to death in the mud. Her palisander wood coffin would not bump against the door frame on its way out. Her son would not put on mourning.

Lenochka dabbed at her tears. The eye shadow had smeared, forming a lacy pattern on her eyelids. She got out her compact mirror and wiped off the smears with her two ring fingers, then went out to join the others. The procession advanced down the corridor with Natalya Petrovna in the lead. Her bright blue jacket, clasped at the neckband with an enormous coral brooch, blazed like an intense ozone morning, her knees danced in and out of her skirt's modest slit. In her wake strode the bearded priest in a high kamelaukion, with an epitrachelion of blazing gold over his black cassock. After them, the ministry staff clattered along in a flickering crowd. They were all eager to witness the sacred ritual.

"How are they going to do it?" Lenochka asked Tolya. She had joined the crowd of coworkers in the reception area. Natalya Petrovna and the priest went into the office; the others hesitated, shifting from one foot to the other.

"What do you mean, how?" answered Tolya solemnly. "First they'll get out a drill and drill holes in the wall. Then they'll insert a little cross in each hole and cover it up."

"Cut it out!" Lenochka interrupted. She knew he was messing with her. The priest would just read some prayers, would sprinkle the corners with holy water and anoint the walls with holy oil. The plaster would gleam with oil; it would give off a churchy smell, and the furniture would absorb the incense smoke from the censer. They would light a candle and make the sign of the cross once in every corner, and three times over the mirrors and photos. Darkness and devilry would be banished. The portrait of the sovereign over the desk would wink indulgently down upon them. "Live and be fruitful," it would seem to say. "Russia is advancing. Our goals are clear, our tasks unequivocal. Our armor is strong, our missiles swift. Peace, labor, paradise." And would flash a gleaming white smile.

Lenochka thought about the former wife of the man in the portrait, the first lady. The omnipotent ex-spouse, it is said, had given her away after the divorce to a gallant lieutenant colonel half her age, supposedly for love. But there had been no legal wedlock; it was just a honey trap with twenty-four seven surveillance. Everywhere she went, there, too, went the lieutenant colonel. Rumor had it he had a real family and children on the side, and this thing with the former first lady was just a work assignment. Just a job. Top secret.

From the office came the droning sounds of prayer. The voice that a priest uses when he chants the recitative is described as velvety. Lush silk, the fabric of kings. Muted and tender like the touch of a butterfly's wing. The prayer lulls the crowd. Half of them have already entered the office, where the censer chain is clinking. "In the name of the Father and the Son and the Holy Ghost, with the sprinkling of this holy water let all evil demonic deeds turn to flight . . ."

Lenochka thinks of her mother. She works in a kindergarten, where every morning prayers are read over the cooking pots. Not a single intestinal infection, not a single staphylococcus or vibrio cholerae can resist the power of the Holy word. Bacteria explode like party poppers; there used to be a hundred thousand, now only one thousand are left. The children's food is prepared using the sanctified water. Lenochka's mother patrols amid the kindergarteners' lunch tables, with their Khokhloma tabletop designs: great bunches of strawberries in bloom, red birds nestled in the corners. The china bowls of kasha clatter. "No one gets up until it's all gone!" commands her mother.

Her palms are dry and yellow with age. Her hands are heavy, like stones. Lenochka recalls her mother's fists thwacking her on the back of her small head. For burning the soup, for getting a D, for staining her tights, her mother would grab Lenochka tightly by her thin hair and in a frenzy of frustration and rage would bang her forehead against the wall. It made a blunt pounding sound, DOT-DOT-DOT. In Morse code, that's "E-E-E." At the noise, her father, immobilized with vodka, howled curses from the next room. His short life had faded and burned out at a top secret chemical factory, which had been shuttered. Left with nothing to do, with no income, Lenochka's father was swept into a boozy world of drinking buddies and garages. His shirts reeked of motor oil and marinated garlic. He would come home angry, completely hammered, and would take it out on her mother, and scarlet lilies would burst into bloom on her cheeks.

Nights like that, Lenochka would creep under the kitchen table to escape from the fray. She would cower down there by the radiator, with its brown cockroaches rustling underneath. Eventually her father would calm down and reconcile with her mother in the matrimonial bed, and by morning he would be sprawled on the foldout sofa, emitting labored snores, with his great terrible arm dangling over the side. Her mother would cover the bruise with a thick lock of hair and would go off to work as though nothing had happened. Back she would trudge at the end of the day, exhausted, lugging heavy, bulging bags of potatoes and loaves of black bread. And Lenochka would be punished for some new offense.

One time the clumsy child scorched her mother's best dress with the iron; the synthetic material wrinkled and pleated like an accordion, and a triangular-shaped gash gaped traitorously on the bodice. When her mother came back she lashed Lenochka with the iron cord, beating her calves painfully with the heavy plug. "Cry, go ahead and cry, you little piece of shit!" shrieked her mother, infuriated at her soulless daughter's stoicism. She finally wore herself out, at which point she gave her daughter's belly one last kick with her slippered foot, and then desisted. Lenochka gasped and fell with a plop onto her tailbone, and her mother went off to the neighbor's.

The plastic heels jutted out from her scuffed soles; her ankles reeked of poverty. And when the leatherette door slammed shut, only then did Lenochka's tears begin to flow.

"To the Creator and Maker of the human race, to the Giver of spiritual grace, to Him who granteth eternal salvation . . ." chanted the priest, and the nostrils of the ministry staff, desiccated from paper dust, workplace tedium, and toxic ink, quickened and came to life, breathing in the sacramental fragrances. The worm that had been eating away at Lenochka's insides mellowed, stretched its coils playfully, and loosened its grip. She felt better, calmer, and her heart stirred, sensing the possibility of some as yet vague future joy. At this point, as though responding to Lenochka's thoughts, a woman emitted a loud, shrill gasp, interrupting the prayer. The gasp broke off in mid-breath, with a hoarse wheezing spasm.

"Are you unwell?" asked the priest. There was a pause, then voices were heard, and the rows of the crowd launched into motion. Natalya Petrovna rolled out into the reception area like a living beach ball and toppled into the very thick of the crowd, like an egg rolling out into the grass. Her unseeing eyes stared blankly before her.

"Oh my God," she whispered, shaking her iPhone. "Oh my God! Sent to everyone, to the entire ministry listserv . . ."

"What happened, Natalya Petrovna?" asked her underlings, but she only clutched at her gleaming iPhone and backed away through the crowd, retreating farther and farther until she completely disappeared from view. Two of the office ladies took off after her, and everyone else rushed over to the holy father. But some individuals in the crowd were already cackling and snickering. Tolya stood amid a cluster of mirthful faces. Fingers jabbed at his cell phone screen, mouths gaped open in astonishment.

"What's going on?" asked Lenochka.

"See for yourself!" Tolya summoned her ecstatically and showed her the screen.

The photograph was unbelievable. An unbridled outrage, a flagrant violation of all laws of human decency. A depraved-looking floozy, eyes sparkling demonically, perched enthroned on a tall, one-legged, stilt-like barstool, posing for the camera. The trollop was none other than the new acting minister. Not the Natalya Petrovna everyone knew, but a madwoman, completely unhinged, and straight out of a whorehouse. A colorful boa was tossed over her shoulders, her plump torso was tightly laced in a leather corset, with her doughy bosom spilling out in sumptuous hemispheres over the edges. Her fat legs, sheathed in fishnet stockings, were spread wide like a circus acrobat's; her feet were tucked up, with their sharp stilettos pointing directly at her woman's shame, itself barely concealed under the lace of her black panties. Natalya Petrovna's crimson lips clenched the metal butt end of a whip. "Twenty lashes with the whip means death; a light touch is a tickle," thought Lenochka. She cast her eyes around at her colleagues. They circulated around the reception area in great excitement, poking at their smart-phone screens, googling Natalya Petrovna's name along with key words: "corset," "BDSM," "shame," "kompromat." The priest had already been shown out, but the aroma of the unction oil still saturated the air. Shocked voices exclaimed:

"What the . . . ? A regular Moulin Rouge!"

"Who posted it? Who did it?" others asked anxiously.

"Cut and paste? Photoshop?" wondered others.

"If it was photoshopped, she wouldn't have freaked out like that," Tolya was in hog heaven. "Ha, ha, ha! Someone sent this picture around to all the official addresses. Not to mention the web. Let the party begin!"

Tolya was having his laugh at Natalya Petrovna's expense. She couldn't stand him; his position in the ministry was hanging by a thread. And all because of unrequited advances, rejected kisses—unsuccessful attempts at harassment. Natalya Petrovna was single, Tolya—curly-haired. All he had to do was meet her halfway, to yield, to give himself like a lamb to slaughter, but Tolya just scoffed at his boss's womanly overtures. He mocked her friskily like a boy in a schoolyard. By this point his dismissal seemed imminent; the sword had been raised and the miscreant's head was about to roll, but suddenly it was discovered that Tolya had friends in high places. A telegram arrived, addressed to Tolya, from a sender in the Kremlin. THE Kremlin. Moscow. The gratitude of those at the very highest level for his participation in the youth forum dedicated to the anniversary of the Victory. The telegram was posted on the ministry bulletin board. Tolya was now officially untouchable.

Lenochka's brief moments of joy ebbed; her legs and shoulders began to tremble, and her cheekbones burned as though they'd been rubbed with snow. She grabbed her big lilac-colored coat from the closet and rushed out of the office. She ran down the steps, immured with the flattened antediluvian rubbish of crushed white seashells. The coarse bannisters scratched the skin of her palms. Outside the entryway a young man called her name. He was handsome, tall, with two sheaves of overgrown golden-brown hair. He waved to her and smiled a tender and somehow April-tinged smile.

"Oh!" Lenochka started. "It's you!"

She recognized him as one of the detectives who had come to the ministry that fateful morning when the boss had not shown up to work. Lyamzin's wife had stated at the time that her spouse had left the night before and had not come home. His mistress had stated that she had waited and waited but that he had never shown up. They had found the corpse half submerged in a rain ditch on the roadside. The corpse had bloated up. That's what people were saying in the office, but how could they have known?

The young man's name was Victor; he had questioned Lenochka about Andrei Ivanovich. He had taken notes the old-fashioned way, using a silvery pen, recording her answers in the protocol: "Recently Andrei Ivanovich had been working a lot, he was concerned about the region, about the country. He was worried about disappointing the governor. And of course he had personal problems, too. He was torn between the two women he loved. Someone had been writing him nasty letters, he himself didn't know who . . . No, he loved life, I don't believe he was capable of suicide. His heart? Yes, he was concerned about it . . ." Why had Victor come back? Could it be that the news of Natalya Petrovna's disgrace had gotten out already?

But that's not what had brought the young man this time. He looked at Lenochka with fluffy bunny-rabbit eyes and asked if she'd like to go out for a coffee. Her chest filled with warmth, the Anahata chakra opened its inner eye. Lenochka answered, "Yes." They walked together past the ministry, a mighty cube on a granite foundation with colonnettes running along the facade. It had been built on the site of a complex of workers' barracks like those that still stood in the area and in various locations around town, poking up here and there like inedible mushrooms—ugly planked buildings with leaky roofs and no hot water. But behind one of these shabby eyesores with tradescantia in pots on the windowsills, a charming coffee shop nestled in a two-story house that had belonged to some pre-revolutionary merchant's wife. The barista, a taciturn man with a pomaded beard, worked magic behind the counter; the place smelled of Arabica, and the foam on the lattes featured smiley-face designs made of cinnamon powder.

Victor and Lenochka took a seat by the window. They clutched tightly on to their cups, and shyly avoided looking into each other's eyes.

"Are we friends?" asked Victor.

"Yes," resolved Lenochka.

"You seem to be the only one who's grieving for Lyamzin; even his wife didn't seem that upset."

"What makes you think that?" Lenochka flushed, confused and pleased at the same time.

"I can sense it," answered Victor. "Do you know what adronitis is?"

"Adron-what?"

"Adronitis. Frustration at the amount of time you waste before you can really get to know a person."

"Does that happen with you a lot?" Asked Lenochka, with a note of gentle irritation in her voice.

"What I feel a lot more is onism."

"Onanism?" snickered Lenochka.

"Onism," Victor corrected her, mirroring her laugh out of the corner of his mouth. "It's a sense of disillusionment from having to spend all your time in one body. Just one. And there are no alternatives, like what you get in a computer game for example. And you can only be in one place at one time. It's just unfair. Really annoying. I even feel a little jealous of elemental particles."

"Where do you pick up all those fancy words? I'm losing it! 'Onism' . . . Never heard of it," smirked Lenochka. "What I envy is not being able to turn back the hands of time." Lenochka turned sad again. "Maybe Andrei Ivanovich's life could have been saved."

"From whom?" Victor leaned in close, and his golden-tinged locks flipped down from his high forehead and swung like a pendulum.

"From everyone," answered Lenochka. "They were driving him nuts."

Victor's face was close to Lenochka's. Specks of light from the windowpanes swarmed over his pink cheeks. She gazed at his lips. An arched contour of the lips is a sign of inner dynamism. When the upper lip is just a bit fuller than the lower, the person is a phlegmatic type. A chiseled contour signals groundedness. But Victor's eyes, fringed with downy eyelashes, looked at Lenochka with a kind of mournful passion, like two midnight suns.

"I'm afraid," said Lenochka. "Andrei Ivanovich had been harassed with anonymous notes. And now his deputy, Natalya Petrovna, is getting harassed, too. Today someone sent her a photograph. She's practically naked in it, looks like a stripper. And now it's all over the internet."

"She needs to report it," answered Victor, "to make an official request to identify the person responsible."

"She flipped out and just took off; she even forgot about the priest who was sanctifying the office," added Lenochka, not without a tinge of malice. "She almost had a seizure."

As though in response to her words, there came the plaintive whine of a siren. First a thin, high shriek that swelled and grew louder. Then low, receding, a howling bass. Doppler effect. An ambulance must have sped past the coffee shop. Lenochka's nose began to twitch, and hot tears formed in the corners of her eyes.

"I'm so afraid," she confessed.

Victor took her hand in his. His hand was warm and firm.

"Don't be afraid. Call me if something comes up. Anytime."

"All right," nodded Lenochka. She was thinking about androgynes. Spherical, hermaphroditic primogenitors of the human race from ancient Greek mythology. She had learned about them during a training session for visualizing desires. The androgynes had four legs, four ears, and two backbones. The gods chopped them in two. And now Lenochka had to roam the world seeking her other half.

Lenochka had written down in her notebook the qualities she sought in her other half: hairstyle, height, personality. Lenochka's computer desktop featured a photo collage: a little house, two hearts pierced with an arrow, and a packet of dollars—dreams that had been released into the Universe. Victor was handsome. He still held her hand in his. Could this man be her other half? She suddenly leaned toward him and kissed him moistly on his tangy lips. Her elbow brushed against a teaspoon, which clattered and bounced onto the tile floor. The barista watched them lazily from behind the counter, stroking his fragrant beard with his hairy hand. And the big espresso machine purred cozily behind him.

CHAPTER 7

THE GORKY REGIONAL DRAMA THEATER WAS ablaze in light. A glittering throng of ticket holders shed their outer shells of fur, cashmere, leather, down, and membrane, and fanned out across the red-carpeted lobby. The ladies sparkled with Swarovski crystals; the men's watches and bald pates gleamed. The theatergoers were eagerly anticipating the cultural enrichment to come. Their demeanor, their postures, their manner of walking proclaimed: "We are no strangers to the sublime; we are here for a premiere. We will now indulge in Appreciation of Art."

The crystal spheres in the tiered chandeliers jingled inaudibly under the ceilings; the fat ticket sellers in their cramped booths nibbled at chocolate bars with porcelain teeth. The chocolate, warmed by its proximity to their teacups, melted on their fingers. The box office ladies flapped their mouths. Gossip flew—from the utility rooms to makeup, from makeup to costumes, from costumes to hairdressing, from hairdressing to the dressing rooms. The actor Poluchkin, who had been thrown out of the theater the night before for a vicious, bullying Facebook post featuring the theater's artistic director, had been interviewed by Katushkin, the piece-of-shit internet journalist. He'd loosed a whole volley of complaints, diarrhea of the mouth. Just let fly. Galloping globs of gobbledygook.

What had upset Poluchkin? What had gotten him into such a frenzy? The theater buzzed like a disturbed beehive, savoring every last detail. The artistic director was named Chashchin. His name was repeated over and over like a tongue twister. The dressing rooms hissed: Chashchin, Chashchin, cash in, slashin' Chashchin, cheatin' Chashchin. He had no theatrical or artistic training; he was an imposter, a former Komsomol functionary, griped Poluchkin on the *Siren* site. A Komsomol functionary and failed scribbler. Author of drivel about the lives of Ural natives. *The Deerskin Tent* was the title of his chef d'oeuvre. It had been staged in a single Siberian town and then faded into obscurity.

Now, having taken over the regional theater, Poluchkin claimed, Chashchin had destroyed everything that was fresh and exciting, yanked it up by the roots. The fonts of inspiration had dried up, the repertoire had lost its spark. The audiences were apathetic; attendance had tanked. They had no interest in the deeper experience of art; all they cared about was loafing around on the couch, chomping sunflower seeds, and watching manic buffoons bleat at each other on the idiot box. Audiences were schlepped in on holidays by the busload from various offices and businesses. They brought their own champagne and uncorked it in the stalls. *The bottles gush, the ushers shush.* Throngs of schoolkids were herded in and counted off head by head. The schoolkids crunched potato chips, rustled the foil bags, scrolled down their cellphone displays with greasy fingers. Luminous rectangles glowed stealthily in the darkened hall.

But Poluchkin spilled the beans to Katushkin about way more than that. The region's minister of culture was also in his crosshairs. Word was, the minister and Chashchin had been palsy-walsy for ages. And the minister's daughter had some kind of mysterious job in the theater and no one had any idea what she did. And on the minister's birthday Chashchin summoned his actors and dragged them out like the evil puppeteer Karabas Barabas to perform for his bigshot crony. The actors put on skits: the singers sing and perform fistfights. The prima donna squeezes into a tight décolletage and swoons with a sweet sigh, and her hem hikes up, baring her shapely legs. The comic actor mocks Americans, opening his mouth wide. The acrobat walks around on his hands and does somersaults; the villain leers, wiggling his bushy eyebrows along the creases of his forehead; the buffoon portrays a lovestruck old woman, snuggling up to young men with a disgusting cackle. The minister of culture laughs. His fat cheeks jiggle, his fat double chin quivers. He embraces Chashchin and expresses his gratitude. The theater gets a government subsidy. Instead of rehearsing, the troupe throws drunken dance parties in the cafeteria.

Poluchkin also blabbed that the previous chief director, a young genius of great promise, had supposedly been forced out of the theater, hounded by intrigues and backbiting. He'd made the same mistake twice. The first time was a production he'd staged based on a contemporary play. A comedy, a vaudeville. They'd finally broken even. The production caused great excitement; word on the street was ecstatic, a rave. But some ladies from the Education Administration had shown up at one of the early performances. They beheld a burlesque show complete with dulcimers. Raucous jokes and gags rained down from the stage onto the audience. The ladies went into shock; their lips curled into figure eights. At one point one of the heroines shouted to another in a fortissimo catfight:

"Hey you old bag! Where do you think you're going to go now? Who the hell needs you?"

"I can go anywhere I want!" snapped the other. "I'll go into education, do Fundamentals of Life Safety."

The ladies from the Education Administration went into shock; the gelled curls twitched indignantly at their temples. Outraged by the hooliganism they had witnessed, they sat down and drafted a document on the spot. They demanded that the words be changed, that the shocking lines be cut. The point being: it disparaged the school curriculum.

Poluchkin's second mistake followed immediately on the heels of the first. A production about an explorer, a vanquisher of distant lands, about his encounter with natives in the north. A certain retiree, a town resident, came to the show, ticket in hand. He came alone, quiet, sharp-nosed, and left indignant, swollen up with wrath like a helium balloon. There was a scene in which the traveler, driven half wild from his ordeals, despairing of ever making it home, uses a sacred icon as a board for cutting up a fish. The retiree was shocked and appalled. He penned a letter to the governor, notifying him of an act of desecration of the Orthodox faith. He demanded that the parties responsible be punished and that the show be closed down. The production was condemned as the first step on the slippery slope of extremism. The lunatic—as Poluchkin called the old man—was heeded, the production was shut down, and the chief director was fired. And Poluchkin lost his role as the male lead.

But the actors, half of whom had been on Poluchkin's side, now spoke of him with uninhibited condescension. The poor bastard had gone off the deep end, but life goes on; and in the meantime they had a major production in the works. Knowing the minister's tastes, Chashchin was putting together a great, epic drama and had himself taken the helm as director. A Cossack choir and a ballet company had been engaged. Seamstresses worked around the clock sewing costumes. A gigantic, glistening set piece was to be lowered from the fly loft, a red sun, symbol of Grand Prince Vladimir, the man who Christianized ancient Rus. The show was called *The Grand Prince*.

The third bell rang out, the houselights dimmed slowly as if in a dream, and the spectators coughed and fidgeted in their velvet seats. There was fussing in the stalls, like a great bustling bird settling down in her nest. The fingers of latecomers counted the rows, groped at the numbers on the seat backs. Programs fluttered nervously in ladies' hands. The curtain stirred and billowed but remained lowered, anticipating the governor's arrival. Finally there was a stirring of obsequious figures in the VIP box and a flash of white—the corner of a collar. The governor settled into the darkness of the box, and his consort, garbed in a long, free-flowing jumpsuit, leaned forward and rested her forearms on the sill, demonstrating to the assembled masses the ponderous amber necklace that dangled above her stole. From the neighboring boxes, his subordinates and their wives—the entire ladder of local officialdom—craned their necks and nodded greetings to the couple. The minister of culture, who had met the governor in the lobby, strode jauntily to the first row of the stalls, closely trailed by the floodlight of a massive, lumbering TV camera. Now the house lights dimmed, and the cameraman seized his tripod and lunged off, bobbing and stooping, to the corner of the proscenium. The curtain gave a great shudder and swept upward.

Thunder crashed down from the stage. Wooden spoons drummed a cannonade; traditional Russian gusli and domras struck up a tune; clackers and rattleboxes thrummed, panpipes and whistles tooted, drumsticks rattled against wooden shepherds' barabanki; invisible steeds neighed clamorously. A mass of singing, dancing humanity filled the stage with a great flapping of embroidered homespun shirts. Feet in laced-up leather sandals thumped the floorboards; headbands gleamed, and embossed badges clinked on the men's chests. Amid the racket and music, from an elaborately painted panorama of forests and fortresses at the back of the stage, out strode young Prince Vladimir and his vaivodes, arrayed in chainmail. The audience burst into applause at the hero's entrance.

"O Rusichi, o men of Rus!" exclaimed the prince, and a hush fell over the theater. The bagpipes cut off mid-note. "I have taken Novgorod, and now I will set off for Kyiv, where my blackhearted brother Yaropolk has taken shelter. With me march the great Varangian host! We will cast Yaropolk down from the throne. Along the way I will take Polotsk and will teach Rogneda, his affianced bride, a lesson. The bitch will bitterly regret the day she refused me! Onward to Kyiv!"

shouted the prince, and his powdered face gleamed yellow in the floodlights.

"To Kyiv, to Kyiv!" roared the assembled mass.

Laughter and applause in the hall. Trumpets sounded a fanfare. The sides of the stage lurched into motion: the Rusichi surged asunder, the walls parted, then came together, and in an instantaneous theatrical transformation Vladimir and his suite found themselves in the chambers of the Polotskian sovereign: round, arched vaults overhead, with sunlight shimmering dimly in painted micaceous windowpanes. Vladimir's warriors gripped the Polotskian prince and his wife and sons by their throats, and pressed spears against their chests. At Vladimir's feet, pinned under his heel, lay their daughter Rogneda, her face terrified but defiant, her thickly painted-on brows frowning.

"What did you tell me, Rogneda, when you refused to marry me?" boomed the prince.

"I do not recall!" wheezed the maiden.

"'I will not bend over to unshoe a slave.' Those were your words. As though I was not worthy of possessing you. As though I had come from the dark, thundering horde, unworthy of possessing Rus! Let them look now, Rogneda! Let them watch, at the moment of their death, as by force you become my wife."

Vladimir hoisted Rogneda up and with his free hand ripped her sleeve with a crackling sound. Her maidenly arm was exposed; Rogneda's attendants groaned, their gagged mouths bleated helplessly, but the stage again lurched into motion, chastely sparing the audience the violent scene of retribution. There again arose a living mountain of human beings.

Behind it loomed the great pagan temples, the wooden idols of Perun, Veles, Khors, Dazhdebog, Stribog, and Mokosh. The mountain sang:

Volodimir in Kyiv reigns supreme.
Glory, glory to the grand prince!

On an enormous screen that stretched across the whole back of the stage, a series of scenes appeared in succession: blood gushing, herds of galloping horses, fearless bogatyrs hacking asunder the spines of their enemies, maidens running through a scene of burning huts, their loose hair waving wildly in the air. But suddenly at the very climax of the singing a bell clanged, the idols tumbled down and disintegrated, and the crowd-mountain parted to the sides, and there knelt Vladimir. The stage darkened, leaving the prince illuminated in a single spotlight, and the silence filled with the peaceful pealing of church bells. Behind the prince the tsaritsa Anna, his Byzantine consort, stood reverently, garbed in golden raiment. The prince raised his arms aloft, and on the screen a small cross appeared between his hands and began to grow and expand until it filled the whole screen, and again the whole scene was illuminated, and the people fell to their knees and sang in chorus:

We glorify thee, o saintly blessed Prince Vladimir, we
honor thy holy memory, for thou prayest to Christ the
Lord our God for us.

At the triumphal climax of the scene, there was a stir in the hall, and the audience began looking around. They noticed that the governor had stood up to listen to the singing. Following his lead, others rose; sleek, well-groomed men leapt to their feet, straightening their jackets, and at the front of the stalls, the minister of culture sprang up. At the majestic closing chords, the curtain fell, and the hundred lights of the chandelier flashed on, and each light was as bright as one hundred candles. Intermission was announced.

The auditorium hummed and stirred; the cameraman and a female reporter rushed to set up in the lobby to capture the voice of the people. First they cornered the governor and his wife. The couple radiated a proud solemnity, as though they'd been onstage themselves. The governor wiped his flushed face.

"To be honest, I'm not a sentimental man," he said to the camera, "but I almost broke down in tears. You see, this is our history, our values, the values our ancestors fought for and created for us. And our task is to cherish this memory and pass it down to future generations. So that they can learn from the example set by such historical figures as the Grand Prince Vladimir. This is our most vital task . . . Unfortunately, I have some urgent meetings that cannot wait, or I would with greatest pleasure stay for the second act. I urge all of our region's residents to come to the theater, for culture is light; without it we are in darkness."

"I can only add that I share my husband's emotions," the governor's wife chimed in when the microphone jerked and shifted over to her, "what a marvelous atmosphere, such grandeur, such talented actors, I will come and see it again."

The background of the frame was crammed with gawkers decked out in their finery, each one hoping to be on the evening news. Behind the governor, the minister of culture was beaming. He was praising Chashchin. His compliments gushed forth like an avalanche. Meanwhile, Chashchin, the artistic director himself, was already sitting in the office of the theater manager, an energetic and enterprising woman, with an elite group of honored guests. Champagne flowed all around, bananas were peeled and devoured. The set designer, artist Ernest Pogodin, sat enthroned on the divan, with his fists cupping the ivory knob of his cane, sideburns curling on his cologne-scented cheeks.

"Monumental!" the guests exclaimed from all sides.

They lauded Chashchin, Pogodin, the cast, and, of course, the minister, who had given the production the go-ahead. The minister had already joined the tight little group. In hushed tones, he reported the ecstasy the governor had expressed before he had rushed off to attend to an urgent matter.

"Beyond his expectations! He is thrilled! He said it was as good as anything in the capital . . ."

Exuberant gestures fluttered in the air of the office, tongues and teeth eagerly mauled the refreshments, champagne flutes clinked. At a certain point the guests parted, clearing a path for Marina Semyonova and her companion, Ilyushenko. Semyonova was in mourning; she wore a black headband with a veil over her forehead and delicate lace gloves; her lips were painted carmine red. Chashchin rushed over to her, fell to his knees, and bestowed a reverent kiss on her gloved hand; Ernest Pogodin rose to exchange three kisses in greeting, sending his ponderous cane clattering across the floor. In the ensuing flurry of activity Ilyushenko grabbed a tart from the tray and took a bite, and crumbs from the crust sprinkled down the front of his cassock.

"Thank you, thank you, my dear, for coming! It means so much to us," Chashchin assured Semyonova.

"It's so sad that Andrei Ivanovich cannot be with us now. He would have loved it, I know," lamented the minister of culture.

"Yes, yes, so true . . ." repeated Ernest Pogodin, toying with the cane, which someone had returned to him, and adjusting his glimmering gold brocade evening vest. "What a marvelous man he was. He had seen my sketches and even wanted to buy one of them. A nimbus rising over a Russian field, you know. It will appear in the grand finale, you'll see it."

"It will be stunning!" Chashchin chimed in.

"About Natalya Petrovna . . . you've heard, haven't you?" the manager began suddenly, and the guests turned their faces to her greedily, surrounding her like flower petals. The conversation became hushed and sporadic. "Her reputation is ruined." "She's a grandmother!" "She'll pray it away." "It's curtains for the minister job!"

Marina Semyonova wasn't really listening; she wasn't in the mood. Just before the show her employee Stepan from the construction company had galumphed up to her like a gorilla in his evening jacket and an absurd-looking bow tie. Ignoring all propriety, he babbled incoherently about a coworker, Nikolai, who'd died in an accident, about his bereaved, impoverished family, about whether they might receive some financial help. She thought she detected an unsavory, sketchy gleam in his eyes, a reminder of their drunken amorous episode. Did she really have to spend her whole life paying for a moment of feminine weakness? She turned away and muttered something into her handkerchief, but right then Ilyushenko appeared at her side and hissed:

"Can't you see that Marina Anatolyevna is in mourning? Do I have to call security?"

Of course, there was no security in sight; Ilyushenko was bluffing. Stepan slunk away.

The first bell rang, and the guests in the manager's office stirred, downed their last drops of champagne, and prepared to go back for the second act. Chashchin was exhibiting signs of nerves. Ernest Pogodin was biting his cheeks, distraught that the stage design had not been sufficiently praised. But just wait—wait until they saw what the second act had in store.

In the auditorium people were still dawdling, circulating, taking selfies in front of the shiny golden boxes. The spirit of the theater inundated Instagram. Virtual worlds pulsed with hashtags: #grandprince, #Ilovetheater, #christianizer . . . Marina Semyonova, all in black, tall, slender-waisted, proceeded down the aisle with Ilyushenko waddling after her like a penguin, his cassock sleeves billowing like flippers. Semyonova faced the stage, her short veil quivering like a vaporous cloud, concealing her big eyes. The only thing visible on her face was its lower half-moon with its tightly tensed carmine-painted lips, slightly puffy around the edges (bio-revitalization of the lips, contour correction).

Behind her, though, the theater began to buzz and stir. The ushers clucked and the crowd parted; ladies moved aside, gathering up the hems of their dresses. And now down the aisle toward the stage, lumbering like a hippopotamus, strode

Ella Sergeyevna Lyamzina. She was in her everyday clothes, a simple work skirt and a dark blouse, protruding at the chest; dark blue circles under her eyes betrayed sleepless nights, she had not done her hair, and, lacking its usually carefully cultivated body, it lay flat, prudishly framing its mistress's skull. Angry brown blotches had broken out on the widow's neck. Ella Sergeyevna had already spotted Marina Semyonova's silhouette amid the colorful bustle of bodies, and her entire body, the movement of her legs and thoughts, concentrated on this one human figure. Semyonova turned and froze, her lips parted in revulsion and disbelief. Three or four lurches, and Lyamzina was standing at her side. Ilyushenko rushed over, intending to wedge himself between the two of them, but Ella Sergeyevna gave him a shove, and he tumbled backward onto the velvet barricade of seats.

"You!" shrieked Ella Sergeyevna, reaching out for her rival. A torrent of white-hot, filthy curses burst forth and broke in a great wave over the floozy's head. The veil was torn off, Marina Semyonova's chestnut locks flew every which way, and she stretched her hands in front of her, attempting to defend herself.

"Floozy! Snitch! Ratted on me, didn't you, you slut? Claimed I was out to kill you! It had to be you, couldn't have been anyone else! Skank! Ho! Thought you'd finish me off, did you? Get your grubby hands on Andrei Ivanovich? Well, you sent him to his grave, didn't you, you mangy bitch! After his money, weren't you, you shameless gold digger?"

Ella Sergeyevna's fingers clawed into Marina Semyonova's head, and Marina, writhing with pain, shrieked for help:

"Get her off me!"

Breaking away, she scratched Lyamzina's cheek, drawing blood; women screamed, and people rushed from all sides along the narrow aisles to help. Ilyushenko, clambering up out of the seats where he'd been wedged, grabbed at Lyamzina's fat sides and clutched and tore at her thin blouse—it ripped open, baring the band of her linen brassiere. Friends and strangers alike, dignitaries, all crowded around, pushing and shoving, and tried to separate the brawling ladies. The minister of culture ran over and took Ella Sergeyevna by the wrists in a gentle but firm grip, forcing her to release her hold on Marina Semyonova. Finally the she-enemies were disentangled, leaving a few strands of chestnut hair clinging to the widow's palms. The third bell rang, the usher ladies scolded and cursed, and a first-aid kit with sedatives was brought over from the manager's office. Marina Semyonova, trembling, dusted herself off and adjusted the straps on her dress. Ilyushenko crawled around in the aisle looking for her veil; it was recovered—dusty, trampled, its headband mangled. The theater manager rushed up to Semyonova, embraced her, and led her off to put herself in order. The second act was delayed.

"Ella Sergeyevna, we understand what a blow it was, the loss of your husband, and the problems with the teacher, but still, what does Marina Anatolyevna have to do with it?" jabbered the minister of culture, shielding the blubbering Lyamzina under his jacket. "Why make a scene? In front of everyone, on this festive occasion, it's our big premiere, after all . . ."

"I don't give a shit!" roared Ella Sergeyevna, suppressing a sob.

She had come completely unglued. The feral force seething within her suddenly ebbed and evaporated into thin air. Her shoulders under the minister's jacket drooped, and she stood mournfully with a paper napkin pressed to her wounded cheek.

"She's the one! It's her! They came and seized my laptop ... the case against the teacher ...." repeated Ella Sergeyevna.

They dosed her with tranquilizers and led her away. The ruckus subsided. The gawking crowd dispersed, exchanging exclamations and conjectures.

"It's a good thing the TV guys have left already," commented the minister of culture's aide as they headed back to their seats.

"There's been plenty of filming here without them," snapped the minister.

Chashchin, who had been cowering in the parterre boxes, tugged anxiously at his tight starched cuffs:

"They've defiled the premiere . . ."

"Don't get all worked up," Ernest Pogodin soothed him. The scandalous scene had cheered him up. "It's good advertising. Just you wait, the whole town will be beating down the doors."

Marina Semyonova returned to her seat, unruffled, her head held high. Her hair was pinned up neatly again, her nose powdered. People popped up from their seats to get a better look at her, some even broke into applause. Ilyushenko, smiling, stroked his friend on the elbow as if to help her bear up, and at the same time to encourage her to join him in showing some lighthearted sympathy for the poor widow who had gone off the rails. Semyonova nodded to him and broke into a sad smile.

At last the murmuring and coughing in the hall fell silent, the ushers closed the heavy gilt-decorated doors and drew the drapes. The house lights dimmed, and the curtain swept up, baring once more the gleaming depths of the stage. A Cossack choir sang and danced, waving their sabers in the air.

> *The holy ones of Russia await victory!*
> *Rise to the call, o Orthodox host!*

Steep-sided cupolas gleamed behind and on both sides of the singers, and from backstage came the sound of church bells, chiming in with the Cossack basses. In the depths of the stage, banners and spears were raised high, and the miters on the heads of the priests and bishops gleamed with precious stones. A church processional was underway.

> *Rus raised its head on high:*
> *Thy face shone like the sun's gold,*
> *But victim of foulest villainy,*
> *Thou wert betrayed and sold . . .*

sang the Cossacks, and their trouser stripes blazed in a rainbow of color, their round fur hats cavorted, their earrings danced. The choir parted slowly, opening the way for the procession with the icons, and the sprightly tune fell silent and yielded to a triumphant *kyrie eleison*. As the solemn voices rose in prayer, there came from the depths of the stage a clattering of real live horses' hooves, and a gray steed pranced onto the stage, shying delicately at the onslaught of light and sound, and astride it, the Grand Prince Vladimir in a magnificent crown. Over his chain mail was draped a sable-collared cape.

"Swear allegiance to me, o people! Expand, o Orthodox Rus!" exclaimed the sovereign. The actors' mouths opened wide, baring a sea of scarlet palates, and emitted a great throaty shout, "Hurrah!" And the hall burst into an ovation, echoing them.

And the show went on.

CHAPTER 8

LENOCHKA GAZED OUT INTO THE MORNING. The window was damp and covered with slush. The wind raged and beat against the window frames, clawing the remnants of leaves from the tree branches. Lenochka's cold heel touched Victor's warm calves. He slept, cuddled in a cocoon of covers with his mouth gaping open like a child's. The house was partially wooden, with three rooms and a cellar; it used to be his grandmother's. After her death, a damp old-womanish spirit lingered on, permeating the cotton duvet covers, the lace doily on the television, and the rust-colored photos on the shelves. Old crystal vases gathered dust in the sideboard, and an orange wobbly clown toy goggle-eyed at Lenochka from its place atop the chiffoniere.

It suddenly struck her as strange that she was alive, and that she was a human being, and her name was Lena, and that she was lying here next to a young man, a detective, and this man had brought her home to spend the night with him. That she, Lena, had had a boss, and her boss had died suddenly.

Had been murdered or, per the official version, had died from a ruptured aorta. The other day at work people had been dropping hints that her time in the minister's reception area was drawing to an end. Instead of Natalya Petrovna, a lipless, bald economist with a stern, deeply wrinkled face had been appointed minister. He had his own people and had no need for an assistant.

Her coworkers had been avoiding her. They buried their heads in their papers and averted their eyes, turning their necks as though to spit across their shoulders to keep the devil away. Lenochka was a marked woman. As one of the late Lyamzin's people, Lenochka would be replaced, disgraced, would be cast down into a cramped little office with cheap government-issue furniture. No more bracelets and scarves from the boss, no more bonuses slipping past the payroll office. Her lingerie would wear thin; the last coating of gel polish would chip off her nails; the money for business lunches and karaoke would run out, her mascara would dry up, her boots would get scuffed. Say goodbye to belly dancing, to man-catching lessons. A string of impenetrable, boring days would begin, and every day it would get harder to go home at night, to go in through the spit-spattered entryway of the shabby hulking high-rise looming amid the wooden shacks.

Her mother, deprived of her annual vacations to Turkey (four-star hotel, all expenses paid) would blimp out and go to seed. They would have to live like the neighbors. Used clothing donated by the church, half her salary going just to cover the rent of their communal apartment. They'd be back to foraging for cheap groceries at wholesale markets and scrounging from people's garden plots. Back to the days of scraping black dirt from unwashed carrots, mashing dingy heads of white cabbage to pickle for future use; her fingers would go completely stiff. The cupboard shelves would swell with containers of cherry preserves, her tablet and fur coat would go into hock; a wrinkle would form across the bridge of her nose.

Lenochka did not want to go back to the dark pits. The very thought of her old trolley stop, drowning in mud, made her eyes glaze over. Could it be that she, Lenochka, would be back to counting out kopecks to pay for tickets like ordinary people? Back to patching her nylons, using tea bags instead of fragrant cream to soothe her temples? True, there were people in town who lived worse, in barracks without gas or toilets; they had to go out, rain or shine, to a flimsy, drafty booth in the backyard with a crooked, ill-fitting door that lacked a bolt and flapped open. They balanced precariously over the reeking pit, shivering and swaying in a half-squat, straining their ears in case someone was coming. They gripped the door from inside, yelling, "Occupied! Someone in here!" In winter they tried not to slip on the spilled frozen urine; in the summer, they had to fend off buzzing green flies, bury their noses in their sleeves to avoid inhaling the shit-poisoned air . . .

Yes, Lenochka was spoiled. She had been the assistant of a wealthy man, had collected business cards from his associates, had swept along viciously potholed roads in a taxi, had gone to the best movies, sat in the best seats, and, dining in restaurants with her girlfriends, would casually toss tips onto the table for the handsome waiter with the cute mole on his upper lip. Was it really over? Was it all squalor and poverty from now on?

Victor turned over in bed, mumbling something incoherent, and the mattress springs squeaked, reminding her of the passionate night before. They had burst in after midnight, excited and drunk, had fumbled around in the dark, it seemed like forever, for the circuit breaker, and the creaky floorboards had laughed and sung. Lenochka had played the seductress; she had tipped her head coquettishly to one side so he could see the kidney beans of her nostrils; she had breathed heavily through her nose and moaned, chewed on a thin lock of her hair, which left a woolly taste in her mouth. Victor was insistent, and finished quickly, and afterward walked shamelessly about his grandma's bedroom, wiping his chest with a towel and letting his now limp prick, its hard work done, dangle and flap.

Lenochka didn't recall when she went to sleep, and she regained consciousness early in the morning with a burning, sticky dryness in her mouth. Next to her on the bedside table, the remnants of yesterday's mineral water played in the thick facets of a drinking glass. Its smooth rim was smudged with traces of yesterday's lipstick. The capacity to the bottom of the rim was two hundred milliliters, to the brim, two hundred fifty. In kindergarten the kefir had been brought from the kitchen in tumblers like this; their blanched-out transparent surface swelled up with the fermented milky bubbles. Lenochka lunged for the glass, downed the water in two gulps. A little dumbbell rolled around inside her head, just behind her forehead. She fell into thought.

Tolya had vanished for a couple of days. Just tweeted that he had been summoned to the authorities for a conversation. A tweetstorm followed, with his followers and commentators weighing in. Then a couple of men in civilian clothing came to the ministry and had a conversation with Tolya's bosses in the Business Development Department. This was discussed in hushed voices at the daily briefing.

Tolya had screwed up big-time. He'd reposted on his social media page the scandalous photo of Natalya Petrovna. But the photo had been altered. A crazy doctored image had been patched in. On one side was a shot from Natalya Petrovna's pilgrimage last year to a nearby monastery, to a holy water spring there. The water is bubbling and spraying out in healing streams. Surrounded by monks, Natalya Petrovna holds up a bottle just filled with holy water, showing it to a group of journalists; a light blue scarf flaps up on her head, and her free hand clutches a small icon. On the right side, the scandalous photo has been pasted in: Natalya Petrovna in a corset, legs splayed wide, but instead of the whip, an enormous eight-pointed cross, with its slanted footboard below and a small crosspiece above, juts out of her debauched mouth. "First we bear the cross, then we suck it."

"Why did he do this?" The staffers at the briefing were indignant. "Why?"

"They took into account their appreciation for his work in the youth festival . . ." noted the department chief. "He's getting off with a fine."

"The law on 'Offending Sensibilities,'" clucked the women.

"Yes, offending the sensibilities of religious believers. Article 148, Part 1. And I would ask you not to repeat his mistakes. They are paying particular attention to the ministry these days. And the sports festival is coming up, important guests are expected from Moscow. Maybe even he himself . . ."

The chief's Adam's apple stiffened, his shoulders under the Italian tweed jacket swelled with resolve. Maybe he, too, would be fortunate enough to catch a glimpse of the Guest! There were already some indications it could happen. Special meetings were going on in the governor's office. The mayor was on the warpath over the public utilities; he swore, rushed resolutely from one facility to the next. Repairs continued on the wires that had come down in the rainstorms. The central street was being hastily patched, which entailed sealing the manholes and stormwater grates with asphalt. The citizens cursed and grumbled that after the Guest left, a fleet of mine-sweepers would have to prowl the streets with metal detectors, to clear the gratings and manholes and open them to the light of day.

They knew that just before the official jet landed, loiterers would be rounded up, the streets would empty out, advertising flyers would disappear from the intersections, and litter would be cleared away from the roadsides. Tow trucks would prowl the town, snatching up ugly, rusty old cars and spiriting them off to impound lots, leaving only the most expensive and sleek ones on the streets.

Workers in orange vests would wash the concrete columns clean, would restripe the streets, toss green netting onto the bodies of dying buildings, like water nymphs, to make it look as though there was construction work going on. The sick, moldy facades, pitted with efflorescence, would be sheathed in colorful painted screens depicting windows with decorative shutters against a background of rustic timbers.

The Guest would visit the stadium and the sports facilities that had made such a rich woman of the insatiable Marina

Semyonova. The government officials' faces would be focused and solemn; their lips would writhe, repeating the Guest's every word, as in a prayer service. Inspection of the fruits of tireless labor. Anticipation of praise, dread of reprimands.

They would of course visit Horizon, the area's only thriving industrial enterprise, which produced electric kettles, electricity transformers, interference-suppressing filters, and, most recently, thanks to the efforts of the late Andrei Ivanovich, sanding machines. The workers would be assembled, numbers would be rattled off. The Guest would promise a raise in the minimum wage.

"We continue to make strong progress," he would state approvingly. "The economy is on the rise. We have passed the worst of the crisis. The gold reserves are growing."

Nervous, happy titters and words of gratitude would be heard. The Guest would be bestowed with a pair of blue workers' overalls. One of the workers, flustered, would ask a well-rehearsed question: "How much longer will we have to endure the reeking breath of the monsters encircling Russia? Isn't it time to launch a response?"

"Well, if you will support me . . ." the Guest would flirt, smiling.

"We are with you! Just say the word!" The crowd of burly proletarians would open their gullets and roar.

It had all happened before. The first time, too, the manholes had been paved over, fresh zebra stripes had been painted on the crosswalks. A load of new computers had been delivered to the municipal hospital—on loan for a few days; the pitted linoleum had been suffocated under carpeting, doctors had been drilled on the right answers to give if asked about their salaries. Patients had been stashed away out of sight, and hospital personnel had put on pajamas and occupied the beds. The benches on the central square were hastily repaired, tree trunks were painted white, and tractors rumbled through the streets at night, keeping the citizens awake. Trucks, spewing great clouds of exhaust, hauled in loads of fresh, powdery snow.

The town had spent a week primping, so as to sparkle for a single day, only to plunge back into decrepitude. After the Guest's departure, in the hospital the loaned carpets were rolled up and stored; the computers were disassembled. The crosswalk stripes faded away, the benches sagged, the trash cans again emitted nauseating miasmas from beer bottles.

Lenochka narrowed her eyes. Her dream was to appear in the Guest's field of vision. She would flash her special, enchanting smile at him: first flit your eyelashes oh so slightly and lower your eyes, then turn them enigmatically to one side, and then suddenly shoot a passionate, fiery gaze directly into his eyes. Yes, yes, just get into his field of vision. Dress up as a worker and find a way into the factory, then merge into the crowd gathered there to greet the motorcade. He would fall for her instantly.

"Who are you?" he would ask, helpless with love.

"I am Lena," Lenochka would reply, "Thank you for everything. If you need an assistant . . ."

"I do," he would answer, overwhelmed by her lush feminine aura. "My assistants are such airheads. Come back with me now to the Kremlin."

And off they would go. They would get into the car and sit next to each other, and right there in the darkness behind the tinted windows she would feel his taut muscles, the heat of his rugged torso. Off they would rush together, and Marina Semyonovna would be green with envy. And that would be the end of Tolya's sarcastic remarks. He'd mocked her when she had been crying about Andrei Ivanovich. "Lost your master," he'd jeered. Serves him right; that's what he gets for his cheekiness.

"Who ratted him out?" wondered Lenochka's coworkers. "The photo was reposted at least forty times and they didn't touch anyone else. Why pick on Tolya?"

"It had to be Natalya Petrovna who finked on him," snickered others. "She hates his guts. Supposedly she's getting some kind of medical treatment now. For what, is the question."

"The clap, gotta be," chortled a guy from PR.

"Why are you ganging up on her all of a sudden? You used to be all over her, licking every last hole, and now look at you . . ." Lenochka broke in.

Hisses all around, everyone turned on her.

"Who do you think you are anyway? Just making an ass of yourself!"

"You're next, just you wait and see, bitch!"

Lenochka retreated in a huff. Her knees shook.

Now, lying in bed with Victor, she opened her eyes again and cast a happy, triumphant look over her lover. In the evening they had gone to a khinkali café. The savory meat broth dribbled out of the boiled dumpling pockets onto the plate; he had picked up the khinkali with his bare fingers, scalding them. The dumplings deflated and tipped over onto their sides like parachutes landing in a field. The adjika sauce was speckled with yellow tomato seeds. The sides of the vodka carafe clouded over with condensation.

"This thing with Tolya is no big deal. Now if they were slapping him with Article 282, incitement of hatred or enmity . . ."

He leaned his elbows thoughtfully on the table, just missing a greasy blotch of boullion that had spilled. His golden brown locks framed his face like ears of rye.

"Is that worse?" asked Lenochka.

"More people go to prison for it," answered Victor. "But they're in the hands of the FSB guys. Fun and games. Extremists, terrorists . . ."

"Are they dangerous?" asked Lenochka, rapt.

"Better believe it." Victor slurped the broth, finishing the khinkalis. His cheeks went slightly concave, like a trumpet player's. "They picked up one recently; he'd been plotting to blow up the stadium at the sports festival. An anarchist. They shook him up a little. Next thing you know he's dashing off messages to Moscow, complaints to journalists and lawyers. Like he's some kind of lamb, completely clueless, the charge is trumped up. He says they tortured him with electric shocks, zapped him right in the nuts. Can you picture that? Bashed his teeth in, poor bastard. But what else could they have done? They couldn't just kiss his ass."

Lenochka burst out laughing.

"How did they catch him?"

"They have a whole network there. A cell." Victor smacked his lips and refilled her glass. The carafe bowed, doffing its hat politely. They clinked their glasses. Lenochka held her breath and drained her glass. She exhaled and fastidiously speared a pickle with her fork. Her thin face grimaced. Victor also frowned, chased the vodka with a swig of cranberry mors and added, "They were tracking their communications."

"Can they do that?"

"Sure they can, on social media, V Kontakte," nodded Victor.

"I don't associate with anyone on there," for some reason Lenochka assured him. "Just watch movies."

"About love, I suppose," grinned Victor.

"More like Horror."

"Aha, you should come work with us!" he smiled. "You'll get your fill."

"What's so bad about it?" Lenochka shrugged. "Drunken knife fights? The mail carrier who stole pensioners' checks? Involuntary manslaughter in the kitchen?"

"What would you prefer? Psychos, maybe?" smirked Victor.

"I like it when it's a mystery, no one can figure it out," admitted Lenochka. Her hand twirled a lock of hair, her lips invited him. She knew that Victor was scrutinizing her, imagining her with no clothes on, and she liked it.

"So that's what you're like," he said slowly, and his voice seemed to deepen. "Strange things have happened, I've experienced it. All kinds of things."

"Like what?"

"Well take last year. They found a guy out in the woods, seven kilometers from the cemetery, with his head torn off. Like he'd been run over by something."

"What a nightmare . . ."

"His clothes were torn. Looked like he'd been running

through the woods; there were shreds of his shirt hanging on tree branches, bushes, everywhere."

"So what had happened?"

"No one could figure it out. But the night before he died, the guy had gone to visit his father-in-law's grave. They'd been pals, used to get drunk together. Anyway, so the father-in-law kicked the bucket. And the guy decides to go pay his respects. He picks up a quarter liter, a couple of glasses, and some munchies, and off he goes. They found his motorcycle at the grave. Something must have really freaked him out. Six kilometers through the woods!"

"What scared him so much?" Lenochka's voice quavered. Victor didn't answer, just munched on his pita. His eyes wandered.

Lenochka took a piece of khachapuri. She picked at the pointy edge with her fork, and a gooey strand of melted cheese oozed out, clinging on to the fork.

"You know," she said, without waiting for him to answer, "they say there's this spot somewhere behind your ear. If you press on it, you won't feel hungry anymore. Convenient, isn't it? It's somewhere in the indentation behind your ear . . ."

Lenochka's fingers dipped behind her ear, as though seeking that special spot. But Victor reached out and grabbed her elbow, drew her hand to his lips and kissed her wetly on the wrist, nipping gently at it with his teeth. The kiss sent thin streaks of lightning through Lenochka's body and filled her loins with drops of lava. She leaned over toward Victor, ready to join her lips to his, but he had already released her hand, and had resumed eating. The muscles on his face moved restlessly, like a child's.

"The ear, that's nothing," he said, chewing. "What really works in an interrogation is to treat it like a game. The guys in the police know how to do it, the secret police . . ."

"Like a guessing game?"

"No. Look. You catch some dude. You tell him this and that, we have your bro in the next cell over. Can you hear the groans? Admit everything or we'll shlep you out into the woods, rip off your arms and legs, and leave you out there. For the bears."

"Scare the guy," responded Lenochka.

"No kidding. And if it doesn't work, you get out the stun gun. It hardly leaves a trace, just little dots. Or you whack him on the kidneys with something heavy."

"Like a bat?"

"Even a plastic bottle, you can beat the crap out of him. On his right side. Just make sure it's full of water. The son of a bitch will be peeing blood, and it doesn't leave a trace."

Lenochka recalled the bottle of holy water that Natalya Petrovna had been holding. Maybe the poor thing was already in the convent. Like a disgraced tsaritsa. Wonder how many kilograms a bottle like that holds. Two or three?

Lenochka commented: "Our neighbor said that when he was in the army they beat him with a bar of soap in a sock. And also with an iron in a felt boot. That didn't leave a trace either."

"Soap is kindergarten stuff," Victor assured her. "Here's how you do it: tie the motherfucker up with rope, cover him with a wet towel, and just beat the hell out of him. There shouldn't be any bruising. This cop buddy of mine told me about it. He punctured one Article 282 guy's eardrum. Using an ordinary pencil."

Victor laughed, and the tabletop jiggled under his hands. The carafe chimed like a little crystal bell.

"And there's the 'baby elephant,' too," continued Victor. "Also a fine method. You put a gas mask on the bastard . . ."

"Oh, right, so he looks like a little elephant," giggled Lenochka.

"Yes, it's like a trunk. So you're sealing out the oxygen. Or spray some bug killer into the mask. Let me tell you, it's a scream. Your guy starts to barf, right into the mask."

"Ugh," Lenochka cut him off. "Have you seen it?"

"I saw them tying one up. Folded him like an envelope. Legs behind his back, head down. They used cable, and I helped with the questioning."

"So is it painful?"

"You better believe it! Just try doing the splits without stretching. The guys ligaments are about to rip, he screams. He'll sign anything you put in front of him."

"Do the cables leave any marks?"

"We put a towel underneath," smiled Victor. "Hey, are you recording this?"

In the light of the khinkali café's pendant lamps his face radiated a kind of blissful tenderness, like a child's face at Christmas. He took her hand again.

"Of course I am; I've got wires all over me . . ." she responded.

"So sexy," he leered. His crumpled, greasy napkin dropped onto his empty plate. Like a Japanese crane. Maybe it's true? Fold a thousand origami cranes and your wish will come true . . .

The mattress shifted again. Victor turned his young face to Lenochka, puffy and disoriented from sleep.

"Not sleeping?" he rasped. "What time is it?"

"It's still early," answered Lenochka and reached over to him. He grimaced and moved aside.

"No smooching, baby. I'm mean as a dog in the morning. Don't be mad."

He lowered his feet, warm from the quilt, onto the floor, felt for his slippers, and shuffled out of the room. The morning light illuminated the reddish fluff on his backside. He didn't even turn around when he reached the door. The faucet spat and sputtered. It strained, growled, and emitted a couple of brief spurts like a water hose. A second passed and then there came an even hiss. The water had finally started to flow.

CHAPTER 9

LYAMZIN'S HOUSEKEEPER, TANYA, GOT STUCK in the elevator. The lights went out. The elevator was cramped, and the stuffy air smelled of cigarette smoke. Someone, violating all the rules and regulations, not to mention basic common courtesy, had smoked an entire cigarette in here and stubbed out the stinking butt—as Tanya had noticed when the lights were still on—on an ancient flyer that was posted on the elevator wall. The flyer, which had appeared God knows when, before the last local election, maybe, or maybe it was the federal election, anyway, it was urging residents to go to their local polling place, where they could get groceries at reduced prices. Eggs—two rubles apiece; bread—from five rubles a loaf; chicken—ninety rubles a kilo. During the election campaigns, volunteers from the Board of Elections had gone through the halls banging on doors in an effort to get out the vote. The residents cursed back at them from behind tightly locked doors.

That had been a stressful time for Tanya's boss, Ella Sergeyevna. It's no easy task to ensure 100 percent turnout from the school staff. A meeting of the Teachers' Council was scheduled. Those who failed to show up were threatened with black marks on their record and loss of their jobs. Every staff member had to commit to bring four more people to the polls. The campaign extended to parents. Ella Sergeyevna's nostrils flared with civic zeal.

Ultimately, her fervor and enthusiasm brought results: on election day, the school, which had been transformed into a polling place, buzzed like a fair; the electorate teemed in the lobby and festive red balloons bobbed about under the ceilings. Folding tables had been set out, and a lively trade was underway in vegetables, sugar, woolen mittens, straw sauna switches, and decorative saltcellars. Behind the tables, people emerged reverently out of the curtained booths. On the porch a clown performed various antics, amusing the voters.

The number of ballots was unusually high; each mark nestled in the proper box under the solicitous supervision of the school ladies, their hair done up in beehives, their nails painted magenta. Ella Sergeyevna was summoned to the Party Committee and awarded a special badge. A celebratory feast was planned. Tanya the housekeeper was ordered to bake a salmon and to have the driver deliver it to the school, straight to the principal's office. It was one of Tanya's specialties— scrumptious salmon in rosemary cream sauce.

That evening, though, Ella Sergeyevna grumbled under her breath and arched her tattooed brows petulantly:

"How could you, Tanya! You really let me down this time! You usually get the fish to come out so light and delicate. I bragged about you to everyone. The ladies from the Education Administration came, they were so eager to try it.

And what they got was inedible slops, not the delicacy I'd told them about!"

"It was no such thing," Tanya was hurt. "It's just that you can't find the good Norwegian salmon in the market because of the sanctions."

"The slightest little thing and off you go about sanctions." Ella Sergeyevna bristled. "It's not the food; the problem is you're just lazy. I'll have to get a new cook. Keep that in mind."

And now Tanya was stuck here in the dark elevator, fuming. The darkness pressed in with its terrifying sides, tighter and tighter, threatening to trap her under its arm. The human eye adapts to darkness in sixty minutes. How much time had passed?

The push-button phone wasn't getting a signal. "I'll dial emergency," decided the prisoner, but at that moment the light flashed on, and Tanya's vision returned. Her fingers darted along the worn keys on the panel and pressed the red emergency button. But the dispatcher didn't respond, and the elevator didn't budge. Its rubber lips remained firmly clenched together, and it just rumbled, swaying in the void, buzzing with its invisible cable. Sunflower shells crunched underfoot.

Tanya cursed and pounded her fist on the sticky metal door, which was painted in an orange wood-grain pattern. Somewhere in the distance a dog barked—the old Doberman, black with spots, withering away in the downstairs neighbors' studio apartment. His insufferable whining tormented her every night. She would shuffle downstairs, knock at the neighbors' door, curse at the Doberman; on the other side of the door the dog would growl. The other residents would emerge onto the landing in their robes, giving the whole scene the look of a hospital. One time they even called the police. The officer had protested:

"With all due respect, I have more important matters to attend to. I can't be wasting my time with dogs. If you can't stand it anymore, then just hunt him down and effing kill him. What do you expect me to do? Give him some dark chocolate—he'll croak in three days."

But Tanya sleuthed out a more reliable method. She went to the drugstore and bought some tuberculosis pills, ground them into a powder, mixed in an anti-nausea concoction, and stuffed the poison into a pungent-smelling Polish sausage. The filling showed blood-red in the gashes where the sausage was cut. The cur was doomed. But the plot failed; they couldn't get to the Doberman. The sausage went bad and had to be thrown into the garbage.

"Emergency, hello!" the dispatcher's voice finally came through. Tanya shouted, "Hello! Save me! I'm stuck, call the repairman! The address . . ."

"Do I give a shit?" the dispatcher cut her off.

"Huh?" Tanya faltered.

"Get a life! What are you all worked up about? Our grandfathers went through the war, and you can't spend a single hour in the elevator. I have ten more buildings on the line."

Tanya was stupefied, paralyzed in mute outrage.

"How dare you?" she finally managed to speak.

"I do dare. Just put up with it, don't shit yourself. You are many, and I am one . . ."

Tanya seethed with rage:

"Don't get smart with me . . . Send the repairman over here this minute!"

"Goodbye!" the dispatcher interrupted, and hung up.

"Crazy bitch!" erupted Tanya. "I'll see you in court!"

For a second she thought she was going to faint; the filthy walls of the elevator lost their solidity, they wrinkled and shivered, like cloth. And Tanya saw her son's face, plastered with a shameless smile. He was demanding money.

Her son was a drug addict.

First her father's war medals had disappeared from the apartment. Then the collection of Melchior nickel spoons. Her son was kicked out and ended up in the clutches of a long-nosed slattern. The woman was some kind of singer, or said she was. She sang in a cabaret in one of the wings of the Department of Internal Affairs building. Her act began with her entrance onstage in a traditional Russian folk headdress; at the climax she performed the cancan wearing only a bustier. Her arms were stick-thin and you could play her ribs like a xylophone. She lived on amphetamines and never slept.

Tanya gave her son an ultimatum: either your mother or the drugs, not both. People reported that he'd found work and had even had some success. He wore thin black neckties. Spells of backbreaking labor alternated with furtive binges. Ultimately he crashed and burned. The son returned to his mother contrite. He wept, vowed to reform. He said that he'd left the singer. That the diabolical crystals and powders were a thing of the past. He wore long sleeves, concealing the blue marks inside his elbows. Tanya cleared a place for him on the sofa in the living room—her son's former room was already being rented out to a student. In the morning, when she left for work, she stroked him on his sleeping head. His hair had thinned out, pimples bloomed on his cheeks. Deep wrinkles ran from his nose to his lips, framing his mouth; his shoulders were skin and bones, and the blades poked out like hinges.

When Tanya came home that evening, her lodger, the student, was distraught and sobbing. Her son had gone through all the cupboards and tried to pry open the locked hutch, looking for money. The hutch had been hacked in two with an axe. A picture had disappeared from the living room. It was a print of *The Girl with the Peaches*. There was a pale rectangle on the wallpaper where the picture had hung.

How had her son mutated into this nightmarish stranger? Tanya tried not to think about it. His very existence had become a festering wound. When she ran into his former friends outside, she averted her gaze, crossed to the other side of the street. Her sleep had become fitful and disturbing. She dreamed that her son was calling to her from a whirlpool, and she was riding past on a boat, and he was drowning. His hand spiraled and descended into the vortex. Tanya would wake up with a guilty scream rising in her throat.

She had had a similar dream twenty years before. She heard the sound of an alarm, and colonels with shoulder stripes were dragging her son away by force. The dream recurred. At the time the Draft Board had been after her son. The draft board craved a fresh, young body to throw into the crucible of war. At the word "Chechnya" Tanya's legs buckled under her. She gathered up her chains and earrings, all the gold she'd accumulated over her lifetime, put it all a bag, and took it to the Draft Board. The greedy Moloch of war devoured her offering and spared her. But six months later the pressure resumed, worse than before. Moloch roared back to life, demanding a sacrificial victim. The hunt was on. They could seize him on his way out of the building and throw him into the meat grinder. Tanya rose up like a mountain. She kept her precious boy inside, didn't even let him out to get a loaf of bread. They thought of staging a suicide attempt, to get a psychiatric exemption. But her son was afraid they'd give him enemas.

"They'll poke around inside me with a hose! In front of everyone, the neighbors, they'll totally humiliate me. I'll never live it down my whole life . . ."

They decided to overwhelm the doctors with poetry. Her son stated during his medical examination that he wrote poetry. The psychiatrist asked him to share some, and he declaimed some dramatic Futurist poem. It made an impression on the psychiatrist. The military colossus released the youth, and its clay legs stomped off to the next victim. Tanya recalled how she had ordered her son to lie next to her, had run her fingers through his hair, which was lush and thick back then. And had drifted off to sleep like that, with a death grip on her offspring, what if they came and tried to kidnap him, take him away . . .

Her head was still spinning. Somewhere from above came the sound of male voices and the clanking of metal on metal.

"Help! I'm trapped!" cried housekeeper Tanya, as though waking up.

"Calm down in there, no hysterics!" came a shout.

Liberation was at hand. Something that looked like the bent end of a crowbar came poking between the elevator doors. They cracked a centimeter, and then flew open, and Tanya beheld a pair of mud-spattered rubber boots—the elevator man's. Next to them fidgeted the shoes of a curious neighbor.

"How are you?" he asked with tender concern. "The electricity went out and all the elevators stopped working."

"Managed to stop smack-dab between two floors," grunted the elevator man.

They reached out, grabbed Tanya, strained, and yanked her up with one great tug. She panted and wiped the dirt off her knees.

"Damn it! I just about nearly croaked in there, do you hear me? And that dispatcher of yours is a bitch! Give me her name immediately!"

The neighbor laughed. The elevator man frowned and huffed.

"So that's how it is. You save someone's life, and instead of thanks they want to kill you. Next time I won't bother coming at all."

He gathered up his tools, turned, and made for the stairs. His back disappeared briskly downward, step by step.

"I'll find it out myself! I'll file a complaint!" howled Tanya after him.

She had the sudden thought that the snotty dispatcher might somehow know everything about her and her son. And was picking on her on purpose.

"I can try casting a spell," she thought. The night before, she had heard about a concoction you can make. She'd gone to the clinic to see the doctor and had gotten into a conversation with some other women in the waiting room. First go to church and buy a candle, then use the change to buy some cheap bread at the store. Cut the bread into small pieces using a small knife acquired on the ninth day of the month (she'd have to wait for the right day and go to the store then). Then add in a crumbled Easter Communion wafer, soak everything in holy water, and add seven eggs and a pinch of Maundy Thursday black salt. Tanya already had the theurgical salt, she kept it in a linen bag. On the Thursday before Easter she had heated up the coarse-grained salt on a frying pan, using a wooden spoon to mix it with rye flour until it turned black, chanting, "Maundy Thursday of the Lord! Protect me from every foul reptile and malady."

So now all of these ingredients had to be mixed together, baked into oladyi pancakes and fed to her son. Then, while he was eating them, she had to chant, "I go, crossing myself, blessing myself with the holy prosphora, girding myself with Holy Thursday, melting with the salt. Begone, o toxin, melt into air, never to return. Amen, amen, amen."

But Tanya needed to hurry. She had lost a lot of time already, and she had an important matter to attend to. On her way down the stairs, she had heard a door click behind her; a girl's head had peeked out from the apartment next door and immediately popped back inside. It was Nikolai's daughter; he was the man who'd been killed by the truck. There was a time when Tanya couldn't stand him, him and his snarky wife— their prosperity, their smug little mannerisms. Nikolai's face had still looked fairly young, but his body had gone south. His ears poked out to the side like a sow's, his leather man-purse beat against his flanks, and his fancy car woke up the neighbors. And the wife! Her whole goal in life had been to make sure everyone in the building knew how much swankier their family was than the others. When he left for work in the morning she used to fling open the apartment door, calling out pompously so everyone could hear:

"Kolechka, sweetie, did you forget to put on your tie? The one we brought back from Italy!"

Once the stuck-up bitch had been rushing off somewhere with a girlfriend, and when they ran into Tanya on the stairs, she didn't say a word. Just brushed her in passing with her mink sleeve and wafted a cloud of perfume her way. Her fur coat, tossed on like a snowdrift, gave off a grayish-brown shimmer. Tanya pressed sideways against the filthy banister. But the two snobs just flounced on their way, didn't even notice her.

"The upstairs neighbor . . ." Tanya heard as the voices receded, "her son is a drug addict."

Tanya turned black with rage and launched a toxic glob of spit after the snooty bitch: "A curse on you!"

The spit flew down the stairwell, branding the snobby neighbor with her victim's pain. Let her pay the price for gloating over Tanya's misery! She hadn't noticed anything at the time, just felt a scratching at the back of her head. And then, bam, her husband had died out on the street! And she had to sell her elegant fur coat.

Tanya stood at the bus stop waiting for the minibus. Around her women waddled like penguins. The bus stop seethed with quiet discontent. The PAZ bus didn't come and didn't come. Today Tanya's workday was short, so she had some leeway, but she was in a hurry. She had to rummage around under the Lyamzins' bathtub. The big iron tub with lions' paws beckoned to her like a cradle. The late Andrei Ivanovich used to like to soak in this tub. He'd lie there with the pine-scented foam rising all the way up to his flabby chin, and only the soft carapace of his sleek tummy poked up out of the froth, and little bubbles swelled and popped around his belly button.

"Tanyusha, my robe!" he would command, and she would run over with a waffle-weave robe bearing the logo of some swanky European hotel. The robe had been filched from the hotel like some business-trip trophy.

The night before, Tanya had dropped a diamond ring in the bathroom. It had bounced under the iron paws, clinking its carbonium facets. The ring wasn't hers, it belonged to the lady of the house. Tanya was brewing a plan to steal it.

"I'm no thief," thought she, scrutinizing the numbers on the minibuses as they passed. Now at last hers pulled up, and the passengers mobbed the door. Tanya managed to press her way in and plopped down on a seat with a ripped cover; yellow stuffing puffed out of the cracks. "It's just that I need the ring more; I have a son, and debts, and Ella Sergeyevna is a viper and a greedy cheapskate."

Her war with Ella Sergeyevna had begun shortly before her boss's death. One time Ella Sergeyevna had been getting dressed for a reception at which Marina Semyonova, her husband's lover, was expected to show up. She tried a dozen outfits, one after another. None of them were good enough.

"Bring me the mink!" commanded Lyamzina. Tanya rushed to the walk-in closet and came back bearing a lush, fluffy cloud, which snuggled up to her like a kitten.

"Take it back, you imbecile!" screamed Ella Sergeyevna. "That's the black one, I need the white one!"

"But you didn't say that," Tanya was about to counter, but her mistress hurled her new, wobbly high-heeled shoe at her, point-blank. Ella Sergeyevna always teetered when she walked in those heels, which resembled stalks of some strange giant sea plant growing out of the ocean floor. The projectile hit its mark—it thwacked Tanya on the shoulder blade. It didn't hurt, but the tentacles of humiliation took hold and sent their filthy roots deep into her soul.

No, Tanya isn't the kind of person that some no-good Ella Sergeyevna, some sham pedagogue, can just push around. So what if she tries to butter Tanya up with presents, brings her fancy souvenirs from duty-free after those trips to see her son—a silk scarf, high-class eau de toilette. Let her fly off the handle, then back off, then get all lovey-dovey and call sweetly to Tanya, with open arms, like everything's fine, like there'd never been any screaming and yelling. Just let her try.

With every passing day, Tanya got more and more upset. After a fresh round of insults ("moron," "leech"), Tanya said some spells over a domino and tucked it behind the portrait of Andrei Ivanovich Lyamzin that hung on the wall in the living room. And the picture, from which the distinguished man frowned down upon the room, became pregnant with a secret.

After his death Ella Sergeyevna had gone completely satanic. On Tanya's day off, officials had come to the widow's home and executed a search; they suspected her of something. Now nothing met her approval, everything ruined her mood, everything drove her crazy. On her flabby neck, a blue vein beat wildly in a panic.

The woman threw constant tantrums. An alpaca throw lay on her bed, with a long stretch of nap bristling up the wrong way. Tanya had been tasked with combing it, fiber by fiber, but the wool still poked out in tufts. It was hard to believe that at one time this soft wool had been part of a living creature, and it had roamed through the Andes, had nibbled at mountain grass, had flapped its double lip, flipped its ears in the air. The creature had given its life so that its white wool would adorn Ella Sergeyevna's bed. And now the alpaca's wool had been combed, but Lyamzina glared at it and snapped that she would dock half of Tanya's pay for such sloppy work. In her bitterness she reminded Tanya of an old cup that had been broken at Andrei Ivanovich's wake:

"You're the one who smashed it. It was my mother's! To smithereens!"

Tanya went home that day with a terrible weight in her chest. She seethed with fury. The elevator was broken; the stairs in the entryway reeked of urine. On the third landing, a pair of leaden, powerful hands suddenly gripped her by the throat and slammed her against the grimy wall. They were her son's creditors, mean thugs with bulldogs' faces half hidden in the gray darkness. There were two of them, but only the first one spoke; as they left, he communicated the likely prospect that they would be back. Tanya's neck ached and her temple convulsed. It was then and there that she decided upon her crime.

Ella Sergeyevna kept her jewels locked up in a safe, but a few rings were usually lying on the bedside table. Toward evening the mistress's fingers would go numb and swell up, and hot, red marks around her fingers marked the places where the rings had been. One ring had been forgotten on the nightstand. It shimmered with light; the white stones danced in their tiny platinum sockets. The ring slipped easily into the pocket of Tanya's work smock. By comparison with Andrei Ivanovich's bulky guns, it would be easy to steal. To steal and sell for some real money. Five-figure sums danced in Tanya's head, dizzying her.

The day before, the opportunity had arisen. Atypically, Ella Sergeyevna had not yelled at Tanya or found fault with her work. She lay on the sofa in the living room staring mutely out the window, where wet snow was falling in great flakes. Winter was coming on, and a terrible lump had lodged itself in the silent widow's heart like a toad, and lurked there, croaking. It was the Toad of Dismay and Fright. Ella Sergeyevna had been dismissed from her position as principal. She lay there stunned and limp. Not a peep out of her.

Meanwhile, Tanya slipped into the bedroom, grabbed the mistress's precious ring from the nightstand, and ducked into the bathroom, where she lifted her booty up to the LED lamp to get a better look at the diamonds' facets. Just as she was about to tuck the ring into her bra, into the sweaty fold between her breasts, which were flattened out like two pancakes, she heard Ella Sergeyevna emit a phlegmy cough. Tanya twitched, her insides heaved and shuddered, and the ring fell and bounced under the bathtub. The mistress walked in. The mistress had decided to treat herself to a cold shower. Tanya was banished forthwith . . .

The stop came into view. Tanya clambered out of the van and headed straight into the quiet lane leading to Andrei Ivanovich's house, concealed behind its tall fence. Webcams peered out into the alley. She rang at the gate. Snowflakes stung her face, melting along the way, and she pulled her polyester hood farther down onto her nose.

Tanya was being watched, and not just by the security cameras. Nearby, a three-hundred-horsepower automobile perched by the curb, and, sitting in its cozy, warm interior, Marina Semyonova looked out the window at Tanya. The radio gurgled almost inaudibly in the speakers. Semyonova was waiting for something. She saw how Tanya rang and rang the doorbell, and finally, losing her patience, took out her own keys with a clatter. The door squealed and swung open. Tanya's polyester back vanished through the gate.

Semyonova got out her compact mirror and gave herself a good inspection. The little sponge hovered above the bridge of her nose, ready to make a quick pass over the fine white skin of her face. But suddenly there came a knock on her window. It was the young detective; she recognized him immediately. She lowered the glass wrathfully:

"What are you doing here? Why are you spying on me?"

"You're the one who owes some answers. Why are you spying on the Lyamzins' house?" grinned the detective.

"Who do you think you are?" Marina asked, flustered.

"I am Victor, Marina Anatolyevna. You and I are already acquainted."

"Go away, leave me alone!"

"Ella Lyamzina attacked you in the theater. Now you're lying in wait outside her house. What for? Why? Whatever for?"

"Don't you dare!" Semyonova erupted. "Do you have any idea who I am? I will go straight to your boss, Kapustin!"

The glass slammed up furiously and the motor roared. Outside, Victor was still talking, waving his arms. The smile lingered on his handsome face. His hatless head was freezing under the furious onslaught of snowflakes. Semyonova wheeled the car around.

Meanwhile, Tanya made her way to the bathroom. She figured that the mistress had left for her country house; she'd said something about it the day before. The old security guard had gone AWOL and a new one hadn't yet been hired. The house was empty. Ella Sergeyevna had completely lost her grip, had slackened the reins. As her bitterness grew, her reason grew feeble, and the house fell into neglect. "And here she picks on me for the pettiest things. Counting the strands of wool on the blanket," grumbled Tanya.

She opened the bathroom door and froze to the spot. The bathtub was full to the brim with completely brown water. The ceramic floor tiles were spattered thickly with blood. And above the surface of the water Ella Sergeyevna's head poked up, staring straight at Tanya, dead.

CHAPTER 10

IT WAS MARINA SEMYONOVA'S FIRST BIRTHDAY without Andrei Ivanovich. Her living room seethed with activity; hired waiters in snow-white shirts and bow ties dashed about, gesturing dramatically like orchestra conductors. Lids were swept with great flourishes from enormous serving plates, revealing entire sides of pike perch on beds of onion lined with lemon slices, beef tongue in walnut sauce garnished with feathery cilantro and parsley, baked pork with red potatoes. The dishes breathed steam, like dragons.

Gilded plates and bowls were laden with small open-top pastries with herring and red caviar, rolled crepes, marinated garlic cloves, pickled cucumbers, carrot stars, stuffed tomatoes, eggplant rolls, and all kinds of salads—French bean, pine nut, and roast pear, imported Parmesan.

The guests held out their porcelain sectioned plates, rotating them to receive a variety of hors d'oeuvres. Aged wine bubbled in champagne flutes. Conversations were born and died; loudest of all were the voices of Ilyushenko and a little man who always turned up at this kind of occasion. He had been an adviser to the former governor but now headed some utterly obscure public institution. His hair bristled in a graying crew cut, and a GTO "sports and country" badge gleamed on the lapel of his jacket. As usual, they were arguing about Russia.

"Peter, Peter, at what point did you turn revolutionary? One minute you're living your life, happy as a clam, espousing ecumenism. There's a slight turn of the screw, and suddenly you're leaping up onto a tank! What you're saying is just ridiculous: autocracy . . . what kind of autocracy do we have here?"

"But why did they come after me?" Ilyushenko frowned.

He had been unable to get his bearings after a recent surprise visit by goons from the Internal Ministry's Counter-Extremism Directorate. They had come to question him about appeals for all-Christian unity he had posted on the internet.

"So you're saying that we have to bow down to the Western church?" the goons had pressed.

"What do you mean, b-b-bow d-d-down?" Ilyushenko stammered. "This is about unity of faith among equals under God's commandment."

"But you do understand that they are our enemies, don't you?" the goons persisted. "What you are calling for is collusion with the enemy."

At the end of the conversation they had strutted around his apartment with their elbows stuck out; they complimented the silver clock that hung over the doorway (a present from Marina Semyonova), then made their exit, leaving Ilyushenko in a state of abject terror.

"They came to sort things out," replied the little crew-cut man. "What if you're spreading heresy? Stirring up the masses? It's their job; they have to maintain security. Especially with the sports festival about to start."

"So now I have to sit all night long in fear and trembling, 'awaiting dear guests, rattling like shackles the chains on the doors'?"

Hearing the familiar lines from Mandelstam's poem, the crew-cut man winced and leered, drumming his patent-leather dress shoes on the parquet floor. "Oh, no. I can't stand it! This is the last thing we need. Please, no crazy speculations! 'Chains on the doors' . . . It's some kind of fad you've picked up, going around scaring people. Enough of these bugaboos — Stalin, the year 1937 . . . It's downright laughable!"

"Well, it wasn't the least bit funny for me." Ilyushenko twitched his nose, offended. "I sure didn't feel like laughing."

"What did they do, rip out your tongue? Send you off to Siberia? Here you are lolling about in the best company, drinking French wines, dining on roast grouse, and you have to jump on the bandwagon and cause a panic. Peter, Peter . . . I assumed you had more brains than that."

Marina Semyonova, her face flushed, perched herself on the armrest of an enormous chair next to the crew-cut man. She was wearing a sparkly black dress, and an exquisite necklace glimmered in her deep décolletage.

"Are you on again about politics, boys?" she asked reproachfully.

"We're talking about you, Marina Anatolyevna, about you!" The little man beamed and draped his hand lasciviously around her waist.

"We are talking about . . . the predicament I'm in," blurted Ilyushenko.

"Oh, that . . ." Her eyes dulled momentarily, then she beamed. Someone had called her name; a new gift had arrived. She fluttered up off the armchair and darted to the door to greet the newcomers.

The crew-cut man's eyes followed her for a few moments, spellbound. Then he picked up where he had left off, as though nothing had happened. "Well, judge for yourself. Take Stalin's staff shake-ups, for example. What was that like? A complete bloodbath! One guy gets his head chopped off, then another, a third, and an entire family is hauled off and shot. What do we have here? Some minister or governor gets caught with his hands in the till, and it's all off the radar—no muss, no fuss, no one lays a hand on him. Maybe someone gets fired—that can happen. Or maybe someone gets hauled off to court. But then it fizzles out. Zilch, diddly. The son of a bitch might even get transferred to a new job, one that's no worse. Rainbows, butterflies, and unicorns. 'Life has become better, comrades. Life has become happier!'"

"All right, but take your basic Ivan Ivanovich . . ." Ilyushenko began, but the man wasn't listening.

"Humanity in general is becoming better. Overall, on earth as a whole. People aren't getting their guts ripped out; no one's being shot or hauled off to the gallows. Except maybe in the Middle East. But even there, there's no comparison. Take a look at *A Thousand and One Nights* . . ."

"What's with the literature lesson?" asked Ilyushenko. "No one's getting hanged, but that doesn't mean people aren't terrified. Why did they come after me? I know I'm not the bravest guy in the world, maybe I am too wrapped up in my own problems, but don't look at me like that—this is no laughing matter. Instead, tell me, why this concern for security, this focus on invisible enemies like in the old days? They're afraid of phantoms, but they're going around terrorizing actual people, citizens. Me! They're terrorizing me personally!"

An enormous basket of red roses was brought into Marina Semyonova's living room with great ceremony, generating a wave of excitement that drowned Ilyushenko's lamentations. The birthday girl skipped and hopped along in its wake, clapping her hands like a child.

"They're from the mayor!" she announced.

The basket, which was of staggering dimensions, became the center of attention. The guests crowded around, and there was a great clicking of iPhones. Semyonova laughed and posed, the golden necklace radiating sparks from its nest in her cleavage. Ernest Pogodin abandoned his glass and fell into a kind of artist's trance, contemplating the picturesque scene—the beauty sniffing the roses—his head tipped slightly like a bird's, the white knob of his cane gleaming between his knees. Chashchin, the theater's artistic director, kept repeating rapturously: "There are easily five hundred of them, no less. I have an eye for it. Believe me, this is way beyond what actors get."

The construction firm executive flashed his dentures in delight; the manager of the Wildflower Aesthetic Clinic, a woman of indeterminate age whose lips had been inflated into a pair of sleek cylindrical bolsters, focused her cellphone lens on the basket and exclaimed hoarsely: "Whoa sister, get a load of them roses!"

When the excitement died down, the little man cried: "You see, Peter? Everyone is happy! No one is afraid!"

"What's this all about?" Pogodin was curious.

Not without a note of triumph, the crew-cut man gestured at Ilyushenko. "Peter here thinks someone's going to squeal on him!"

Guffaws all around. The beauty clinic manager's puffy lips parted, and her shoulders quivered in mirth. Marina Semyonova administered a loud, jokey kiss on Peter's forehead. "Don't be afraid, Petya. Why get your knickers in a twist? Nothing's going to happen to you."

"Nothing?" Ilyushenko shot back. "What do you mean, nothing? Something sure happened to Lyamzin. And his deputy. And his wife, too."

"Shh, shh . . ." Hisses came from all sides. "You'll ruin the party."

Chagrined that he'd let himself run off at the mouth, Ilyushenko fell dumb. He stood guiltily stroking the massive cross that hung over his belly.

"Relax. Don't worry!" The hostess soothed her guests. "I know that's all anyone can talk about, about poor Ella Sergeyevna. I personally have nothing against her. I even wanted to make up with her. But I was too late."

"Who ratted on her?" asked Chashchin, extending his glass to a waiter for a refill. Everyone started talking at once.

"The school . . ." Everyone had a fact to share. "Teacher . . . fired . . . her husband . . . She slit her wrists . . . The maid found her . . ."

"I've got people squealing on me, too, and I couldn't care less!" declared Ernest Pogodin, looking up from his boiled shank roll.

"What, you, too? What could anyone say about you?" Marina Semyonova flirted.

"That I debauch boys, my models."

That stirred up the guests, who'd been getting too serious.

"Ha, ha, ha!"

"Boys!"

"Right there at the easel!"

"A pedophile artist!"

"You got it," nodded Pogodin, appreciating the attention. "Recently I did a portrait of the governor's wife. And during one of the sittings she comes out and says, 'Ernest, if I'm to believe the rumors, you are completely depraved; I would not allow you to paint my son.' Quote unquote."

"She bought the slander?" whispered Chashchin.

"Whether she did or not," snickered Pogodin, "the lad had already signed up for a portrait. Decked out as a cadet."

The guests sat side by side at the table, rapturously devouring the refreshments. Their molars ground and pulverized; their canines chomped; their incisors bit and tore.

"It was terrible what happened to Ella Sergeyevna," Chashchin confided, masticating. "Completely unexpected, to be honest. She was a real tough one. Like a bulldozer, that woman. Must have been the psychological shock. You've seen the YouTube videos that people took in the theater. Quite the bitch fight. Ten thousand views! The filth, the language! People like us—creative artists, public figures—we're used to that kind of thing, but what must it have been like for a peaceful, decent public servant like her?"

"I looked into this thing, wrist-slitting," Pogodin noted, taking a loud swig from his glass. "Did you know, for example, that the blood's velocity through the vessels is forty kilometers an hour? That's just insane."

"And?"

"Picture how it all just poured out into the bathtub—five liters. She basically drained herself out completely."

"Yes . . . I feel sorry for their son," sighed Chashchin. "An orphan, alone in the world."

"Completely loaded, though. Set up for life." Pogodin winked.

The living room grew lively again. New guests arrived: the prosecutor Kapustin with a bouquet and a mysterious little blue box tied with a ribbon, along with two detectives. One was the guy with the mustache who had questioned Lyamzin's widow about the history teacher. The other was Victor.

"I'm here with my entourage," announced Kapustin, and, kissing the birthday girl, he murmured into her ear: "I have received the money and the papers."

Semyonova nodded approvingly. The waiters bustled about, brandishing wine glasses and directing the guests to the refreshments tables.

"Forgive us for coming late," said Kapustin in his bass voice. "We were at the movies. Our entire team, so to speak."

"Why the movies?" snickered Marina Semyonova.

"Under orders," clarified the mustached detective. "They had us go to a patriotic Russian film. Very inspiring."

"On the eve of the sports festival," interjected Victor.

Indeed, the town was festooned with banners. The festival was to showcase traditional folk games. The competitions would begin on the main town square, then various events would be held in sports facilities all over the region. Athletes had been invited from China, Zimbabwe, Turkmenistan, and Venezuela. With all the excitement, the governor had taken to adding several drops of hawthorn extract to his evening cup of chamomile. The mayor was racked with insomnia. The minister of tourism and sports had lost two kilos from worry.

The little man, who had been arguing with Ilyushenko up to this point, suddenly spoke up. "Let's drink to Marina Anatolyevna! Our precious treasure. The manager from her construction company is here tonight. These fine people, ladies and gentlemen, have poured their energy into rejuvenating and modernizing our town. They've built an ice arena, a new bridge—and all of this has come about thanks to the vigor, brains, perseverance, and of course beauty of our very own Marina Semyonova. Well, as Horace said, 'Life grants nothing to us mortals without hard work.' And she is our hard worker. My dear, I wish you health, love, and may there be, well—you know what I mean—no more tragedies!"

Glasses clinked, the naked cupids cavorting on the ceiling were overcome with emotion, and the guests succumbed to a sweet tipsiness. Marina Semyonova tapped her knife handle against the stalk of her wine glass, silencing the room.

"I have a proposal. Since we're all gathered here together, let's play a game!"

"What a scamp! I'll pass, though," Ernest Pogodin said immediately.

Ilyushenko perked up. "What do you have up your sleeve?"

"Don't you drag me into any games," said Kapustin, his mouth stuffed with food.

"Actually, as chief prosecutor, you'll find this extremely interesting," said Marina Semyonova. "The game is called 'bringing the sphinx to life.' See, I take a match and place it on Petya's eyelid. Like this, right above his eyelash. Now Petya, make sure you don't blink."

"How am I supposed to keep from blinking?" asked Ilyushenko, to general laughter.

"Petya will be the sphinx," she explained. "I have to try to say something that shakes him out of his complacency so he lets the matchstick fall, see?"

"If that's your goal," drawled Chashchin, "all you have to do is yell *hey* at the top of your lungs. That'll do the trick."

"That's just it. I can't. You're not allowed to raise your voice or wave your hands. You have to keep your hands in your lap."

Marina Semyonova sat on the elegant stool opposite Ilyushenko, as the game prescribed. The guests gathered around, so as not to miss the moment when the sphinx would get rattled and drop the matchstick.

"Now then, Petya," she began. "Thank you for coming to my birthday party. I thought you might have been so scared about the counter-extremism guys that you'd completely lose it. Yes, of course there are haters out there—I'm not going to deny it—but no one is scheming to drive you to your grave. Though I'm sure they could come up with a reason if they wanted to."

Ilyushenko sat perfectly still.

"Do you know what people are saying?" She lowered her

voice to a near whisper. "That supposedly you're not into the ladies, Petya. Know what I mean?"

Scattered chuckles.

Ilyushenko's knee twitched, but he remained stoic. On his eyelashes the matchstick quivered like a candle flame.

"What do you have to say for yourself? Stallions and warhorses all around, just one gentle nag for the ladies," Semyonova pressed on, her tone gentle, her words cruel: "You see a nice-looking boy and think, *What a cute widdle bunny wabbit, gonna shag 'im through the back door.*"

The guests lost all restraint and guffawed raucously. Ernest Pogodin wriggled his sideburns mirthfully and let fly: "Bugger! Bum chum! Queen! Pansy! Fruitcake! Gayboy! Faggot!"

The matchstick quivered, then toppled into the folds of Ilyushenko's cassock.

"That's not fair!" he flushed. "First of all, you're all ganging up on me. Secondly, I'm not allowed to say anything. What kind of game is that—just sit here like a fool while everyone beats up on me?"

"The sphinx has come to life! The sphinx is alive!" purred the birthday girl, ignoring her friend's protestations.

"Your turn now, Marina Anatolyevna," said Kapustin, savoring his dry red wine.

"Fine!" Shooing Ilyushenko off, she settled down in the armchair. "Give me a matchstick! Who is going to try to wake me up?"

"Oh," muttered Chashchin. "What wouldn't I give for a chance like this?" And he plunged his fork into a serving of horseradish aspic.

The mustached detective stood up. "Let me give it a go."

A piece of dill had gotten stuck to his mustache, which gave it the look of a bare hedge in winter with just a single green leaf poking out. The smile vanished instantly from Semyonova's face.

"You're not allowed. You have an unfair advantage!" the woman with the sausage lips squealed saucily. But the hostess took up the challenge.

"So be it. Here goes."

The matchstick was perched on the pedestal of her semi-permanently mascaraed and curled lashes. The detective sat down facing her.

"Allow me, Marina Anatolyevna, to express my deepest admiration for you," he started out with vague platitudes. "You are an extraordinary woman, that's for sure. We all know how much the late minister loved you. And if there is a next world,"—he looked upward, and the guests tipped their heads back and gazed up at the flock of angels on the ceiling—"he's regretting that he cannot wish you a happy birthday as usual."

Victor was sitting by the grand piano, and his fist accidentally slipped onto the keyboard, producing a mismatched do and re in contraoctave. The matchstick on Marina Semyonova's lashes twitched and tipped, but held.

"We know it's not been easy for you," the detective raised his voice. "Your beloved was by your side, but at the same time not with you . . . Tell me, were you the one who sent him the anonymous letters?"

The guests murmured and stirred. The sphinx's eyelashes wavered and dipped, and to a chorus of oohs and aahs, the matchstick tumbled to the floor.

·"You're such a joker!" Kapustin shook his finger at the detective. Semyonova tittered and hunched over awkwardly with her hands pressed to her lips, leaving lipstick smears on the soft tips of her fingers. Victor applauded for some reason.

But at this point the lights went out. Ernest Pogodin sat down at the piano and plinked the notes to the familiar melody. The guests chorused:

Happy birthday to you! Happy birthday to you!
Happy birthday, dear Marina. Happy birthday to you!

A cart glided slowly into the living room, bearing a luxurious, five-tiered cake, proceeding tentatively, like a bride. Each tier was lined with a dense, magical forest of confectionary candles whose flames quivered, sending enchanting shadows scurrying along the delicate, creamy icing petals of the cake's airy bluish-beige sides. On top, a coffee-colored chocolate inscription read, *Happy Birthday, Dear Marina!*

The cake wheeled up to the birthday girl, where it halted and curtseyed like a ballet dancer in a tutu before a fairy-tale queen. Deeply moved, Semyonova leaned over to make a wish, and in the gaps between the candles could be glimpsed the sparkling of her dress, a piece of her chin and neck, and the beguiling cut-out triangle on her full bosom. She exhaled, extinguishing the candles, all except one, whose little flame swayed for one more second in mortal agony before it, too, died, plunging the room into darkness.

The overhead light came on, and everyone squealed, gathering around the extinguished cake, which stood like some exotic beast in a trap. One of the waiters brandished a huge knife. In its mirrored blade the guests' faces, the room's cornices, and the cherubs on the ceiling flashed and jerked. The knife plunged amorously into the cake's soft, spongy insides like a swimmer into a pool, soiling itself in the cream, luring lovers of sweets.

A line of guests holding dessert plates coiled around the cake cart. When they received their servings they stepped back, transfixed like blind men, salivating. Victor indulged himself without the slightest restraint, his golden brown forelock grazing his spoon. Chashchin stood to one side, eating alone; he leaned low over his plate, kissing the cake like a woman. Ilyushenko went for seconds, getting tangled in his cassock along the way.

The waiters circulated, repeating their refrain, "Tea or coffee?" Surrounded by guests, Marina Semyonova flipped through the mass of fresh photographs on her phone. The alcohol had kicked in, infusing her movements with a sluggish languor.

"Music! Music!" she demanded.

The band struck up one of the latest dance tunes. The birthday girl stepped out into the middle of the room, her dress shimmering like a snakeskin, undulating with her movements. A ring of bodies formed around her. The rhythm determined their movements—spurred them on, quickened them, prescribed their patterns. Victor flicked his fingers dashingly, the little man with the crew cut launched into the twist, and the Wildflower manager twerked her sensuous derrière.

She danced up to Marina Semyonova and took her hands: "So, babe, how is it going?" she asked. "Are you thinking about your Andrei?"

"Actually, not anymore," giggled Marina. "I've fallen in love with another."

"O-ho-ho! Tell me right this minute, who is he? Is he here, at the party?" The pillow-lipped aesthetician burned with curiosity. Her paws encircled Semyonova's waist.

"I'm not going to tell you. I'm not . . ." Semyonova gathered up the hem of her dress and whirled around her axis. The music changed to a slow, swaying love song.

"Slow dance time. Ladies' choice," announced Ilyushenko, finishing off his third piece of cake.

Marina Semyonova went up to the prosecutor and gave him her hand. Kapustin flashed a flattered, lascivious smile. They went out into the center. They began the dance, and the others gazed on, entranced.

CHAPTER 11

THE JOURNALIST KATUSHKIN AND THE teacher Sopakhin met in a cafeteria. They clattered their worn plastic trays, scratched with knife marks.

"Get a move on!" commanded the serving woman. The crown of her toque swayed like a tightrope walker over an abyss.

The diners obediently sped up, hastily taking the plates with chicken and noodles, borcht, chicken Kyiv with a mound of mashed potatoes, mimosa salad with salmon and mayonnaise, and glasses of thick, warm kisel. The cashier's hands dexterously tossed the plates onto the scale and clattered the cash drawer open and shut.

"Next! Look lively!" shouted the cashier's lips.

After paying, the customers grabbed napkins and headed for the utensil rack to pick up bent aluminum knives and forks. They stepped carefully, balancing their trays and dodging the rag mop, which the adept janitress was briskly flopping across the floor, and settled down at the tables.

"No way," said Sopakhin, hunched over his bowl, which was empty except for a soggy piece of black bread. "I will not say one bad thing about Ella Sergeyevna Lyamzina."

"I understand," nodded Katushkin, "de mortuis aut bene aut nihil."

Katushkin was a plump man with a pair of small round glasses perched on the bridge of his nose. He was in an old jacket, which he wore winter and summer.

"It's not about the moral side of things," Sopakhin frowned, and the sleeves of his sweater, with its faded squares and diamonds, also suddenly creased, as though in solidarity with their master. "I'm already under a stay-at-home order as it is. Plus a fine. You know yourself what my sentence is."

"You need to protest! The school principal, you know, engaged in litigation and appropriated budget funds, and here you're the one who's answering for it. On a fabricated charge."

"No, no, no . . ." mumbled Sopakhin, "I am not going there. And plus, Ella Sergeyevna is also a victim. I'm alive at least, whereas she . . . I have a lot of people picking on me right now. The mayor is about to tear down a park that was built in the nineteenth century. The only one in town. They're building a business complex there. The people are getting all worked up, trying to get me involved, but what can I do? I'm under investigation!"

"The right thing to do would have been for Lyamzina to pay the fine for you. A half million wooden ones! That's nothing for those moneybags."

"Well it's moot now anyway," Sopakhin brushed it off. "The main thing for me is to get my life together, figure out how to make a living. My wife is threatening to leave and take my daughter with her."

"After the search, you mean?"

"Basically, yes. They barged in at night, broke down the door. And now my daughter can't get to sleep. My wife moved in with her mother. And I'm a criminal. And unemployed. And in debt to boot."

Sopakhin heaved a ragged sigh. His chest sagged, and a long convex fold formed on his sweater, turning the diamonds into equilateral triangles.

Katushkin glanced around at the people munching and slurping around them, at a boy who had erupted into a tantrum and was writhing like a worm on the cold, freshly washed floor tiles. At the pretty young Asian girl in a chiffon apron who was clearing the abandoned trays from the tables. A smile hovered at the corners of his mouth. He was an energetic guy, this Katushkin. At some point in the past, a perpetual motion machine had taken root in him, something like a cigarette lighter or a power cell, a nano-motor that hummed constantly, doing and making things. "Can't sit still," people sneered behind his back; "got a wild hair up his ass."

"But still," he wasn't giving up, "what was it that upset the detectives so much?"

"I . . ." Sopakhin hesitated. "I don't want to say anything about the kids; they supported me. I've been fired, but the students come to see me, and they came to the jail, too. They're asking me to help them prepare for the end-of-school exams; they'll pay me. I'm getting tutoring jobs."

"What are the complaints against you, then?"

"One girl, a tenth-grader, recorded part of my class about the Great Patriotic War. And supposedly I defamed our history. But the main thing was Russian History Week. That was open to the public, so it's a more serious charge and the punishment is worse."

"How did you 'defame history'?" Katushkin pressed on.

"How? Well . . ." Sopakhin blew his nose into a coarse paper napkin. "I was lecturing about the Molotov-Ribbentrop Pact. The joint occupation of Poland by Hitler's troops and the Soviets. How we brought the Baltic republics into the USSR. In short, the annexation. First Estonia, Lithuania, and Latvia, then Finland . . . Anyway, they added that to my case, too."

"They think it's a falsification?"

"Yes. There's this one detective with a mustache. He has a gentle, friendly way of talking. But the other two—they're real brutes; they even whacked me a couple of times. When I objected to something."

Sopakhin reached for his glass of kisel. A fly was drowning in it. He tried to scoop it out with the handle of his soup spoon. The kisel quivered like a live thing and clung to the handle, refusing to yield its victim. The fly was tossed onto the corner of the table. Its wing swayed feebly.

"But how could they object to the facts? What could they say?" Katushkin pressed.

"The usual. That I'm slandering the Soviet state. That the nonaggression pact was a victory for our diplomacy, that it delayed the war for a while. That we saved Poland and the other countries, too. We were the liberators. That Stalin, despite all the excesses of the repressions, was an effective manager."

"So they are admirers of the generalissimus then?" Katushkin fluttered like a bird.

"Not at all," answered Sopakhin bitterly. "Their point is simply that you must never under any circumstances equate

Stalin with Hitler. Or else you're rehabilitating Nazism. And that's a crime. Anyway, they say that I was equating them."

Sopakhin lifted his glass to his thin lips, exposing its ribbed lower edge, and took delicate sips of the gelatinous kisel.

"So what are you going to do now?" asked Katushkin.

"Nothing. I have to find some money. On top of everything else my door has been desecrated. Someone painted 'Fascist' on it. Apparently the neighbors."

"Why 'Fascist'?"

"What do you mean, why? To them it's self-evident from my arrest."

Sopakhin was tired of answering questions. He nervously picked at the pills on his sweater sleeve. His eyes darted in all directions. He looked at an old woman who was masticating a sweet roll with toothless gums. Her skull gleamed through her scant gray hair; brown patches of pigment splotched her forehead and temples. The old woman had just bought this roll with a fistful of coins and had asked the cooks for a glass of hot water. A used tea bag she had snatched up from someone's tray dangled in the glass, clouding the water around it a rusty brown. The old woman was destitute; her pension didn't cover her expenses. Her face expressed detachment, hunger, irritation, tender piety, ecstatic emotion, resentment, humiliation, irritation, belligerence, and resignation. A half of the roll would be eaten; the other would go to the pigeons. Pigeons are doves, the Holy Spirit, bird of God.

"Listen," said Katushkin, leaning over to Sopakhin, "I'm trying to understand. So Minister Lyamzin dies. Out of fear, intimidated by an anonymous informant, right?"

"Could be," responded Sopakhin uncertainly. The big toe of his right foot felt at his disintegrating shoe. A hole had opened up between the toe cap and the sole. Like an open mouth.

"All right," grunted Katushkin, "so the minister was being blackmailed. But for what? For his affair with the gold-digger Marina Semyonova? But that was common knowledge, people just ignored it. Or maybe the anonymous letter-writer threatened to spread the news about how Lyamzin and his lover were siphoning off some kind of capital from the national budget?"

"Giving her tenders, contracts? Yes, I heard something. I read it in your paper, actually, in the *Siren*," nodded Sopakhin.

"So the minister croaks, bam, and the investigation combs through all of his data and hidey-holes. Which leads them to Semyonova, too, right?"

"Most likely."

"But Semyonova was a queen already, and that hasn't changed. She still has the construction company. The bank accounts and real estate, too. But in the middle of it all, there's this dirt on his deputy. A god-fearing woman, in thick with monasteries, and all of a sudden . . ."

"BDSM" Sopakhin interjected.

"Precisely, a photo with a whip. The deputy, who was inches away from her late boss's throne, now in utter disgrace, cuts and runs. Dissolves into thin air."

"Nervous breakdown," noted Sopakhin.

"Moving on. Next, a stone gets thrown into your garden. With Ella Sergeyevna's name on it. There's already enough to lock her up, with all the shady dealings and scams in the school principal's office. Not to mention her husband's real estate holdings abroad, under fake legal entities. But no one even hinted at any of that. She was interrogated in connection with Article 354. You're in the same file with her."

"You think they're connected?" Sopakhin sounded skeptical.

"Why not? Look. Lyamzina is fired. Insult to injury, she attacks her husband's mistress, Marina Semyonova. And accuses her of snitching. You can hear it on the video of the fight."

"Yes," Sopakhin nodded. "Someone ratted on her, wrote that she supposedly threatened to kill this lover of his."

"'Someone wrote . . .' So that same someone makes a habit of ratting on people, are you following me?"

Sopakhin observed Katushkin. The man was sweaty, animated. His glasses were slipping down the crest of his damp nose, like children sledding down a hill. Dark patches appeared under the arms of his jacket. His shoulders shifted impatiently.

"So who might this mysterious plotter be?"

At these words, Katushkin actually bounced up in his chair and pounded his fists on the table.

"That's it, precisely! That is the question: Who? Or maybe there's a whole group? Squealing all over town, it's some kind of maelstrom, an epidemic! Over the last month alone, fifteen denunciations of foreign agents have come in to the Ministry of Justice. Fifteen!"

"Agents in different agencies?"

"Yes, the Association of Ecologists, that's one; the Center of Labor Solidarity, two; the Hard-Labor Prison Museum, three; the Independent Legal Aid Society, four;

and on and on, I can't recall them all. The claim is they didn't report to the Ministry of Justice about money they're getting from abroad. One failed to submit a report; another neglected to post their label as a foreign agent on their website."

"Broke the law, in other words," noted Sopakhin grimly.

"Right you are, I understand the logic. Let the people know that these shady gangs are not striving for goodness and truth; they're just earning their Eurodollars!" Katushkin emitted a little cackle. "And that's not all; they loosed the dogs on me, too."

"Why you? Are you a spy, too?" asked Sopakhin morosely.

"Yes, they're trying to stick me with a charge that I'm a foreign spy working through the media. They denied me accreditation for the sports festival . . . But that's just . . ."

Katushkin suddenly erupted in convulsive laughter; he writhed like a rubber ball with the air being let out, guffawed and jerked his knees, attracting attention from the other diners. Many looked up from their plates and cast alarmed glances at the man's inappropriate display of mirth. A woman with warts on her face, vast as a water tower in her bulk, hissed a rebuke as she swept past:

"Sir, pull yourself together!"

Katushkin immediately placed his finger to his lips, as though to demonstrate his full intent to comply. His twitching subsided at last, and a single tear squeezed out from under his glasses lens and trickled down his left cheek. At that point Katushkin extracted from his pocket an enormous checkered handkerchief, none too fresh, and, having wiped his glasses, blotted his face. It was still flushed, as though he'd been out in the sun. Sopakhin asked:

"Do you really get money from over there?"

"That's just it," answered Katushkin in a voice still distorted after his fit of laughter, "I work alone, with just a couple of guys helping. It's just a small, independent little site. We get funds through crowdfunding, that goes into an open account."

"And?"

"Well, it came to light that our donors include some foreigners. This nice woman from Odessa. And they got all worked up. Launched a full-scale excavation! What's the point all that digging, over a measly thousand rubles? A pathetic sum."

Katushkin brought his thumb and index finger into a circle, squinted his eyes to demonstrate how pathetic. His hand took on the look of a parrot's head, in profile, with a gaping oval hole for the eye and a quivering crest of feathers.

"What do I have to do with it? It's not about me!" continued Katushkin, "I'm just curious as to what's going on; why all the excitement? Center E has sprung into action . . ."

"Well, they're always up to something," Sopakhin muttered, "they were always coming over to lecture my students. To warn them to keep away from hostile sites that attack government officials."

"Aha, yes, right," nodded Katushkin, "They do that. They've come up with lists of activist citizens, yes, that's true. And they've gone around to their homes to warn them. To the tune of, 'If you spend too much effort advocating for your rights, we will send you off to prison, to be a fuckboy. Lousy social justice warriors. Jackals, losers . . .'"

He giggled again and, as though trying to get himself under control, honked loudly into his handkerchief. Sopakhin looked over at where the old woman had been sitting. She was gone. In her place an Asian woman in an apron was wiping down the table with a sponge. Crumbs, puddles of tea, crushed noodles, everything swooped into the trash can.

"Take your trays, no loitering!" commanded the cafeteria server in the distance.

The culinary tongs clicked like castanets. Thus equipped, the server's hand looked like a crab's pincer. She tossed the cutlets onto the customers' uplifted plates with the gracious gesture of a goddess of plenty. Her countenance was intimidating but her hands were generous. The people moved on, their faces expressing a compliant, focused bliss.

Katushkin continued:

"My point is that after Andrei Lyamzin's death, not a day goes by without a search, suspicions. Who are they targeting? Basically everyone, indiscriminately."

"You mean to say," said Sopakhin, still sulking, "that this whole series of events is one man's doing?"

"Not entirely," Katushkin bit his lip. "This anonymous letter-writer sort of set the tone, you see? And the town took up the tune. You know what I mean? A trend, a fashion. Fashion is a controlled epidemic, as someone once aptly noted."

At this last phrase, a family appeared, rising up like a cluster of mushrooms. The man a morel, the wife a boletus, the children little chanterelles.

"Are you intending to stay in this spot forever?" barked the woman. "There's no place for people to sit, and here these guys, feast your eyes, have chowed down and are hogging the whole table!"

The assembled diners again pricked up their ears and turned to cast accusatory glares at Katushkin and Sopakhin.

Ai-ai-ai, how rude! Taking up public space for no useful purpose, how could they! Sopakhin twitched nervously on his chair but Katushkin rose to the challenge: "Calm yourself, madam!"

She was evidently working on a comeback, and undoubtedly things were about to go downhill, but a distant table opened up, and the husband dragged her away. The family vanished.

"What people!" Katushkin slapped at his knee. "Where was I? Oh, right, Prosecutor Kapustin. I'll tell you a secret, I'm working on a monster of an article. It's about a deal I'm sniffing out between the prosecutor and this Marina Semyonova. Something like a bribe in exchange for her freedom, and peace and quiet."

"Suspicions are not enough in a case like this," noted the teacher.

"Well, it's as clear as day; I have the documentation. Dug it up with the guys. We've already posted an announcement about it on the *Siren* site. Stocks for the seltzer water plant. They used to belong to Semyonova, but now Kapustin has them. Presto! Next: Ten hectares of land under construction outside the town line. Semyonova used to own it, but now it belongs to Kapustin's mother-in-law. The town needs the land for growth, so there's a deal to be made. Now: Kapustin's wife's latest acquisition—a diamond-encrusted watch. Posted on her Instagram. We found out what one like that costs— it'd blow your mind. Multiply the prosecutor's salary by one hundred."

Katushkin sputtered and snorted, he was so eager to spill all the dirty facts; but Sopakhin remained listless and unmoved. His face displayed complete indifference.

"I have a student coming over," he interrupted the over-excited journalist. "I have to go do some tutoring. You understand, I'm sure."

His chair scraped against the tiles. The teacher squeezed into his coat.

"Of course, yes, yes. I apologize for taking up your time." Katushkin collected himself. "I have to go, too. They're unveiling a monument on the square near here. I'm going to take some pictures."

They left the borscht-infused air of the cafeteria and went out onto the busy street. The inrush of oxygen set their heads spinning. The shop signs rippled, exchanging visual shouts like peddlers arrayed along both sides of the road selling their wares. A tree's roots swelled up under the asphalt, splitting it into ridged cracks. Sopakhin stepped over them like a superstitious child. Step on a crack, break your mother's back.

"What monument?" he asked. "I've not been keeping up."

"Haven't you heard about the controversy? A monument to Peter and Fevronia. At first they wanted to put one up honoring a local military general, I don't remember which one. You must know, as a historian. Anyway, so then people started proposing a bust of the last tsar. They're doing it in other regions, how are we any worse? But ultimately they settled on Saints Peter and Fevronia. The bishop gave his blessing."

"Aha, family values," Sopakhin nodded. "But why are they doing it in the fall? Isn't their saints' day in July?"

"It was supposed to be in July, but it dragged on and on . . ." clarified Katushkin. "Where are you headed? To the crossroad? I'll walk you that far. As for Peter and Fevronia, my relationship with them is extremely complicated."

For the first time in their conversation, Sopakhin broke into a genuine smile. As though in response, a city bus clattered past, beeping; on its sides a crowd of colorful children brandished hockey sticks—an ad for the sports festival.

"What kind of relationship can you have with saints?" he grinned broadly.

"I'm an Orthodox believer. But those two are not my peeps," Katushkin answered, seriously. "Take Peter for example. First, his brother the Murom prince is not a real man; he's a wuss. This fiery dragon flies in to his woman every night and has his fun with her, up, down, and sideways. And he's like, whatever. And that's just for starters. He gives her advice: when the dragon comes for his fun, be all lovey-dovey, and get him to tell you what he thinks is going to cause his death."

"Well, he was being clever. What should he have done?" Sopakhin wasn't following. "That's how they learned how to kill the dragon. And the princess wasn't running around behind his back; the dragon basically raped her—disguised as her husband."

"First of all, it doesn't add up that it was rape. She was all over the dragon, coming on to him. Secondly, she did see him in his real form. Can you imagine what that was like? To sleep with a reptile like that? Complete depravity!"

"I'll grant you that. But what is it about Peter that you don't like?"

"From where I stand the man's no saint. Just look at the circumstances . . . He chops the dragon in two, right? He's stained with dragon blood, covered with stinking scabs. Anthracnose, must have been. And this voodoo witch, or sorceress, turns up and volunteers to cure him. On the condition he marries her. Just think—a peasant hag! If she'd been a saint, she would have declined any gifts or favors, would have cured him, no strings attached. But no. She just had to be a princess! Now Peter, he's no fool, has no intention of marrying her. By the way, the source says nothing about her looks. Meaning, this Fevronia was a dog."

"You don't say!" Sopakhin burst out laughing. The fresh air had cleared away his despondency. The day was cold, but dry and sunny. The mud at the curbs hadn't turned to slush but had dried, forming a sandy flat surface, etched with tire-tracks and footprints. The wind whirled Katushkin's sparse fringe of hair and blew into his mouth, chilling his tonsils. But he was on a roll. He raised his voice, competing with the honking of cars stopped on the street.

"I'm telling it like it is. A hideous witch! So what if she's young? Imagine how diabolical and calculating she'd have to have been to cure his whole body but leave one wound there on purpose. So that the ulcers would come back."

"Now listen here!" Sopakhin halted in the middle of the sidewalk. "She did it to teach him honesty. Or else, look, he'd be cured, but would pull a fast one and violate his vow."

"He had the complete right to after her trickery," Katushkin took him by the elbow. "She put it like a question: Either marry me or rot alive. Drove the guy into a trap. And then later he was glad to be rid of her. Remember how his brother died and Peter became a prince? And the boyars rebelled, upset that their princess was a commoner."

"Yes, and they proposed that he load her up with treasure and banish her forever, and to marry a girl from the nobility."

"Precisely. But he's waffling, it's neither yes nor no, he's dreaming of getting rid of his wife, but he's chicken, like, what will she do to him if he does? Maybe change him into some animal? A horrible story, just horrible. And that's our model for family values!"

They had arrived at the crossroad. Here their paths parted.

"That's all; I'm off to the left," said Sopakhin.

"It was good to talk. Let's be in touch."

The teacher and the journalist said their goodbyes, shook hands, and went off in opposite directions. After a couple of paces Katushkin turned into an alley to take a shortcut. The courtyards thrummed with their inner life. A woozy wino sprawled against a garden fence. A woman in a window was hanging up laundry. Children poked around in the mud under the carcass of a broken merry-go-round.

Katushkin passed a garage, where he heard a mechanical voice; someone was watching TV and working on a car. His feet carefully skirted a puddle that had been there for an eternity. The puddle was swollen. In its depths lurked forlorn, rejected objects: a torn galosh, a pair of blackened fifteen-kopeck coins, necks of broken bottles, handles from plastic bags, a length of twine in a state of almost complete decay. A wobbling board formed an improvised bridge over the puddle. On the other side a curving path led through to the next street.

Having overcome this obstacle, he heard the rustle and whimper of resolute footsteps behind him. A sudden sharp blow behind his knee threw him off his feet. A firm shoe came down hard on his ear. A second assailant knocked him senseless with his boot. Katushkin's head imprinted itself in the wet earth. His glasses gave an ominous crack.

"Who? What? Help!" howled the victim, but a new volley of punches silenced him and twisted him into a writhing lump of flesh.

His body flailed and coiled, contorting itself in its attempts to escape the kicks. His knees strained to touch his forehead. His elbows squeezed into his belly button. The victim was putting up resistance. He wallowed in the crusty mud like a bug that had fallen onto its back. His curses turned into a groan. He bit his tongue and it throbbed with pain; his pummeled sides stung. Pink bubbles trickled out from his lacerated tongue and lips.

"Listen, asshole, if you scribble anything about the chief prosecutor, you will be a thing of the past. Got it? Capeesh?" one of them rattled off.

"Six feet under, hear? Stinking squeaker!" chimed in the second. Curses churned in his mouth.

Someone walked past—Katushkin heard a rustling in the bushes, a muffled exclamation.

"Help!" he rasped, but the invisible passerby, terrified, scurried on his way. The muscleheads couldn't care less. They pummeled Katushkin on the ribs, extracted a promise:

"You going to scribble or not? Yes or no?"

"No, I am not," hissed Katushkin. His numbed tongue felt a shard of something in his mouth. "A tooth?" The thoughts tumbled erratically through his brain. "Can I afford a dentist?" The assailants continued to batter him with their feet. Reality transformed into a dumb, flickering picture. A broadcast interrupted by static. Everything went dark.

"You will write a retraction! Got it, pussy? An apology on video! And no! More! Articles!" growled the goons.

A woman's shriek was heard; someone had noticed them and started to wail. Katushkin felt one last parting kick on his back, his consciousness ebbed from his half-closed pupils. The knuckle-draggers retreated, leaving the trampled reporter writhing in circles from the pain.

They made their way out onto the crowded street and hurried toward the square, to where the crowd had gathered. There, looking across the citizens' heads they could see the monument, covered with a sheet. Cameras and video cameras chirred at the plinth. The mayor was giving a speech. Individual words could be heard—"loyalty," "chastity." The women in the first rows hoisted their gurgling infants overhead for all to behold.

The bishop stood next to the mayor. His palitsa glistened at his thigh.

And when the thugs' ragged breathing subsided, a momentous, solemn act was accomplished before them. The veil dropped away, revealing the figures of Peter and Fevronia. Under Peter's heel the soaring dragon heaved its dying breaths. The assembled multitude erupted in applause.

CHAPTER 12

LENOCHKA AND TWO OF HER FRIENDS came out of the movie theater holding big paper cups with popcorn kernels rattling along the bottom. The ushers obligingly held their garbage bags open and the cylinders flew in with a gentle clatter.

"So scary! I nearly peed my pants!" babbled the shorter, pudgy one. Freckles peeped through the toning concealer that had been applied to the wings of her nostrils. The girls' stilettos clicked loudly.

"Oh, come on, I wasn't scared at all, we should have gone to a comedy instead," the second girl countered, blowing aside a lock of brown hair that had fallen over her eyes. "At least we could've had a good laugh."

"No, there were some scenes in there . . ." said Lenochka. "For example, when the boy turned into a zombie and attacked his mom. Did you notice the guys behind us? They were scared shitless."

"You mean when they poked their knees into the backs of our seats?" snorted the brunette. "They just wanted to get to know us."

"If they wanted to, there was nothing stopping them," pouted Pudgy.

There were still a lot of people in the mall. Behind the shop windows, salesclerks floated like fish in aquariums, and mannequins—some missing their heads—gawked blankly out at the shoppers. Here fashion was distilled to its quintessence, and everything was aimed at persuading people to doll themselves up. The consumer didn't stand a chance.

"Oh, how I'd love to have that hair styler," sighed Lenochka, stopping in her tracks.

"So buy it already!" smirked the brunette.

"I have one already, I don't want to just throw it away . . ."

They came up to the railings caging off the great cavern of the escalators, with their accordion-pleated steps, and caught a glimpse of the activity on the floors below. All the lower floors looked like exact copies of the one they were on. Mise en abyme.

"Do you know the horror story about the shopping mall?" asked Pudgy, out of nowhere.

"Which one? Is it also about zombies?" smirked the brunette.

"Not exactly. A guy I know told me. A true story. He felt like having a beer one night but there weren't any left in the fridge. So he remembered the twenty-four seven supermarket in the mall."

"This mall?"

"Yes, ma'am. The one in the basement. Anyway, so he comes here. But things feel a little off. The security guard at the entrance has a strange look to him, and the cashiers, too. Anyway, he goes down the aisles, but there's no beer anywhere. Goes down one aisle, then another one. Takes a closer look, and what the hell? Nothing but empty boxes. No actual stuff in them. So now he loses it, tries to find someone to ask, or get to the exit. But it's no use!"

"So what happened to him?" Lenochka was scared now.

"He disappeared and that's all there is to it. He starts walking along the wall. He reaches five corners, turns each time, but still no luck. Suddenly he hears this woman's voice yelling from behind a shelf: 'Help! I'm lost!' He tells her: 'Let's go together and follow the shelf till we get to the end.' But no luck. The shelf just goes on and on. And the woman's voice says, 'I've been in here a whole month, can't get out. And there's no cell reception.'"

"Get out of here!" giggled the brunette. "So how did he escape?"

"He saw the security guard and started running over to him, but the guard bent his head so far out of shape that it was obvious he wasn't a man at all but some kind of hologram. A computer thing. With a hole on the top of his head. Our guy hawks up a big juicy glob of phlegm and spits on him. At this point the hologram closes in on itself, the wall opens up like a pair of sliding doors, and he manages to jump out. You can't drag him back to this mall for anything."

Lenochka laughed: "That's not a horror story. A horror story is when you really can't tell whether it's true or made up. For example, see that kids' play space over there?"

"Yes, and?"

"One time this woman brought her four-year-old here, left him to jump around on the trampoline while she went up to the second floor to buy herself a leather jacket. She comes back in an hour and a half, and the kid is gone. The workers there swear up and down that they've never seen her before. And claim that they had never signed the boy in. She calls the police, but they don't believe her—they believe the workers in the play space. They said she'd offed the kid herself, and then was trying to shift the blame to people who had nothing to do with it.

"So then what?"

"So then two weeks go by, the woman is losing it, and she gets a call from an unfamiliar number, and they say, 'You posted that you lost your son. And we've found him on the bypass. He was standing there by the side of the road, crying. We recognized him from the photo.'"

"But how did they track down her number?" asked the brunette. "Did the boy give it to them?"

"Maybe they googled it using 'lost boy, shopping mall,' who knows?" Lenochka frowned. "Anyway, so they bring the boy, and he's got a scar running all down his side. They did an ultrasound and it turned out he was missing a kidney . . ."

Pudgy grunted into her fist: "Well, if they were organ harvesters, how come they turned out to be so decent? They took out one kidney, then sewed him back up neatly. He still has the other kidney. And his spleen, and whatever else is in there, too!"

"Maybe they weren't killers," objected Lenochka. "Maybe they weren't organ dealers, but just a family whose kid was dying and he needed a kidney. And the boy was the right match."

"You're insane," commented the brunette. "Forget about it, let's just go have a drink."

They turned into a bar on the same floor and found a table in the corner. The only other customers were a couple of pairs of lovebirds and a group of scruffy-looking men.

"Not a single man worth a second look," observed the brunette. "For that you have to go to Moscow. That's where all the bachelors over twenty-five are."

"Yes, by thirty all our guys are potbellied and have a whole litter of piglets," griped Lenochka.

Pudgy sighed. "What, have you got something against children?"

"No, I'm just in a bad mood right now," complained Lenochka. "I've been demoted. They stuck me in Purchasing. I'm telling you, it's the pits."

"What a prima donna! I'd kill half the town for a job like that," noted the brunette, blowing at her pesky lock of hair.

Her finger ran blindly up and down the drink menu.

"Right, piña colada, sex on the beach . . . have you decided?"

"I've had sex on the beach," confessed Pudgy, though no one had asked. "In Turkey, on vacation. Ladies, you should have seen that Turkish guy! Huge eyes. Showered me with compliments every day. 'Me heart,' he'd say, 'no pit-pat wiz-out you.' Can you picture it?"

"We've heard that story," Lenochka said dismissively. "All right, I'll go for a bloody mary. Fits the mood."

"Oi, oi," the brunette perked up. "I've heard about that one, it'll knock you out. My boss tried it in Cambodia. Rice liquor made out of tarantula, can you imagine?"

"Tarantula the spider you mean?"

"The actual spider! They kill him fresh. And they bring another one for you to eat with your drink. Costs three dollars."

Pudgy winced. "No, I'll just go for a good old mojito."

A few minutes later the pockmarked waiter brought their order. A cucumber disk perched on the rim of Lenochka's glass. Her lips puckered around the straw.

"I haven't seen my Victor for a few days now," she announced.

"Where'd he go?" asked the brunette.

"He says he's really busy. Only answers every other text. Yesterday I texted him 'Sweet dreams,' and he answers: 'You too.' With a period at the end."

"No smiley faces?" asked Pudgy.

"No smiley face, no heart. Nothing, basically. Cold." Lenochka's voice trailed off.

"Before that," she went on, "we made a date for after work. He writes me at six that he's held up, he'll get back in touch in forty minutes. And that was the end of it, zip. I wrote him back in an hour, like, 'Sup?' He didn't read it right away. Then he read it, but nothing."

"Whoa, really?" said Pudgy, not without a tinge of smugness.

"Then twenty minutes later he writes, 'Poopsie, I don't know when they'll let me go, I'll text you.' So what about me over here? I fixed myself up, put on a nice dress, and now I'm just supposed to sit around and do nothing? I sat in a café till ten, hoping he'd send word. Downed an entire liter of tea."

"And?"

"And it's already ten, and I'm just sitting there sobbing. Then I get, 'Hey there.' Woke up, I guess. So I write: 'I'm with some friends, hanging out.' So he doesn't think that I'm just moping around because of him."

"So then what?"

"He texts, 'So they'll walk you home then. I'm tired as a dog. Straight into the shower and to bed.'"

The brunette grimaced. "So he didn't even come to give you a ride home?"

"No, I had to cough up the money for a cab, otherwise, you know, I'd have to walk home, in the middle of the night, in my sketchy part of town . . . Better not take the risk. The worst was, I got this moron driver. Kept driving around in circles. Tried to get my number."

Lenochka's phone bleeped and she grabbed at it, lifted the screen to her eyes; her misshapen iris flashed in the LED light.

"Not him," she said, disappointed. "It's my mom."

"Fuck him, this Victor of yours," Pudgy frowned. "He's obviously a wham-bam-thank-you-ma'am type of guy."

"He's not like that!" protested Lenochka. "He's just super busy. They have a lot going on in the Committee right now. And plus, he called me poopsie. It's sweet, isn't it?"

"Poopsie-doopsie," muttered the brunette. "Get rid of him. He's just using you, playing hard to get. Basically, a douchebag."

Over at the scruffy guys' table, one of them, who had been sitting with his back to the girls, stood and rose up to his full height. He was gangly. His body had the look of a carnival barker on stilts.

"Tolya!" exclaimed Lenochka. "I didn't see you!"

Tolya nodded, shifted awkwardly from one foot to the other. His usual energy had disappeared, leaving only a kind of jittery restlessness in his limbs.

"Come join us?" asked Lenochka.

Tolya sat down at their table. The girls eyed him from their corner, giggling.

"Hey," he said hollowly. "These your friends? I'm Tolya."

Introductions. The brunette gave her name and took to slurping up the last drops of her cocktail. It gurgled loudly. She waved to the waiter and lifted her finger, like, bring another glass.

"I'm out on bail, I signed for it." Tolya jumped straight in.

"Out for long?"

"Until the trial. With luck they'll acquit me."

"What exactly did you do?" asked Pudgy.

"Posted a photo on my page. Of the boss lady," mumbled Tolya.

"Aaaah, right, it went viral," noted the brunette coldly. "Anyone who's anyone downloaded it."

Lenochka clarified:

"Tolya did the photoshop. In the original the boss is holding a whip in her mouth, and in his picture it's a cross. They are calling it blasphemy."

"That's not true, Lena, I'm not the one who did the photoshop! I don't know who it was. I saw it on a friend's phone and reposted it. That's all I did."

"'First we bear the cross, then we suck it.' That's your style, isn't it? Or not?" Lena dug in.

"What do you mean, 'my style'? I didn't do it, I'm telling you."

Tolya scowled. Not all that long ago he'd been living the life. His uncle had palled around with the local movers and shakers; from his childhood he'd been friends with a very important person who was in the governor's inner circle. This very important person had granted his uncle some land in a protected forest. The uncle took on the role of master hunter and was constantly hosting high-ranking guests there—former athletes, security personnel, gangsters, goons, bigshots, racketeers, and fat cats, men transformed by a stroke of fortune into generals, ministers, and helmsmen at the wheel of state. Even the governor, even the inspectors from Moscow, even they came out to his property for R & R. To commune with nature, partake of their motherland's natural bounties.

The guests fished and hunted on a grand scale; they shot fowl, moose, hares, and boar. They dragged the carcasses across the white snow, leaving dirty crimson tracks, and the dogs rushed wildly in circles around them with their tongues hanging out. While the campfires were being set up and the cooks' team skinned, dismembered, and chopped up the meat, Tolya's uncle would heat up the bathhouse with his own two hands and settle the weary hunters and fishermen on the hot limewood benches. He would slip armfuls of medicinal juniper twigs under their bright heads, and would lash their sleek thighs and backs with a birch switch. Tolya, his indulged, favorite nephew, would manage the steam. The red-hot coals hissed under the flow of water poured expertly from the ladle. The guests groaned and begged for more. One of them would suddenly rush out and dive with a primeval shriek into the icy tub; the freezing water bit, stung, bristled against his overheated body. Back in the bathhouse vestibule, while the princely banquet was being prepared, vodka gurgled in glasses, crabs turned red, girls frolicked about. Under their wet towels could be seen the rounded contours of their naked breasts.

It was there that Andrei Ivanovich Lyamzin, with hands sticky from chitin husks, with a felt cap on his head and a chest damp with coniferous bathhouse sweat, noticed clever, gangly Tolya and secretly nicknamed him Tapeworm. Then and there the uncle persuaded Andrei Ivanovich to take Tolya on and find him a place in the ministry.

So Tolya was in. Tolya began to go around to youth rallies and congresses. In Moscow Tolya saw famous singers and top government officials. They spoke from the stage, and Tolya stood in crowds of chuckleheads like himself who'd been trucked in from the provinces, and cheered with all his might: "YES! YES! YES!"

Tolya found himself behind the wheel of a Mercedes. And his uncle had already started talking up a girl he'd found for him to marry—the daughter of that very same important person, a graduate of a fancy master's program abroad, an Instagram queen. Tolya tasted additional stratospheric blessings of fate, but shortly before Andrei Ivanovich's death, the very important person was unexpectedly arrested for embezzlement—a billion rubles of state funds. Tolya's uncle was left without a protector and had to make himself scarce. The wedding was called off. The sword of Damocles hung overhead. The uncle's hunting establishment teetered on the brink. Tolya's moment of glory had come to an end.

"I've given a lot of thought to the whole situation, tried to make sense of it all," said Tolya suddenly. "And I figured it out. Marina Semyonova ratted on me."

"*Oho!*" Lenochka stirred.

"Semyonova? THE Semyonova?" asked the brunette, sipping at her second margarita.

"Who else could it be? First of all, I know, people told me she saw me somewhere with Andrei Ivanovich and then called me a 'worthless string bean.' Something about me set her off."

"Does she like anyone at all?" interjected Lenochka.

"Obviously only herself. That's the way it is. And there was something else, too, it happened a while ago. I'm in this swanky restaurant. I look over and see Andrei Ivanovich with her, with Semyonova, at a table on the other side of the room. They're just sitting there, no big deal, everyone knows about them. But then they get into some kind of argument and she throws her napkin at him, thwack, right on the nose!"

"Oho!"

"I'm telling you! She jerks her chair away with a clatter, jumps up, yells something, she's screaming. Hysterics, basically. So I grab for my phone and start filming."

"Show us!" exclaimed Lenochka.

"Yeah, right. The hell-hag saw me. And one of Lyamzin's thugs was sitting nearby at a corner table, eating. She sicced him on me. To make me erase the recording. So I did."

"Then what?"

"She took off. Lyamzin stayed. Anyway, it was awkward, and I tried not to look at him. He's my boss, after all. And in an embarrassing situation. Humiliating. Why am I telling you this? She's out to get me, that's why."

"Like you're even on her radar," mumbled the brunette.

"The main thing is," added Tolya hastily, "it happened the day before Andrei Ivanovich's death."

Lenochka flushed bright red. Electric currents coursed through her thin brown hair, sparks of static across her skin. A hundred-ampere arc ran from one shoulder to the other. The toxin that had accumulated in a secret sac under Lenochka's pink tongue spurted out into the open:

"I'm sure of it, she's the one! Just put two and two together: everyone's getting ratted out, and there's Semyonova up on her high horse! It's got her name all over it. Andrei Ivanovich's wife kicks the bucket. Slits her wrists in the bathtub from depression, and meanwhile what's this slut up to? Out on the town—the theater, parties! She never loved Lyamzin, never!"

A black lump lurched in Lenochka's throat, the straw twirled in her glass and aimed to smack her in the chin. The bartender glanced over at the noise, stroking the beer taps like puppies.

"I hate her," said Lenochka hoarsely.

"She's already got a new boy toy," noted Tolya.

He looked around at his companions, but they had forgotten him and were hooting over something, watching the silent flat screen over the bar. Legs shod in soccer shoes ran across an expanse of crisp, dark green grass. A dozen or so legs and shoes had gotten tangled up together and tumbled like a centipede onto the ground. The official blew his whistle, and the players' faces expressed utter despair. The stands howled mutely. The ball flew out of bounds.

"Who is it? Tell us!" Pudgy was all worked up. "Who's she seeing now? The governor?"

"I heard it's Kapustin," winked Lenochka.

"No way! I saw them myself—in the elevator, at that same restaurant."

"The restaurant again? You sure get around, don't you?" smiled the brunette.

"My uncle took me. I mean, not me, the lawyer. We met, the three of us, to discuss my case. Anyway, I had to, excuse me, go take a leak. Number one. And the restroom is at the far end and you have to walk past the VIP rooms. And there's a separate elevator in that hallway, specially reserved for the people who use those rooms. So I step out into the hallway, the elevator doors open, and there's Semyonova. And she's not alone—she's in there smooching with a guy."

"Smooching!" the fat girl squealed.

"Who with?" gasped the brunette.

"Kapustin?" laughed Lenochka.

"It's not Kapustin, I'm telling you! It was a guy! A young guy! And there they are, sucking face, and evidently with no intention of coming out of the elevator. I wasn't going to let this one slip, and immediately started filming. On my phone! I only got three seconds. First it was all blurry but then came into focus. Hah!"

Tolya was jubilant. The bones at the base of his palm rocked back and forth, drumming some unknown, triumphal song on the tabletop.

"Why? What are you, some paparazzo? Why bother?" The brunette persisted. Her forelock dipped into her cocktail and congealed into a sticky icicle.

"What do you mean, 'why bother'?" rattled Tolya. "I did nothing wrong, and here I am under investigation. To hell with her! A she-thief and swindler, running around loose with pretty boys, not a care in the world. Effing ho."

"Let us at least have a quick look at your video," said Lenochka eagerly.

Tolya got the phone out of his pocket and ran his fingers

over the screen. The icons flashed, a folder opened, and a short video swelled up and filled the screen. The girlfriends hunched over the screen, their foreheads clumped together like three fingers about to pick up a pinch of something. They gawped at the lovebirds. Semyonova was wearing a jaguar-pelt coat, her hair was pulled up into a high do, and its locks spilled over her temples as she gave in to the lover's ardent advances. He greedily gnawed into her neck, his face buried in the jaguar collar. At first the picture was blurry, but then it suddenly came into focus, and Semyonova's beau looked up and pressed his lips into his enchantress's. His golden brown curls flew back from his high forehead, exposing an attractive profile, and with horror Lenochka recognized in the mysterious stranger kissing Semyonova her very own, dearly beloved Victor.

She recalled an incident from her childhood. It was a hot summer day, the dandelions were in bloom. The air was filled with fluff from the dandelions and poplar trees. It clogged her nostrils and sprinkled the earth with what looked like cotton seeds or shaggy cocoons with baby butterflies ripening within. Lenochka took some matches from the apartment and went down into the courtyard to where the kids were playing, to set fire to the fluffy carpet. A blue flame ran along across its surface, leaving a covering of black spots in its wake.

One time a girl showed up in the crowd of kids, a little neighbor. She had come back to town from her grandmother's place in the country, and she was wearing an impossibly delicate dress, ephemeral like a cloud. The girl babbled on and on, and whirled around like a little goat. A piece of fluff got caught in her eyelashes, and her eye filled with tears, but her hand couldn't reach her eye to wipe it away. The girl had a stump in the place of an arm. It had been bandaged up. Her mother later explained to Lenochka that a local policeman had chopped off her arm because she'd taken some candy from the jar, and the image congealed into a viscous horror under her heart that Lenochka bore for a long time afterward.

Another time her father had come, drunk, to pick her up from the playground. He was unsteady on his feet, in a jolly mood, and ready for a good time. He'd bought a huge, venomous-looking crimson cloud of cotton candy. The way home led past the train station, and he got an urge to pop into a filthy beer bar, where some of his old drinking buddies had gathered in a merry crowd on the porch. Their hands with the fingernails fringed in black patted Lenochka on the head. One seasoned drinker reached into his pants pocket and extracted a snow-white lump of sweet sugar, which he handed her with an exaggerated bow. The former builders of socialism stood around the tall bar tables laden with heavy yellow mugs of malty brew, foamy heads spilling over the rims.

Lenochka tried to get her father to leave and take her home, but he just got drunker and cursed at her. The drinking buddies cursed and bellowed with laughter. A feeling of dread came over Lenochka, and she went outside and stood under the awning. There, a band of semihomeless street boys loitered, smoking. They stared at Lenochka with amused insolence. The wildest of them, in a cap tipped rakishly down over his forehead, kept his bag of glue sealed around his mouth and nose. The bag breathed, swelled up like an attacking frog.

"So, daddy left you on your lonesome?" he barked. "Come live with us, you can spend the night on the heat pipes."

Lenochka's teeth chattered with fear.

Another time Lenochka was riding the bus with her mom. There was a traffic jam, and the passengers' bottoms and sharp-cornered bags pressed into her face. Chicken legs and cans of green peas poked out of the bags. The crowd cursed and yelled. Paper money passed overhead as the passengers paid their fares. Suddenly someone, she couldn't see who, grabbed Lenochka's hand tightly. Her heart raced. Her fingers, trapped in the person's grip, jerked in panic, but she was too scared to cry out, to call her mother. Her hand was forced through the metal zipper in someone's fly, pressed against something soft, hairy, and disgusting.

"Lena!" snapped her mother. "Our stop is next."

In the cramped bus, bodies pressed in on all sides, sharp elbows poking into flesh. For another moment, Lenochka's hand continued to twitch and struggle, and finally, with a mighty effort, it broke free. Her fingers tore themselves out of the stranger's shameful private nest, and the flow of passengers expelled her into the open air. The raped hand felt disgusting and vile. Lenochka felt like crying but she was terrified of her mother. If she were to learn about the shameful incident, she would have beaten her senseless with her shoe.

Now the sight of Victor kissing Marina Semyonova's lips gave her that same feeling—nausea and chills up and down her skin.

"It's Victor," she said.

"Victor who?" Tolya didn't get it.

"Victor, Victor, THE Victor!" squealed Lenochka and, knocking Tolya off his seat, rushed out of the bar. Her cocktail glass toppled and shattered on the floor.

"Hey!" yelled the bartender. "You out of your mind? Pay for the glass!"

Everyone in the bar craned their necks and gawked. Pudgy clip-clopped out after Lenochka, leaving the bewildered Tolya alone with the brunette.

"Hey, stop!" she yelled. "Stop, Lena!"

But Lenochka was already racing down the escalator, knocking people out of her way, generating a chorus of hisses. Her coat hem whipped out on all sides. Her bag knocked people in the knees. She rushed out through the revolving door and found herself on the street, fraught with the mystery of the advancing night. Two building facades gleamed, illuminated from below. Central Street. Families strolled along the sidewalks. Music filled the air. Lenochka was overcome with terror.

CHAPTER 13

THE WILY FACILITIES MANAGER OF THE regional art museum had been issued significant chunks of money for repairs, three different times. He swore up and down that they'd redone the parquet. But the floorboards persisted in squawking like sick roosters. Two boards were particular offenders. They were right at the entrance into the formal hall where the temporary exhibits were mounted, and every time someone's shoe stepped on them, they emitted an insufferable shriek, like whipped dogs. And on this particular day there was a plethora of shoes. It was opening day: an exhibit of works by portrait painter Ernest Pogodin. In the far corner, two violinists and a cellist worked magic in the air over the polished wood instruments with their f-shaped sound holes. The bows floated sleepily over the strings, as though they had just awakened and were stretching.

"Welcome! Please come in!" The museum director, a woman at the very pinnacle of her prime, with a mop of pin-curled hair, bustled around the hall. Little drops of sweat glistened in the cleft between her nose and upper lip—the place kissed by an angel—signaling the importance of the occasion.

In the middle of the hall stood a long, narrow, intestine-like table with a row of crystal goblets standing in formation like a line of soldiers. Carbon dioxide gases frolicked in their transparent, shapely bellies. Champagne was being poured.

The portraits eyed the proceedings from under their brows, tilting forward and swaying slightly on their thick wires. Like a fleet of warships, they emerged from the smooth surface of the plaster walls; their baroque frames gleamed like the barrels of polished cannons. In one of them, the local internal affairs minister, dressed like General Kutuzov, frowned in half profile. Two medals on ribbons crisscrossed his chest; a saber handle poked out to the side. The governor's wife sat enthroned in another frame, in the pose of the Princess Yusupova; a black velvet neckband adorned her throat and a cute lapdog was curled up in her lap.

Faces looked down from each canvas: government officials, singers, and athletes, along with their wives and children, all arrayed in uniforms, sailor suits, tournures, and ball gowns from prerevolutionary days. And in the middle of the hall, frowning like some fantastical monster, a monumental portrait presided over the proceedings: the president of Russia decked out as the peacemaker Tsar Alexander III astride a white steed, surrounded by his retinue. Most prominent in the retinue was the regional governor mounted on a dapple-gray horse. His general's epaulets gleamed in the sunlight; his cockade radiated a swashbuckling whiteness; clouds of dust whirled up under the horse's hooves.

Ernest Pogodin appeared at the opening for some reason without his customary cane but in an ornately patterned brocade robe over a traditional Russian shirt and wide Turkish trousers. He had been supplied with an escort, a beanpole of a girl with remarkably long legs. These stunning legs were revealed through the slit in the girl's scarlet dress with every step she took.

Pogodin introduced her. "Angelina," he said. "An up-and-coming actress."

It was no secret that Pogodin had been married some five times and was supporting a dozen or so kids from various women in different towns. His last wife had fled; his artsy exertions had been too much for her. Rumor had it, Pogodin forced her to use special sheets, pillowcases, and duvet covers with her own image on them when she made up the marital bed; portraits from Pogodin's brush were printed on specially ordered bed linens. This particular wife plumped up the pillows and was then banished from the home. Onto the bed sprang a herd of torrid young naiads. And while Pogodin savored Dionysian pleasures atop his wife's various countenances, the actual, real-life wife roamed about under the windows, submissively awaiting the orgy's end.

A microphone shrieked in a frenzy of feedback. The guests clutched at their ears as the rebel was brought under control. The minister of culture approached the microphone with springy steps. His calves twitched with excess energy. His toned shoulders radiated strength. With brash pride he scanned the hall: over there the museum director advanced, eyes brimming with love; over there domesticated reporters from the local news media, their sweaty shirts harnessed in camera straps; over there the bulldog-like faces of government administrators, bowing floorward before the grandeur of the portraits; and, sprinkled throughout the crowd, the ubiquitous connaisseuses of the arts, ladies whose charms had faded an eternity ago.

"Ernest Pogodin is our Dalí," began the minister. "He is our mirror and our chronicler."

The minister's speech took on momentum and scope. It soared like Pegasus. "A triumph of originality. The mystery and precision of art. A brilliant personage. Now, undoubtedly, our museum is the envy of the Metropolitan and the Louvre."

"It is a joy and a privilege to be a contemporary of this man, Ernest Pogodin," concluded the minister.

He saw that his portrait was admiring the original from the side wall. In the portrait the minister was outfitted in a Lomonosov wig and a red doublet. He held in his hand a goose-quill pen; by his side could be seen the dark arc of a globe. He was writing to some future reader, foreseeing through the darkness and storm clouds ahead the rise of a new Russia.

Applause. Next the museum director sailed up to the microphone. The curls wobbled on her head, each one of them holding in itself the mystery of life, the Universe, the Milky Way, compressed energy, the light at the end of the tunnel, the waxing and waning of the Moon, the papillary whorls on the human palm, and the rise and fall of cyclones. The director's speech overflowed in expressions of gratitude. Gratitude to the minister oozed out of her like yeasty dough from a tub. Her words were fortified with sugar, caramel, nutmeg, cardamom, cinnamon, and treacle. They smelled of a baklava bakery. They oozed melted butter and honey syrup.

"And of course," she bleated, "it is a huge honor for us to receive the paintings of the great Ernest Pogodin."

The artist's name pierced the hall. Again the microphone emitted a burst of feedback. There were pockets of applause but then, overcoming it, an enraged voice arose from the back:

"It's fraud! A swindle!" cried the voice. The crowd parted, revealing as its source an ancient ruffian with a sparse gray beard.

"What does not meet with your approval?" inquired the minister with a smile.

"Defrauding the people! You know how much tickets to this exhibit cost? It's outrageous!"

"How did he get in here? Who let this bum into the gala?" snarled Pogodin.

The director took a wide-legged goalie's stance and called for security, but the minister felt like having a little fun. He kept nipping at the old man:

"So tell us, what's too expensive? Do you begrudge spending money for good art?"

"I'm an artist myself!" rattled the old man. "And this is not art! Not only is it total crap, but these are not even originals—they are photocopies!"

A murmur rippled across the hall.

"The bosses have the originals," howled the rabble-rouser. "And this stuff is who the hell knows what. You can draw on this paper. Look, I'm going to write the letter X on this supposed piece of art, right here and now!"

And the would-be vandal pressed forward like a prize-fighter, straight toward the featured canvas. Pogodin rushed to intercept him, the women who served as monitors sprang into action, the security guards trotted up, and the ill-fated artist was collared, folded in two, and escorted from the hall in disgrace.

"Crooks!" he wailed in a broken voice as he disappeared from view.

"Jealous, that's what they are, these people," lamented Pogodin. The sapphires blazed on his brocade robe.

The crowd grumbled. The reporters rubbed their palms. The leggy girl craned her neck, gazing silently in all directions, with her mouth forming a perfect "O."

"Oh," her full lips seemed to say, "Ko-ko-ko. Ro-co-co. No-no-no."

The cello and violins resumed their sawing. The goblets were passed around, and they filed along the walls past the pictures, like torches in some nighttime procession. The minister of culture, having cordially shaken hands with the honoree, made his exit, after which the frock-coated bureaucrats evaporated as well. The great artist was besieged by journalists. Pogodin swaggered. His fists pressed firmly into his crimson-clad sides, filling the space around him.

"I am resurrecting the cruelly violated grandeur of a bygone age," he pontificated. "I am clearing off the dust from the ages. Under my brush, the true, genuine Russia is coming back to life. But she has new faces—living, modern ones! These are not merely portraits. This is a musical score that will serve a future historian as he plays the symphony of our time. As he tells of those who were renowned in our town, in the region, in the country, who contributed to its prosperity and enabled it to flourish."

"Can you tell us why we don't see a portrait of Andrei Ivanovich Lyamzin here?" asked one of the reporters.

Pogodin hesitated, cleared his throat.

"Come now!" he said hoarsely. "I am not putting all my works on exhibit. I have three thousand of them. Not to mention, the canvas is currently in a home that has been orphaned. That has lost both its master and its mistress."

"So it's not photocopies hanging here, then?" timidly asked the reporter.

"Photocopies? Are you out of your mind?" the artist flared up. "Who have you been listening to? Lumpen? Bottom-feeders? Shitheaded hell-raisers? Didn't you see that vandal about to attack my canvas? And did you take note of who was on that canvas? Can you imagine it? It's an attack on . . ."

He broke off, unable to go on. His nostrils vibrated. The reporters withered in silence. An awkward pause hung over the crowd.

"Now where," a girl from the press got her bearings, and held out a Dictaphone to Pogodin, "Where and how do you find the inspiration for your sublime works?"

Pogodin warmed up.

"Baby," he beckoned to his tall companion, who was standing to one side with her glass, "come over here. I am inspired by this woman here. Angelina. A budding actress."

Angelina's mighty leg emerged from the slit in her dress, giving all the cameras the opportunity to rise lustfully along its full length from her Louboutin toe, up along the ankle, the soft knee, and onward and upward, to the titillating thigh that receded into the fold of her dress, like a gigantic beanstalk into a scarlet cloud.

Having had their fill of the spectacle, the cameras retreated to the walls to capture the guests of the opening at the most thrilling, most intimate moment of their experience—the contemplation of the works on display.

"Looks like him," said some.

"Doesn't look like him," asserted others.

Someone took Pogodin under his tender wing, patting him on the shoulder with a familiar touch. It was one of his friends, the same little guy with the crew cut and GTO badge who had let himself go at Marina Semyonova's birthday party. He was prissily sipping his bubbly.

"Congratulations!" he greeted Ernest Pogodin. "You are a genius!"

"I am a genius, and this is my muse," agreed the artist, introducing Angelina. Judging from the fidgeting of Angelina's sleek eyelashes, which had been enhanced with sable in the Wildflower Aesthetic Clinic, the muse was getting restless. She was looking forward to the culmination of the evening, the banquet, the intimate gathering afterward, the bestowal of golden offerings, the opportunity to rub shoulders with the featherbrained elites and trendsetters of the town. She couldn't wait to make her escape from the museum.

"Divine, just divine," the man winked to Pogodin. His approval of the artist's escort, however, did nothing to dampen his feverish state. His entire being pulsed with electricity. A rolled-up newspaper poked out of his jacket pocket.

"What have we here?" Pogodin nodded toward the newspaper. "Something in there about me? About the portraits?"

"Guess again," gesticulated the man. "It's something different, brace yourself!" In his excitement he spattered some champagne onto the newspaper, and the paper darkened. Pogodin chuckled:

"Did you know? One time the French came up with the idea of waterproof newsprint. So you could read it over breakfast and lunch. If you spill your egg on it, no problem. Get some coffee on a page, no big deal. The paper could take anything you gave it. But there are people—and here he poked Angelina's bare neck—who don't even know what a newspaper is. Am I right, babe?"

He leaned over to his date and tickled her rosy cheeks with his scented sideburns. Angelina's perfect teeth made an appearance. The girl was showing emotion.

"Lion cub, go play awhile," Pogodin commanded abruptly, and, giving his escort a gentle slap on the bottom, he turned back to the crew-cut man. The scarlet dress billowed like a sail and swept off in the direction of the musicians.

"How about that beanpole of mine? Not bad, is she?" he asked boastfully.

"Magnifique!" the crew-cut man went for French. Then he unhurriedly extracted his newspaper.

The grayish paper unrolled, revealing a banner spreading across the top, its print slightly blurred from the incident with the champagne.

"A national newspaper!" exclaimed the man. "It's about Lyamzin's murder!"

The artist grimaced, glanced around. The hall was humming with life. The enthralled dilettantes continued to mill about under the paintings. An art scholar stood, hushed, at the underbelly of the main canvas. The whirling paints were refracted in the thick lens of her glasses. The pirouettes and cabrioles of individual splotches blended into the overall mass of the corps de ballet. The woman was frowning.

"What do you mean, murder? Why bring it up at my opening? Can't it wait?"

At Pogodin's words the museum director materialized next to them. Her ovine face radiated ecstasy.

"Success. A smashing success!" she puffed. "We're completely sold out! We're going to be mobbed in here tomorrow!"

"Delighted, very glad," said Pogodin. "The people here are no strangers to real culture."

"No strangers indeed! We'll have to charge extra for selfies with the pictures, what do you think?"

"Absolutely," agreed Pogodin.

Another reporter popped up, a clingy one, overflowing with softball questions, and the plump director, grimacing, hastened to be interviewed. The towering curls on her head quivered as she minced away, threatening to fly off in all directions. The crew-cut man absentmindedly drained his glass.

"Well, what have they written there?" asked the artist, unable to control his mounting curiosity. "Let's step out into the foyer."

They left the hall and went over to a window overlooking the alley behind the museum, where an epic panorama unfolded before their eyes. The alley was clogged up with a brown slurry. A sewer pipe had burst the night before and had been spewing a seething river of fetid goo ever since. A woman in an anorak and rubber boots was fording the stinking stream, holding her nose. Pogodin and his companion glanced down at the woman's contortions, then turned their attention back to the newspaper. The headline was disturbing, mysterious: "Mistress Murders Minister?"

"Hold on just a minute here. What?" muttered Pogodin. "Meaning, she killed him? But didn't Lyamzin have a heart attack?"

"Now look at this," began the man, screwing up his eyes. "Here it says: 'Our editorial offices have received photographs from an unnamed source, who wishes to remain anonymous...' blah blah blah ... Aha: 'The assumption in the region is that the minister died from a sudden rupture of the aorta, but the photos that have come to light suggest that there's something fishy going on here...' That's what it says, 'something fishy.' These hacks have completely forgotten how to write."

"Go on, go on," barked Pogodin.

"All right.... 'From the photos, which were taken on a cell phone, it's obvious that on the evening of his disappearance and death, the late minister of economic development, Andrei Ivanovich Lyamzin, was near the home of his mistress, Marina Semyonova, the owner of a number of assets in the region.' Right..."

"We don't need those pen pushers to tell us where the poor guy spent the evening," noted Pogodin. "Brilliant deduction."

"But Marina insists that the minister never showed up!" The crew-cut man gesticulated. "Anyway, then, blah blah blah ... Aha, here it is: 'In the photos in our possession, despite the dark time of day and the cyclopean downpour...' What the...? What the hell even is that, 'cyclopean downpour'? Can a rainstorm have eyes, or even one eye?"

"Focus, my good man!"

Having ascertained that they were alone, Pogodin got a pair of glasses out of his robe pocket and mounted them on his nose.

"Damned farsightedness," he whispered self-consciously. The man continued:

"Right. 'Despite the dark time of day and the cyclopean downpour, a figure can be seen running from someone in the pedestrian area. Next, the figure is seen standing next to a Toyota Camry. In the fourth photo the man turns, and we can see that it is none other than Regional Minister Lyamzin. Lyamzin gets in the car. And that's the last time anyone saw the minister alive.'"

"Wait . . ." mumbled Pogodin. "Who took the photos?"

"Could have been anyone," snorted the man. "Just someone who happened to pass by. But listen to what comes next! 'The license number of the mysterious automobile can be discerned in the photos. To verify the information in the anonymous letter, we ran the plate number through the database. The results are shocking and alarming. The Toyota's owner turns out to be Nikolai N., an employee of Marina Semyonova—who, we remind you, for many years was the minister's mistress and his partner in a number of unsavory financial deals. The regional media resource, the *Siren*, recently published an exposé about these dealings.' Et cetera, et cetera . . . Then there's some stuff about Katushkin's article. All right, hold on . . . Aha, here it is: 'Nikolai N. worked in the Procurement Department of Marina Semyonova's construction company. The anonymous source who sent us the photographs commented that Lyamzin and Semyonova had been having some issues . . .' Holy effing . . . they're at it again! 'Issues'? Who are these hacks? All right, OK, I'm reading. Next: 'You have to agree, there's something downright strange about the fact that the man behind the wheel of the automobile carrying Andrei

Lyamzin off to his imminent death is an employee of the man's mistress. Might this so-called 'accident' actually be more like a contract killing? Are the local investigators hiding something? Might Semyonova have paid them off?'"

The crew-cut little man looked up from the paper and glanced out the window. Reeking sludge continued to spew into the alley behind the museum. And that same woman in the rubber boots was slogging through it, only now in the other direction, and with a child howling and screaming on her back. The man followed her with his eyes to see if she would manage to stay upright and make it to the other shore with her fidgety burden, then turned back to Pogodin. He was reading the article to himself, moving his lips as though trying to catch invisible flies in his mouth.

"Listen!" he exclaimed. "Just look what they're writing! The owner of the Toyota was killed in an accident the day after Lyamzin's death. He ran into a truck at an intersection. 'According to the anonymous source who sent us the photographs, Marina Semyonova most likely had assigned her worker Nikolai N., the owner of the fateful car, to do the job on Lyamzin. But something went wrong. Maybe Nikolai N.'s conscience tormented him and he wanted to go tell the police everything. So then Semyonova decided to take him out. What criminal would not want to get rid of an unwelcome witness, the instrument of her crime? On the day of Nikolai N.'s death, Marina Semyonova had shown up unexpectedly at her construction company, which she hardly ever visited. Let's suppose that the possible killer and the possible person who ordered the killing had a fateful conversation on that day. Might she have slipped Nikolai N. some kind of soporific or other drug that sent the poor man to his grue-some death?'"

Pogodin finished reading and adjusted his glasses. His interlocutor watched and waited. Several guests walked past them on their way from the hall to the exit, exchanging heart-felt farewells. The museum director looked over at them:

"Now we're going to my office for refreshments!"

"Yes, yes, right away," answered Pogodin.

"Well?" the man asked him at last, when the crowd had passed. "What do you think? It's in the national news, in Moscow! They'll loose the dogs, don't you see? They'll say it's a cover-up. I can feel it, they're digging a hole under Kapustin, the chief prosecutor. It's not random, it's a signal! Kapustin's on his way out!"

Ernest Pogodin, who'd been listening with disapproval, stretched and even yawned, signaling the sheer pettiness and insignificance of the newspaper exposé.

"It's nonsense! Baloney! Complete hokum! Come on: if this Nikolai is a killer, then why did the prey run straight to him? Meaning, why would Lyamzin get in his car? He had chauffeurs, bodyguards!"

"He'd dismissed them . . ." the man began, hesitantly.

"I don't believe any of it. It doesn't add up. It's a gutter rag, not a newspaper. Yellow journalism! Why did you even spend money on it? You can get all that shit for free on the internet!"

"I'm an old-fashioned guy," the little man objected. "I like the real thing. And then, I'm not the only one who's gotten worked up about it. The clouds have been gathering around Kapustin for a long time. He'd been lining his pockets for way too long; things being what they are, it was well past time for him to spread the wealth around."

"I was commissioned to do his portrait," said Pogodin. "We had just three more sittings left. Don't you know how to read the signs? If the artist Ernest Pogodin paints someone's portrait, it means that that person won't be coming down from Olympus anytime soon. The soonest would be five years."

"For real? It's a sign?" The little crew-cut man was impressed.

A chubby fellow emerged from the hall and approached them; he was a young guy, a low-level staffer from the Ministry of Culture. He had lingered at the opening in the hopes of partaking in the refreshments and was now casting his eyes around the room, hoping to sleuth out the way upstairs to the invitation-only reception in the director's office. Noticing the newspaper lying inside out on the windowsill in a kind of crumpled, irregular polyhedron, he manifested an unseemly degree of joy:

"Oh! You're reading the article! About Marina Semyonova being a murderer!"

"You seem know a thing or two," sniffed Pogodin.

"Who doesn't? I got a link on Messenger this morning. Crazy stuff! Just nuts. Semyonova can sue them for real money. It's libel!"

"What if she really is a murderer?" noted the little man.

"Hardly likely, but what if? Even then it's all pretty crazy and stupid. Why show all your cards? She can read it and get rid of the evidence, or run off to Thailand or somewhere. It's not Marina they're after. It's Kapustin. It's a signal to our chief investigator in Moscow, along the lines of, get the hell rid of

Kapustin. No, no, not even that! It's actually the chief investigator sending us a message, using the article."

"A signal? Through some tabloid? That's absurd." Pogodin shrugged. "You know what rags like that write about me? That there are virgins lined up under my windows. That they flock in from the countryside to offer me their chastity." Pogodin broke into a sugary smile. "Now that's just plain . . . practically untrue, my dear friends. Hey, what's happened to my Kolomna beanpole? My muse! Someone could make off with her."

The muse, as if on cue, materialized by his side. Her dress was a little tight. The material quivered under the pressure of the muscular body it contained. The body craved fresh air.

"How much longer, kitty cat?" she purred into the artist's ear.

"Just a minute, my darling, we'll just take a peek upstairs, have a bite to eat, then off we go. Go powder your cute little nose."

The beanpole girl nodded and retreated, leaving a trail of aromatic perfume in her wake.

"I envy you, the great and mighty," confessed the dumpy fellow, following her with libidinous eyes.

The little man picked up the thread again. "So what do you think about Kapustin? You think he's in any danger?"

"He's not the victim, he's the one to watch out for!" laughed Dumpy. "Did you see the reporter, Katushkin, apologizing? Did you see it? I almost died!"

He got out his smartphone, poked at the screen with his fingertip, and held it up to his companions. On the bright display, against the background of a wall with peeling paint, loomed the head of the journalist Katushkin. A ridiculous-looking cap with the logo "Olympiad-80" had been pulled down low on his head, as though to cover something. There were dark shadows under Katushkin's red eyes. He blinked nearsightedly. He stammered:

"I would like to apologize to the chief prosecutor of our region . . . I was wrong . . . I received money from foreigners and simply wanted to make myself useful to them. To stomp with dirty boots on our home, on our Russia . . . I slandered and told lies. I betrayed my homeland. But I repent. Forgive me for wanting to sully your good name . . . You do so much for law and order, without sparing yourself . . ."

Katushkin's swollen lips twitched as he strove to manage his words. A purple bruise showed through the stubble on his cheek.

"Enough, that will do," scoffed Pogodin. "Why waste time with that dickhead?"

"How about that?" Dumpy exulted. "Brought that asshole to his knees. Now they'll close down the *Siren*, I bet. I have a lot of confidence in the State Media Supervisory Committee."

"What about Marina Semyonova?" the little man was still anxious. "Is she involved in what happened with Lyamzin or not? Where's the truth in all this?"

The remaining guests began to fill the foyer. They surrounded Ernest Pogodin. Their minds were on the invitation-only reception that awaited; they could already taste the tartlets and the bitterness of the cognac. Panegyrics flowed.

When the crowd, continuing to shower praises on Ernest Pogodin, reached the formal staircase, the artist espied

Marina Semyonova advancing briskly toward him, rustling her sequined hem; Ilyushenko waddled along in her wake, with her jaguar furs draping from his elbow.

"Ernest! Ernest!" called Semyonova. "I'm sorry I couldn't come earlier. But I couldn't miss your exhibit!"

She radiated contentment, flaunting the splendor of her outfit, face, and bearing. Dumpy blinked rapturously, the little man stroked his crew cut, and Ernest Pogodin bent to kiss her fragrant hands.

CHAPTER 14

THE SPORTS FESTIVAL WAS GETTING UNDERWAY. The town square danced and screeched. Booths offered fried oladyi pancakes and corn on the cob; sbiten and mead were being sold by the glass. Playing fields had been set up directly on the square, and popular entertainments were underway. Hurlbats clattered together like fencing foils. Teenagers chased a bandy ball around, cheered on by passersby. People dressed up in traditional costumes called out, recruiting players for Russian folk games like lapta, piggy-back, and dodgeball. Rosy-cheeked youngsters were wheeled about in their strollers like doges overseeing their subjects; little tricolor Russian flags tumbled from their loosed palms onto the bumpy asphalt. Traditional ditties tumbled one after the other from great black speakers on the festival stage.

Finally a voice blared out onto the square. The governor was giving the opening address. Underlings flanked him on both sides. In just a few moments, the most magnificent, spectacular competitions were about to begin in all the stadiums of the region.

"When others take up arms against our country," roared the governor, "when filthy stories are told about us, about doping, year after year, when our athletic teams are accused of cheating, when we are banned from international competitions, we do not sulk and whimper like beaten dogs. We manage on our own! We have our own traditional, deep-rooted games. We have our own Russian boxing, our wall-on-wall fighting. And we're masters at everything else, too! The supplest gymnasts. The strongest musclemen. We will not let anyone hound us. They do it out of fear, am I right?"

The square roared and cheered. Lenochka stood in the crowd, waving her lilac-colored balloon in the air. Her entire ministry was here. The night before, the office team-building chief had gone from floor to floor, making it clear that every last staffer was strictly required to show up. Lenochka did not resist. The crowd was boisterous, in high spirits. A muscleman walked around the square, performing a routine with dumbbells. A lady clown was passing hoops out to plump middle-aged ladies, challenging them to compete to see who could spin them the longest. Some of the streets around the square had been blocked off and were lined with booths selling pastries and flags.

Pavilions showcased different ethnicities. There was an exhibit of minority nationalities in native costumes. Tatars selling chak-chak, Uzbeks boiling shurpa, Bashkirs pouring cups of koumiss, Tajiks serving plov, Chechens giving out servings of khingalsh. Huge pots steamed over lively wood fires, filling the air with appetizing aromas. People dressed in ugly, scary costumes representing balls, badminton rackets, and discuses line-danced through the crowd, gathering swarms of kids along the way.

A rumor spread across the square. Lenochka listened as her colleagues passed the news from neighbor to neighbor. Shocking news: Marina Semyonova, Andrei Ivanovich Lyamzin's mistress, was under arrest. The details metamorphosed as they passed along the crowd's "telephone" lines. Some said that the hussy had been picked up while coming out of the art museum. She had been walking down the stairs toward her fancy car, when a SWAT team had swept in from all sides and clicked handcuffs onto her tender wrists.

Others swore that Semyonova had been seized while taking a relaxing aromatherapy bath. Men in black balaclavas had burst into the Wildflower Aesthetic Clinic and Cosmetology Spa. The villainess had been lying naked, basking in warm water mixed with milk, honey, and patchouli essential oil. They'd dragged her from the tub, spraining her hand in the process.

Others said that Semyonova had come on her own and turned herself in after confessing to the late Lyamzin's spiritual adviser. That he had persuaded the sinner to repent before the earthly judge. That Semyonova had walked on foot to turn herself in, through potholes and mud, across the entire town, dressed in ordinary jeans and a jacket. She walked, whispering:

"Forgive me, forgive me, forgive me . . ."

Lenochka went numb from all the rumors; her ears burned, her imagination painted one scene after another of Marina Semyonova's shame. She recalled one time when she'd seen the trollop in profile, looking up slightly from below. From there she could see a fleshy bag, like an iguana's, under her chin. Miss Perfect had a flaw! How could Andrei Ivanovich not have noticed?

Marina Semyonova, a dropout and a social climber, had always wanted to appear smarter than she was. Once when Lenochka had gone to her house on an errand for Lyamzin, Semyonova had been watching a movie. It was a recording. She had pressed "stop" and the screen had frozen on a mysterious black-gray image.

"Do you know what the Kuleshov effect is? You don't? Oh, what ignorance. It's when—you following?—two shots are juxtaposed during montage and it adds new meaning."

She wanted to show Lenochka up. She liked to learn new words and then use them constantly out in public.

"With you, Lenochka, I always experience a kind of jamais vu. Why are you blinking? Jamais vu, I'm telling you. The same as déjà vu, only the other way around. I've known you for such a long time, yet your dimwittedness never ceases to amaze me—just like the first time."

"Hylozoism," she'd say. "Anthropic principle." "Wilhelm Reich." "The theory of the leisure class." "The global village." "Apatheism." "Stochastic process." Without always understanding what it all meant, she tried out each phrase, each word, for its taste, like some delicacy on her tongue. Ilyushenko was her own personal supplier of intellectual trivia. They often got into arguments about maneuvers and manipulations that could be put into play to capture someone's love. One time Lenochka had overheard part of one of those conversations.

"You, Marisha, are such a fisher of men," Ilyushenko said, munching on a cookie as usual. "You're a regular Benjamin Franklin."

"What do you mean?" asked Semyonova.

"I mean you don't order people around; you make requests. When you ask someone for a favor, he readily complies, again and again."

"What else makes me charismatic?" asked Semyonova, thrilled.

"What else? Fascination."

"What do you mean?"

"Fascination—you have the ability to charm people. And your victim is deaf to all other signals—morality, for example, or reason. You have the victim in your snare. And he likes being there."

Sometimes Marina Semyonova came to Lyamzin's office at the ministry. He would be a little nervous. He preferred neutral territory.

"Andrei Ivanovich is with someone," Lenochka would say.

Semyonova would toss her elegant ostrich-leather purse onto the sofa and would go over to the mirror and begin fussing with her hairdo. She had a special mousse that she used to add body to the roots of her chestnut locks. The reception room would fill with the smell of musk.

"Who's he got sitting in there, some motley gang?" she would inquire, projecting authority. And Lenochka, suppressing her irritation, would chirp, "It's about the land development plan."

Sometimes Semyonova would be in a generous mood. One time she gave Lenochka a cosmetics bag. The bag wasn't to Lenochka's taste and she tossed it into the trash. The same with Semyonova's edifying moral lessons. Though it is true, one piece of advice did take root in Lenochka's head, like a mantra that she had been required to memorize in self-improvement coaching sessions:

"If a guy insists on having his own way, then make him sleep in a separate bed. He'll be eating out of your hand before you know it."

Semyonova had applied this separate beds tactic with the late Lyamzin. One time the minister had been separated from his lover's body for two whole weeks. He pounded on her door, phoned, snarled, begged and pleaded, but she held her ground. She kept her peace, and the door remained tightly shut. It had been over some pathetic little thing. She had wanted to travel with her lover around Europe, openly, like husband and wife. And she wanted to be showered with presents, to go to the opera and restaurants. Lyamzin had waffled. He was afraid of letting it be so obvious. When he thought of his wife or the governor, he lost his nerve. The region had taken a firm stand on family values. A jaunt to Europe could bring on some serious consequences. But now the minister was dead, and the festival was in full swing. The mayor was at the podium, and his shaggy cheeks filled the huge screen like a giant's.

"In just one year our town has acquired ten brand-new jungle gyms. We care deeply about the athletic development and personal health of our younger generation . . ."

The square buzzed. No one was listening to the mayor. His speech was a mere accompaniment to all the little conversations and greetings going on in the crowd. From where he stood, the townspeople looked like an expanse of multicolored gravel, shifting around, as in a kaleidoscope, in response to someone's invisible will. A pink one slipped off somewhere to one side, a blue one floated upward on a diagonal curve, a brown one whirled in a circle.

But suddenly from amid this Lilliputian kingdom that spread out before the stage, a schismatic voice rose up:

"What do you mean, 'we care'? You're destroying our park!"

The voice came from a megaphone. How had they managed to get a megaphone through the metal detectors? Who was the traitor?

"Who do you think you are? Why are you disrupting the festival?" snarled the mayor. The crowd heaved. The megaphone voice initiated a chant, and a patch of trigger-happy hellions took it up, supporting the ringleader:

"OUR PARK! OUR PARK! OUR PARK!"

There was a flurry of activity on the stage. A wall of security guards rose around the dignitaries, and special police units—"cosmonauts"—from different ends of the square plowed through the crowd, making their way toward the ruffians.

"We demand an end to the destruction of our historic park! It is our culture, our lungs. What are we leaving for our children? Let us now, all together, demand an answer from those who are exploiting us. Instead of repairing the broken sewer lines over there by the art museum, they're doing who the hell knows what!"

The protesters burst into applause and whooped, but the troublemaker's voice suddenly broke off; the "cosmonauts" had surrounded him and his two dozen supporters like a black funnel cloud. The megaphone was torn from his hands, and there came the sounds of women's screams and expletives.

Lenochka strove to see what was going on but people all around her were stampeding, elbowing one another and blocking her view. All she could see were the round tops of police helmets and a turbulent mass of bobbing heads. The unexpected defenders of the park were forced off the square. Some random festivalgoers seemed to have been arrested along with the group. An old woman could be heard cursing like a sailor.

"Fellow townspeople!" The governor addressed the crowd. "Do not be taken in by provocations. They are trying to ruin our long-awaited sports festival! But we will not allow the hooligans that satisfaction. We will continue to enjoy ourselves, and to take delight in our celebration."

In response to his words, there came the sound of a brass band, the soundtrack of the old Soviet song:

> *The heat will rise up to the skies,*
> *We sing our heroes' victory;*
> *The brightest athletes win the prize,*
> *And shine with pure integrity.*

"What's going on? What's going on?" Lenochka kept asking.

"It's a protest for the park—what else could it be? They've already been taken away. They'll get fifteen days each, most likely. Like people don't have anything else to do!" answered one of her colleagues from the Procurement Department. "Let's go, Lenochka, how about we have a donut?"

"Who was the guy with the megaphone?" people in the crowd were asking.

"They're destroying the park, but what can you do about it?"

"You can't help by starting a war."

"Hooligans!"

"The mayor, did you hear? He didn't say a word about the park. Didn't have the guts!"

The seed of revolt, fed to the crowd, sent forth thin shoots and sprigs. Excited mouths poured commentary into wide-open ears. Lenochka heard:

"The guy was telling the truth . . ."

"Remember when the mayor announced a flash mob? For the best photo taken at the monument to Peter and Fevronia. He said that the winners would get trips to the sea, valuable prizes. But ultimately the only people who got prizes were members of the town administration. They played the people for fools!"

"They opened a bordello in the Veterans' Home. And are selling furs there, too."

"They're taking down the park so they can build offices there; meanwhile people are living in barracks."

"Our house is in a dangerous state; the roof is disintegrating."

"Hooligans! Rabble-rousers! Where'd they get the megaphone!"

Lenochka saw some people she knew coming her way. They nodded to her. She waved to someone. But she felt a hammering inside her head. Was it true what they were saying about Semyonova? How was she going to get past Victor's betrayal? Was it really her, Lenochka's, fate to keep struggling to make ends meet in the Procurement Department?

Their way was blocked by a full-size stuffed puppet, a brown Mishka teddy bear. Mishka wanted a hug. Lenochka turned away, but her coworker ended up in the bear's armpit, flashing a broad smile. Fine wrinkles spread from the corners of her eyes to her temples. Onstage, the song culminated in a jaunty chorus. The disturbance on the square subsided. The beast hid his horns. The lion retracted his claws.

Or did it just seem that way? Here and there, from different sides of the square, loud voices shouted:

"Our park!"

"Hands off our park!"

The minister of sport, for some reason garbed in an Olympic uniform from the time of the Crimean conquest (featuring the logo "Sochi 2014" on the trouser striping), completely lost his bearings and choked up. But he kept on reading from a piece of paper, ignoring the insolent shouts:

> The first soccer match was played in our country in 1898, in Petersburg. And the first national soccer championship in Russia took place in 1912. Moscow crushed Kharkov with a score of six to one. The first dedicated Russian skating rink was opened in Petersburg in 1838. The first World Figure Skating Championship in pairs was held in our country in 1908. As for skiing, our chronicles mention an army ski regiment as early as the fifteenth century. And beginning in 1704, we even had a special postal service on skis. The first Russian ski championship took place in Moscow in 1910. Our women also made their mark in ski competitions. In 1935, five wives of Red commanders covered the

distance from Moscow to Tyumen, 2,132 kilometers, on skis, in ninety-five days. In 1936, ten female electrical plant workers skied from Moscow to Tobolsk—2,400 kilometers—in forty days. And in 1937, five Komsomol female athletes skied from Ulan-Ude to Moscow. That adds up to 6,065 kilometers.

"Hands off! Don't touch the park!" The voices in the crowd got louder. But the minister of sport droned on:

The first hockey match in our country took place in 1899, in Petersburg, on the rink by Tuchkov Bridge, between the Russians and the English. The match ended in a tie, four to four. But then, as you know, we became number one in the world, defeating even the Canadians. In cycling . . .

"Our park! Our park!" the crowd chanted, much louder. Again police helmets flashed in the crowd.

"What is the meaning of this?" stammered the minister of sport. "Have you lost your minds? The ringleaders will face terrorism charges right here and now! You are disturbing public order, interfering with the festival! Enough squawking, comrades!"

The minister of sport looked helplessly around at his colleagues. The governor was nowhere to be seen, but the minister of culture rushed over to help. He was wearing a white knit ski cap.

"Fellow citizens, calm yourselves!" he appealed to the crowd briskly, taking the place of the dazed and confused minister of sport. "Like you, I grew up in this town. I played in that park. As your minister of culture, I care deeply about preserving our heritage. And the health of our children, of course. Please do not believe these paid hacks! No one is planning to destroy the park! It is simply undergoing upgrades, do you understand? Stores and cafeterias will be built, and a business center. Cultural life will flourish in the park. You will thank the mayor yourselves!"

"We don't need upgrades!" an older man in a cap yelled in a bad falsetto, but he was immediately collared and dragged from the square by "archangels" who'd been patrolling the crowd.

"For shame! For shame!" a dozen men shouted.

"Stop disturbing the peace, and no one will touch you!" continued the minister of culture. "Do not allow them to stir you up! Can't you see that you're being manipulated? You are being specially targeted. They are fanning the flames. Think who benefits from this. Why have you gotten all up in arms about the park? Who started it? Just a couple of so-called activists. But if you were to scratch them . . ."

"Scratch yourself!" Lenochka heard a voice beside her. She turned to look, but couldn't make out who the heckler was.

Sensing danger, people began to move their children off the square, taking them by the hand or pushing them in their strollers. The festive music changed tempo. Fortissimo and agitato notes mixed in with the allegro. The minister of culture continued orating. He got carried away. His hands traced crossing lines and sharp angles in the air.

"All misfortunes begin with disrespect for history!"

"What about the park? Isn't that history?" grumbled some ladies in berets to the right of Lenochka. Lenochka's coworker lost her temper and completely forgot about the donuts.

"Idiots!" she raged at the park defenders. "Why are they muddying the water? The festival was off to such a great start!"

But things were falling apart. The more people were seized and taken away, the louder were the voices of protest.

"Give us back the teacher Sopakhin, that will show some respect to history!" shouted a scowling young guy standing nearby.

"What, is Sopakhin under arrest again?" she asked.

"Who the hell cares?" responded her coworker.

The guardians of public order—black knights in glittering helmets with rubber truncheons at their thighs—elbowed past, on the prowl for rabble-rousers. Lenochka's coworker was pressed aside and hidden from view behind their armored backs. The ministers also vanished from the stage. Now a man in epaulets stood at the microphone trying to prevail upon the horde of humanity heaving before him, like a hypnotist or a street hawker selling discounted down jackets:

"Your actions are unlawful. Cease your aggressive behavior. Do not prevent peaceful citizens from enjoying their leisure."

Lenochka hastened her steps. The lilac-colored balloon tore itself from her fingers and soared into the sky, tracing first a circle, then an ellipse, then shrinking to an ink drop. She found herself out on the street, where the festivities continued, despite occasional ripples of unease. There was a line at one of the booths, manned by a cook serving Central Asian food. Samosas were baking on the sides of a tandoori oven. The hot triangles were scooped out of the oven using a special net and served, piping hot and sizzling, to the ravenous merrymakers.

"What will you have?" heard Lenochka. Someone touched her shoulder. She turned. Behind her stood Victor, looking at her with a sly, hurt, and at the same time guilty expression. Lenochka tried to make a break for it, but Victor grabbed her by the shoulders and stared straight into her eyes with big puppy eyes.

"Baby, wait! Don't run away, listen!"

Lenochka fluttered weakly in his grip. But Victor held on tight, and she softened and yielded.

"What are you up to, anyway? Why don't you pick up the phone? Why this whole drama?"

"What do you mean, 'why'? I wrote you, you know everything!" Lenochka sputtered. Around them the line clamored. The samosas were fished out and served, fished out and served; their greasy sides glistened, sesame seeds stuck in the crowns of their triangular heads.

"It's about Semyonova, isn't it?" Victor shook her. "I explained everything! I was grooming her! Do you understand? I was playing a role! Leading her on, capeesh?"

"Has she been arrested?" mumbled Lenochka.

"I laid the groundwork myself!" rattled Victor quietly, half whispering. "I spotted her lying in wait in the car at the Lyamzins', on the lookout for Ella Sergeyevna! The same day that the maid found Ella Sergeyevna dead."

"At Ella Sergeyevna's house?"

"Yes, yes!" I had been tasked with earning her trust. Poopsie, you read me? And here you are throwing a whole hissy fit. Baby, are you listening?"

"Did Marina Semyonova murder Ella Sergeyevna?" muttered Lenochka dumbly.

"No, but look, that's not the point. But the article . . . Did you see the article in the Moscow paper?"

"The car . . . Nikolai N."

"Yes, yes, we ran it through the database; he was officially Semyonova's employee. He's the one who took Lyamzin out to the bypass."

They flung their arms around each other. They stuck together like Siamese twins. They murmured sweet nothings, burned each other with their hot flaming whispers. The cook demanded that they give their order, and moments later they were handed a couple of paper plates with doughy, meat- and lentil-filled envelopes. Victor counted out the money, and Lenochka took a couple of napkins from the tray. They stood at a plastic table next to a young family—parents and mischievous offspring—who were gobbling down belyashes. The child writhed like a worm, emitting a prolonged, heartrending series of peevish whines.

Lenochka gripped her samosa awkwardly in the napkin by its crisp corners, trying to find the best place to bite first. The monotonous appeals for calm from the PA fell silent. Music started up again. And on the crosswalk, behind the shooting gallery and the archery pavilion, stood a line of paddy wagons. The arrested rabble-rousers were being packed into the metal armored vehicles.

"You were kissing her. In the elevator," said Lenochka, swallowing a tasty mouthful.

"I was earning her trust, it's my job!"

Victor was not backing down. And even now he kept his grip on Lenochka. With one hand he held her by the shoulder; with the other, he held his samosa.

"Nice job you have there. And you slept with her, too, I presume?"

"It's not about it being nice or not," snapped Victor. "You don't understand!"

"Do you have to do that kind of work often? In bed with your suspects?"

They went back and forth like that, but half-heartedly, more like a couple of little songbirds who'd come upon a bread crust they had to share. The loudmouth brat was dragged away by the scruff of his neck.

The kid pummeled the air with his feet. The family's place was taken by two grumpy women with poverty written all over their sour faces. Hunching over the table, they bitched and moaned, addressing each other and, at the same time, everyone around them:

"They just had to ruin the festival!"

"And did you hear how the sheep in the crowd chimed in? 'Baa-baa-baa.'"

"What if they haul our kids in again? They don't have any sense, putting their own heads in the noose. Takes nothing to set them off."

"Tomorrow we'll devote a class to it. As part of moral instruction."

"Yes, let's. As if that damned Sopakhin weren't enough. You can't even let kids out on the public square to hear the governor."

Lenochka pricked up her ears. She thought she recognized the teachers from the school that Ella Sergeyevna had been principal of.

"Do you know Sopakhin?" asked Lenochka.

The grumpy women seemed to have been expecting the question.

"We worked with him! And we're still dealing with the consequences!" one of them bristled.

"I had told Ella Sergeyevna that he was leading the students astray!" seethed the other. "He just had to devote a whole lesson to that nonsense! I stopped in his class one day and you know what I heard?"

"What?" exclaimed the first woman.

"'Holodomor'! Can you imagine? He spun this creepy tale about the supposedly artificially induced Ukrainian famine of the 1930s. Claimed that they took grain from the peasants. Talked about this 'Law of the Three Spikelets.' Why on earth, why?"

The teacher was completely bent out of shape. There were deep furrows between her brows.

"Is it bad to talk about the famine?" Lenochka asked, just to be sure.

"To lie! It's bad to lie, young lady! It's just wrong! Disinformation! Bald-faced lies!" interjected the first woman.

"By 1929 our country, thanks, by the way, to the efforts of the government leadership, for the first time in the history of the human race had completely eliminated unemployment, do you understand? Through a planned economy, industrialization . . . they completely liquidated it! In Ukraine, Stalin built the DneproGES Hydroelectric Station, gave them electricity, and instead of 'thank you,' they just whine and curse. Spread fables about the Holodomor. And this Sopakhin of ours did the same thing, just had to go and spit into his own well!"

"Somehow under the 'Soviet occupiers,'" the first woman added venomously, "the Ukrainian population doubled. And the moment the USSR collapsed, the demography went straight to hell. All they want to do is slander and ridicule us in other countries' embassies. And this Sopakhin has to go and play the same tune, and in front of the children, no less! Let him sit in prison and think about it. Serves him right."

"Well he probably was paid. By the Americans, maybe. He'd do better to study up on that beloved America of his. During those same 1930s, seven million people starved to death over there. There's Holodomor for you."

The teacher's voice trembled. In her dry palms, tea steamed in a paper cup.

"We're not arguing with you," said Victor. "We agree."

He finished his samosa, and now he reached out and held Lenochka tight, with proprietary confidence. Lenochka did not resist. She now wanted to belong to Victor. She listened to the festive music, in which an affettuoso note had begun to dominate— "voluptuous, passionate, impetuous, oh so tender." Lenochka rested her head on Victor's shoulder. And her belly and chest filled with sweet bliss.

CHAPTER 15

AFTER THE DEATH OF HER ALCOHOLIC FATHER, Lenochka's life changed, but not for long. Her mother snared a rich guy somewhere and brought him into their home. The source of the man's capital was vague and suspicious, but he introduced an era of sunshine and plenty into their decrepit apartment building, which was permeated with the smell of pickles and the foul exhalations of drunkards. The beau was a muscle-bound, bull-headed hulk. A violet-colored carpeting of tattoos—dragon scales, crosses, female bosoms—adorned his back, amid a sprinkling of sebaceous cysts. He would vanish for a month, and then would burst in suddenly with a flash of light and sound like a big firecracker. They would be inundated with cartloads of goodies and boxes of gifts. Her mother got a mink. Lenochka acquired a computer, which immediately catapulted her to the top of the class pecking order. A huge refrigerator appeared in the kitchen, and it bulged with freshly butchered meat, fish, and red caviar.

That summer, her mother's sugar daddy settled Lenochka with her aunt and grandmother in a dacha—a splendid house in a lakeside resort. A tutor was hired to help

Lenochka prepare for university entrance exams. Even now Lenochka's heart swelled with a warm, dull ache at the memory of those rainy August days. It seemed that vacation had only just begun, and suddenly it was autumn, and it was time to go back to town and start school. The air was dense with an earthy, mulchy smell. The red currant bushes, damp from rain and cold dew, gave off a distinctive, mournful aftertaste. The birch leaves were fringed in yellow—highlights, a hairdresser would have called it. Balayage (back then, Lenochka had been in the habit of collecting fancy words). She finally got her ears pierced, defying her grandmother, who claimed that the holes in her earlobes would ruin her eyes. Malarkey, basically, nonsense. Lenochka still had great vision. She could even count the black polka dots on Sopakhin's collar.

Sopakhin was her tutor. Lenochka had a hard year ahead of her, test prep. So Sopakhin had been brought in. Reddish hair, thin fingers that seemed to tremble slightly. Vegetarian. A real talker. Lenochka's grandmother was immediately smitten, but her detested aunt, a spinster who had long ago lost her freshness and youth, took a dislike to the man.

"I can't stand vegetarians," she muttered one time after he'd left. "They're always complaining about something. The wife of one of my college friends gave up meat. Then fish. Then all her food had to be raw. Ultimately she joined the Hari Krishnas and ran off and cloistered up with them somewhere."

"Sopakhin eats eggs," interjected Lenochka, but her aunt just sniffed.

And there really was something pathological about his fixation on what he ate, and how it should be cooked. But Lenochka was flattered by his way of treating her as an adult.

One time when they were going over ancient history, he corrected a mistake she had made. They had been talking about food.

"*Ab ovo usque ad mala*," Sopakhin purred. "It means 'from beginning to end.' Literally from the Latin, 'from eggs to apples.' The ancient Romans used to begin their meals with boiled eggs."

"I can't eat more than one at a time," Lenochka picked up the thread, happy for any distraction.

"Have you tried deviled eggs? Hard-boil some eggs, scoop out the yolks, mix them with something—spinach, mushrooms, or liver pâté . . ."

The door squeaked and her aunt poked her head in.

"You are not being paid to give cooking lessons!" she reprimanded the tutor.

Sopakhin blushed, started, grabbed the test book, and clammed up. They spent the rest of the hour reviewing the emperors up to the fall of Byzantium.

Was Lenochka attracted to Sopakhin as a man? Hardly. He was too old, too pale. Though Lenochka could only guess his age based on the stories he told. His face gave little in the way of clues. A beige birthmark on his neck, a wrinkle at the bridge of his thin nose. When they discussed Peter the Great's decree establishing punishment for wives who dragged their soused husbands out of the state-owned taverns, he suddenly leaned back in his chair and confessed, with particular bitterness:

"My wife was an alcoholic. I can tell you; you have a receptive mind. You have great potential. Organic, like sourdough starter, or something . . ."

Lenochka felt herself blushing, but she sat up straighter and tried to assume a serious and concentrated expression. She was wearing a pretty orange sundress and she pictured herself as the girl at a bride-viewing. Sopakhin was the suitor, she imagined, who had lived through a lot, who had suffered at the hands of a sinful, bad woman, and who had come to Lenochka for salvation, as to an anchor in stormy seas.

The more she thought about it, the more evidence she found to confirm her suspicion. Her aunt, especially when her grandmother wasn't around, would say particularly vicious things about Sopakhin. She must have sensed that he was sweet on Lenochka, and naturally envied her, and was scared.

"How long do you intend to go on tutoring for a living?" she asked point-blank one day when they were out on the terrace having tea.

"You know I can come here just because I live nearby. If you add it to my school salary it's a perfectly livable wage. Enough for two, even," reported Sopakhin.

"You wouldn't know by looking at the kind of shirt you're wearing," she cut him off rudely. "And what's 'just because I live nearby' supposed to mean? Do you have so little respect for us?"

"Did I say anything about disrespect?" he laughed. "You always twist my words around. I'm going to have to ask your niece to defend me."

"A mere child?" exclaimed her aunt, leaping out of her chair and fake gasping.

Lenochka was offended, hurt, annoyed. This over-the-hill, dried-up feminist had to stand by and watch Lenochka come into bloom and was burning with envy. Her aunt had asked her one time when they were on their way to the market:

"Why did you put on heels, Lena? We're in the country, not at some reception. Where's your sense of measure?"

"I felt like it, and I put them on," mumbled Lenochka, weakly.

"Or maybe you're hoping you'll run into your tutor? He's a strange, untrustworthy man. Giving history lessons at his age! Scraping by on a teacher's salary . . . and why doesn't he pluck that hair that sticks up on the bridge of his nose? It drives me crazy. I can't even look him in the eye because of it."

One time some of Lenochka's girlfriends came from town to visit, and they went down to the lake. The rains had passed, yielding to a hot, relentless sun, and it seemed that school was a long time away, that vacation would go on forever. The girls dived off the wooden pier into the deep, cold water. And Lenochka felt so womanly in her two-piece bathing suit, with her stud earrings, which gleamed with a seductive violet-colored light. The young guys floating by in their boats waved at them, and the girls laughed like madwomen.

When Lenochka was walking them back to the bus station, they ran into Sopakhin on the path. For some reason he seemed extremely happy to see her, and called out in a loud, joyful voice,

"You look so pretty! Swimming is good for you, Lenochka!"

He came over to her, grabbed her around the waist and lifted her into the air, then set her down, waved to the other girls, and disappeared. It was so unexpected that it took Lenochka's breath away. Her friends took note, of course.

"What was that about? Your tutor? No way!"

Lenochka came home beaming with pride. With a premonition of something momentous about to happen. At home they seemed to have figured it out. Her grandmother was distracted, and her aunt acted strange at dinner and went straight to her room after the dishes were done.

The next day, when Sopakhin came for her lesson, he was solemn and even looked sad. Not a trace of the levity from the day before. They came to the section about the Russian Revolution. In the middle of the lesson he suddenly turned his full attention to Lenochka and said: "You know, your aunt treats you like a child, but you and I can talk as equals. You understand me. That's very rare . . ."

Lenochka froze. It was like in the theater. Her heart raced, though she was able to observe and admire herself from the side.

"I have to tell you that I'm in love. I thought that after my first marriage there was no way I'd ever . . . But here I am, trapped again, hook, line, and sinker. And glad about it!"

Lenochka stared at Sopakhin with uncomprehending eyes.

"I want to get married," smiled Sopakhin.

All night Lenochka tossed and turned, suffered, bit her fingernails. She was scared, disgusted, and at the same time pleased. She had read parts of *War and Peace*, just the parts about Natasha Rostova, and Natasha had also been fifteen when for the first time . . . She'd run straight to her mother and cried, "Mama, Mama, he proposed to me!" Lenochka had found the scene terribly awkward to read. And here she was in the same position. A grown man, who had already been married, had fallen in love with her, a schoolgirl! It was awful, but sweet, too. What if she said yes? She'd have to wait until she turned sixteen. The age of consent. But at the very thought of it her mind clouded over.

The next morning, sluggish and weary, Lenochka came out to make breakfast. Her aunt and grandmother were in the kitchen. Her grandmother looked distracted, but vibrant and happy. Her aunt, who was standing over the sink rinsing eggs, turned to Lenochka and said:

"Dearest, I'm getting married. Sopakhin proposed yesterday."

It took Lenochka forever to come to her senses after the blow. So she'd imagined everything? So the object of his love was not her, not a young girl, but this old crow! And her aunt actually did marry Sopakhin and even bore him a child. What must she be feeling now! Shitting bricks, no doubt: wife of a falsifier of history, a criminal, blasphemer, desacralizer, traitor to the motherland, and convict.

Lenochka was always unlucky at love. Even her first love. In books on the list for extracurricular reading, first love was different: lovestruck, high-born boys. Girls with tender fingers, thin faces, and heroic impulses. A dark forest, a shriek, gasps, his strong arms, a rescue . . .

Things were different in life. A rust-stained bathtub with drippy faucets. Chronic disorder, a dark cave-like room, ugly china cabinets. Old crystal glassware and ubiquitous fragments of junk: broken stilettos, used ear plugs, parts from broken furniture, dead batteries. Her mother, before her fleeting romance with the rich capitalist, had been constantly in a bad mood, grouchy after her shifts in the kindergarten, rustling plastic bags and popping pills. That was a couple of years before Sopakhin. Lenochka had still been awkward and plump, and she wore unattractive, cheap tops bought wholesale at the market. Her skin was pallid and honeycombed with acne. The biology teacher had once called her coloboma a mutation. The other children picked up on the label, and when they saw Lenochka they would yell, "Mutation! Mutation! Radiation!"

Scrawny, pimply, awkward Lenochka had the misfortune to develop a crush on Siga, whom everyone adored. Siga was a tall, lanky boy with long dangly arms. An irrepressible troublemaker with an active mind. The class supervisor called him a good-for-nothing Romeo.

Lenochka suspected the class supervisor also had a crush on Siga. And all the other girls, too. He was already even dating one clueless girl, and Lenochka tormented herself imagining them in various romantic scenarios. Lovebirds. But Lenochka had no desire to actually be Siga's girlfriend. Something fleeting and secret—but real—would be enough. She fantasized how they would be walking together to school and would get into a conversation and stop at a crosswalk, just so they could keep talking. Lenochka would be wearing a beautiful skirt from a fashion magazine. mascara. Clear skin. And Siga would touch her shoulder and say, "Oh, Lena, you're such a . . ." And that would be all. And he would walk away.

As though he was so overcome with emotion, he couldn't finish the sentence. Lenochka would imagine the whole scene at night. She would cry and pray, not really understanding to whom and for what. And then she secretly got ahold of some lucky Chinese coins and whispered over them and tossed them, trying her fortune on hexagrams. The Book of Changes, the I Ching, is the ancient covenant of the tortoise. Her mother, lying awake, heard the coins jingling; she showered Lenochka with curses:

"Viper! Straight to bed with you! How are we supposed to get any sleep?"

Lenochka knew Siga's exact address. Which building, which entrance, which story. Just two blocks from the school. In the evenings she would go there and stand outside the building, trying to figure out which windows were his apartment and his room. He seemed to sense that he was being stalked. They'd run into each other several times in the courtyard.

"Mutation-Radiation!" he would yell. "You lose something here?"

Shock, happiness, bitterness, and pain—they all mixed together in Lenochka, filled her to overflowing, and she would blurt something about the store, or about her girlfriend who lived in the building, but Siga didn't listen and would just go on his way.

When she was around him Lenochka ran a temperature. At least that's how it felt. There was a ringing in her ears, and her hands quivered. Her deskmate sneered, "You've been Siga-ed, haven't you?" They all gossiped about her, of course. In the locker room after gym, they talked and snickered about her behind her back. One Saturday, when Lenochka was sitting at home finishing an assignment, she got a phone call from a stranger who said he was a friend of Siga's:

"He really likes you but he's afraid you'll say no. He asked me to call for him . . . Anyway, come to the back of the school in half an hour; he'll be waiting for you there."

Lenochka answered that she didn't believe him, but the blood rushed to her head and drops of sweat trickled down her back. What if? What if? She had to go, but maintain her dignity. Give the impression that she'd just been walking by. Just catch them out, that's all. And if Siga was actually there, then it would mean . . . She found her mother's old compact with the remnants of something beige stuck to the sides. She patted her face with her fingertips. Put on her new pants, the ones with appliqués. Rushed outside. There was no one at the school. Her chest was hammering. She took a leisurely stroll around the building, trying to seem casual, just in case someone was watching.

At the school gate she froze. She heard a shriek, and a cheerful, breaking adolescent voice yelled something obscene, filthy. Right next to her. Other voices chimed in, howling with laughter. Lenochka thought she was going to faint. She started rushing about, trying to figure out where the voices were coming from, but then she heard the thud of footsteps, voices whooping. The jokesters rushed past, doubled over with laughter. Five or six of them.

She knew them all from school. The last one, all red and sweaty, was him—Siga.

"Hey, Siga!" his friends joked as they fled. "What are you waiting for, grab her! Poke her deep, up to the balls!"

Lenochka pinched her own sides to keep from bursting into tears, and yelled, "Perverts, scumbags!"

But now, so many years later, Lenochka was happy at last. She wore fine lace lingerie; on the table by the rug were slices of fine cheese and a green bunch of grapes.

And Victor, who loved Lenochka, clinked crystal glasses,

filling them with semisweet bubbly. They had been sitting and drinking, and Victor was getting more and more impulsive, more and more aggressive, like an animal. It excited Lenochka, set her afire.

"I want to harness you to the radiator!" whispered Victor in her ear. Lenochka's clothes lay scattered around that same bedroom where she had undressed that other time, and that same plastic wobbly clown toy gawped blankly down at her from the chiffoniere, like before.

"Do with me what you will . . ." she answered, aflame.

He took her by the nape of the neck, turned her toward him, and dragged her over to the stream radiator, her slender arms bent backward like a swallow's wings. The handcuffs clicked. Lenochka panted, waiting for Victor to resume the caresses he had begun on the rug. But he just breathed heavily, staring deep into her catlike iris. His palm kneaded her narrow neck.

"I want you . . ." he said hoarsely. Lenochka smiled seductively, with sultry, languid desire. She dreamed of crude surrender, of lace torn off in handfuls, of bringing the ceiling down.

"I want you to give me some answers," continued Victor in the same low, testosterone-saturated voice.

"Yes, yes, answers!"

Lenochka closed her eyes. Her body melted, was ready to surrender, to gratify, to be naughty.

"You're the one," uttered Victor in an intimidating voice, like a prosecutor's, "you are the one who brought Andrei Lyamzin to the brink of suicide."

Lenochka's eyes flew open. "What? What? What is this about?"

"Yes," continued Victor, sternly and methodically. "You tormented him for an entire year with letters from anonymous addresses. You were ready to grind him into a powder out of malice. And all because he loved Marina Semyonova, and not you."

Lenochka jerked, but the handcuffs cut painfully into her wrists.

"Let me go! What are you talking about?" she howled in terror.

"Don't try anything. Or you'll get one in the face, you bitch!" snapped Victor. "We know everything. The whole chronology. One year ago Lyamzin fucked you while drunk. And you came to who knows what conclusion. You began pursuing him. Tender messages, selfies from the bathroom. He didn't know how to escape but kept you on. He realized that you were crazy and that you would run out and tell the whole world about your little roll in the hay!"

"You're the crazy one! You pig, scumbag, brute! I'll go straight to the police!"

"'Go to the police!'" Victor howled with laughter. "They're on their way over here! It's an open-and-shut case, they have all the evidence. When you realized that Lyamzin didn't give a damn about you, that's when you started your little blackmailing campaign, sending anonymous messages from different email addresses. You stalked him. Lurked outside Semyonova's house. You're the one who took the video of him getting into the Toyota! You're the one who sent the materials to the newspaper! You're the one who informed on Ella Sergeyevna and on the teacher!"

"Lies, lies, all lies!" shrieked Lenochka.

"Right, so then what are all those anonymous email accounts doing in your iPhone storage, the ones you used to harass the minister—is it just coincidence? Those shots of Lyamzin in the rain in your photo folder—is that also just random? All those notes bombarding him on Messenger from shady SIM cards? Also a lie? Don't try to resist, you yourself took screenshots of your entire correspondence as a keepsake, it's all there in that very same iPhone. Remind me what you wrote him that last night? 'I can see you. You're wearing your favorite jacket, you're getting out of the cab, you're going up to your mistress's house. You've let your chauffeur go. I'm not giving up; I will write the governor about the shady deals you made for your slut.' And on and on, every five minutes! Lyamzin couldn't take any more. His heart burst. And all because of you!"

"No, no, no! There's no way you could get into my iPhone! You couldn't have found out!" snarled Lenochka.

"What do you mean I couldn't get in—I did! Right here! In this very room! On our first night. While you were sawing logs, I pressed your finger to the sensor. And everything unlocked. You had your work email in there, too—Andrei Ivanovich's, which you managed, as his assistant. Natalya Petrovna, fool that she is, sent her crazy vamp photo to this email address. Whip, corset, the whole package. Apparently she was trying to trap the boss, too. So with everything going on you downloaded the photo and put it in circulation, sent it around to the entire ministry list. For everyone to admire."

"You pig! How could you! It's against the law!" protested Lenochka. She wasn't shouting, more like barking. Her voice broke like a teenage choirboy's.

"Nikolai! Ella Sergeyevna! Natalya Petrovna! Tolya, your colleague! It's all your doing! And if you try to deny it, I'll smash your snout in, you grasping whore!"

Lenochka was in shock. She howled incessantly. She writhed, strained her vocal cords, twisted and turned. The handcuffs clanged against the radiator. Victor stood in front of her and gripped her hot crotch with his hot claws.

"Oh baby . . ." he began, breathing heavily, "You're so sexy when you're mad. You're getting me all excited."

"I . . . I . . ." stammered Lenochka. Her chin trembled. "I did not kill the Lyamzins, they did it themselves! I was scared when Andrei Ivanovich . . . I loved him! I thought that it was Nikolai who offed him. I was hoping he would confess!"

"Is that so?" Victor began tenderly, passionately, stroking Lenochka on her pubis. "Did you also text him from an anonymous number?"

"No, no, I was scared that they'd be onto me. I printed the note. An actual note, like in the old days. He's guilty, not me! He's the murderer, not me!"

"No, honeybunch, you are the murderer," muttered Victor, with feeling, continuing to press his fingers along her body, from her moist beaver up her sweaty belly, to her flat chest. "You went mental over your infatuation and you messed up your boss's mind. And everyone around him, too. His wife, his mistress, his deputy, his protégé . . . Do you have any idea what you're up against, cutie pie?"

"I'm not up against anything! I'm innocent!"

A slap. Lenochka's temple slammed against the wall. A scarlet imprint of Victor's palm burst into bloom on her cheek.

"You sleaze, you'll tell everything!" declared Victor. "About the husband, and about the wife, too. You have to, you sent them both packing to their graves. Him and her both." His golden brown shock of hair seemed to darken from the nervous strain. He went over to the table and took a swig of wine.

"You will now give me a detailed description of how Lyamzin impaled you on his dick," he said, popping a grape into his mouth.

Lenochka whimpered, spluttered. Her memory flew back to that night. After an official ministry banquet, Andrei Ivanovich, blue in the face, bleary-eyed, had slammed the lobby door shut and locked it from inside, and had started dashing from corner to corner, back and forth. Like some kind of pendulum. A sewing machine needle.

"You know what I want," he declared. And her entire being filled with a mixture of fear and joy. Could he be cheating on his chic, fancy Marina Semyonova with her, with Lenochka? And who was this "he"? The minister himself!

He shoved his assistant with his belly, pressing her onto the table, yanked up her skirt, ripped her stockings. The actual moment of their coupling was terrible, painful. Lyamzin did not kiss her. He entered her on the table, like a prostitute, and then went into his office without a word. The next day Lenochka received a gift—an elegant phial of perfume, and for Lyamzin that was the end of it. Case closed. Semyonova reigned triumphant. Lenochka was spurned. Again.

But didn't Lenochka deserve love? Didn't she have a right to revenge?

"Marina Semyonova was a thief . . ." she said, stumbling at every word. "She should not be let out of prison!"

"You idiot, what makes you think that Marina Semyonova was in prison? Those were just rumors. Lies. I lied, too. So you, lowlife, wouldn't try to make a move."

"Wait, what?" cried Lenochka. "What—she's not in prison?"

"Of course not. She is at home. Drinking coffee with cream!"

"Aaaa!" wailed Lenochka, completely distraught. Strands of her chestnut hair spiderwebbed across her face. Her body, shackled to the radiator, heaved.

"Go ahead and scream, no one will hear you!" sniffed Victor.

He was overcome with thirst. He kept taking sips from the wine glass. The weeping Lenochka was pathetic, disgusting, like an insect who'd been crushed but was still alive. Still crawling, wingless, mortal. He perched on the bed, felt at the freshly washed patchwork quilt. His phone beeped. New texts semaphoring in his Messenger.

- "We know who the exemplary detective Victor is dating. And it's not the floozy Semyonova. It's the debauched libertine Ilyushenko," proclaimed one. Victor froze. He flipped through the rest of the messages.

"Vitya, you're into butt-fucking," another one followed up.

"Here's how the priest and the detective do it," announced a third. This one came with a video file. Homemade, filmed on someone's phone. Victor is lying completely naked on Ilyushenko's bed. Ilyushenko's voice is heard offscreen, crooning sweet nothings. The angle switches to a frontal view. Now they're both visible on screen. They bring their faces together, rub noses . . .

Stupefied, he turned off the video. His hands launched into a St. Vitus's dance. He cast an unseeing glance over at Lenochka, who, still bound to the radiator, continued to jabber and sputter incoherently. Her figure in the lingerie had a rectangular look: chest, waist, hips—all the same dimensions, on the same plane. Purple varicose veins branched out on her thighs. Bones poked out on the sides of her flat feet.

A siren blared under the window. A clamor, footsteps, and into the room burst Victor's buddies, armed operatives on assignment to arrest Lenochka. Lenochka wailed, flailed about:

"I loved Andrei Ivanovich! I didn't want it to happen! Go arrest Marina Semyonova instead!"

Victor broke away and ran out of his grandmother's house. Cold, almost frozen air lashed his face. He dialed Ilyushenko over and over, but the calls kept breaking off. He was about to hurl the damned device onto the ground, shatter it against a rock, but suddenly the display lit up. Someone was calling— from an unfamiliar landline.

"Hello?" shouted Victor at the top of his voice, in a desperate baritone.

"Vityun, Vityunia!" Ilyushenko's voice keened. "Someone broke into my iCloud! I can't use my phone now. Vityush, can you hear me? They broke into my cloud storage! Vityush!"

Victor emitted an unprintable, bone-chilling curse. He turned in the direction of the birch forest that began outside of town and so didn't see the shackled criminal Lenochka being brought out of the house with a great ruckus, with oaths, thumping, and crashing. He did not see her bare feet kicking out right and left, or the lilac-colored jacket that she had thrown on over her expensive lingerie.

Victor's aorta throbbed in his panicked chest. Lenochka was arrested, but the virus of calumny and backbiting permeated the town. Neighbor spied on neighbor; Cossacks patrolled the town, cracking their whips in the air, on the hunt for anyone who might desecrate the nation's symbols, or attempt to undermine its founding principles, or defile anything holy. The region's residents began breaking off mid-sentence; they became careful with words, took to glancing apprehensively around them; they worried they might blurt something out on social media, or ingest some foreign food by mistake— Australian meat or French cheese—or allow the devil to lure them onto some banned website through a VPN, or accidentally advocate for something inappropriate. But an inspiring song rose above the rooftops. A march was being rehearsed for the Day of National Unity. A saxophone played out of tune. And in the low sky there soared, making its escape upward to freedom, a single fugitive, plump balloon.

Thank you all
for your support.
We do this for you,
and could not do
it without you.

DEEP
VELLUM

PARTNERS

pixel ||| texel

LIFE IN DEEP ELLUM

EMBREY FAMILY
FOUNDATION

COMMON DESK
COWORKING

ALLRED
CAPITAL MANAGEMENT
of
RAYMOND JAMES®

ADDITIONAL DONORS, CONT'D

Mark Haber
Mary Cline
Maynard Thomson
Michael Reklis
Mike Soto
Mokhtar Ramadan
Nikki & Dennis Gibson
Patrick Kukucka
Patrick Kutcher
Rev. Elizabeth & Neil Moseley
Richard Meyer

Scott & Katy Nimmons
Sherry Perry
Sydneyann Binion
Stephen Harding
Stephen Williamson
Susan Carp
Susan Ernst
Theater Jones
Tim Perttula
Tony Thomson

SUBSCRIBERS

Alan Glazer
Amber Williams
Angela Schlegel
Austin Dearborn
Carole Hailey
Caroline West
Courtney Sheedy
Damon Copeland
Dauphin Ewart
Donald Morrison
Elizabeth Simpson
Emily Beck
Erin Kubatzky
Hannah Good
Heath Dollar

Heustis Whiteside
Hillary Richards
Jane Gerhard
Jarratt Willis
Jennifer Owen
Jessica Sirs
John Andrew Margrave
John Mitchell
John Tenny
Joseph Rebella
Josh Rubenoff
Katarzyna Bartoszynska
Kenneth McClain
Kyle Trimmer
Matt Ammon

Matt Bucher
Matthew LaBarbera
Melanie Nicholls
Michael Binkley
Michael Lighty
Nancy Allen
Nancy Keaton
Nicole Yurcaba
Petra Hendrickson
Ryan Todd
Samuel Herrera
Scott Chiddister
Sian Valvis
Sonam Vashi
Tania Rodriguez

AVAILABLE NOW FROM DEEP VELLUM

MARIA GABRIELA LLANSOL • *The Geography of Rebels Trilogy: The Book of Communities; The Remaining Life; In the House of July & August* • translated by Audrey Young • PORTUGAL

TEDI LÓPEZ MILLS • *The Book of Explanations* • translated by Robin Myers • MEXICO

PABLO MARTÍN SÁNCHEZ • *The Anarchist Who Shared My Name* • translated by Jeff Diteman • SPAIN

DOROTA MASŁOWSKA • *Honey, I Killed the Cats* • translated by Benjamin Paloff • POLAND

BRICE MATTHIEUSSENT • *Revenge of the Translator* • translated by Emma Ramadan • FRANCE

LINA MERUANE • *Seeing Red* • translated by Megan McDowell • CHILE

ANTONIO MORESCO • *Clandestinity* • translated by Richard Dixon • ITALY

VALÉRIE MRÉJEN • *Black Forest* • translated by Katie Shireen Assef • FRANCE

FISTON MWANZA MUJILA • *Tram 83* • translated by Roland Glasser • *The River in the Belly: Poems* • translated by J. Bret Maney • DEMOCRATIC REPUBLIC OF CONGO

GORAN PETROVIĆ • *At the Lucky Hand, aka The Sixty-Nine Drawers* • translated by Peter Agnone • SERBIA

LUDMILLA PETRUSHEVSKAYA • *The New Adventures of Helen: Magical Tales* • translated by Jane Bugaeva • RUSSIA

ILJA LEONARD PFEIJFFER • *La Superba* • translated by Michele Hutchison • NETHERLANDS

RICARDO PIGLIA • *Target in the Night* • translated by Sergio Waisman • ARGENTINA

SERGIO PITOL • *The Art of Flight* • *The Journey* • *The Magician of Vienna* • *Mephisto's Waltz: Selected Short Stories* • *The Love Parade* • translated by George Henson • MEXICO

JULIE POOLE • *Bright Specimen* • USA

EDUARDO RABASA • *A Zero-Sum Game* • translated by Christina MacSweeney • MEXICO

ZAHIA RAHMANI • *"Muslim": A Novel* • translated by Matt Reeck • FRANCE/ALGERIA

MANON STEFFAN ROS • *The Blue Book of Nebo* • WALES

JUAN RULFO • *The Golden Cockerel & Other Writings* • translated by Douglas J. Weatherford • MEXICO

IGNACIO RUIZ-PÉREZ • *Isles of Firm Ground* • translated by Mike Soto • MEXICO

ETHAN RUTHERFORD • *Farthest South & Other Stories* • USA

TATIANA RYCKMAN • *Ancestry of Objects* • USA

JIM SCHUTZE • *The Accommodation* • USA

OLEG SENTSOV • *Life Went On Anyway* • translated by Uilleam Blacker • UKRAINE

MIKHAIL SHISHKIN • *Calligraphy Lesson: The Collected Stories* • translated by Marian Schwartz, Leo Shtutin, Mariya Bashkatova, Sylvia Maizell • RUSSIA

ÓFEIGUR SIGURÐSSON • *Öræfi: The Wasteland* • translated by Lytton Smith • ICELAND

NOAH SIMBLIST, ed. • *Tania Bruguera: The Francis Effect* • CUBA

DANIEL SIMON, ed. • *Dispatches from the Republic of Letters* • USA

MUSTAFA STITOU • *Two Half Faces* • translated by David Colmer • NETHERLANDS

SOPHIA TERAZAWA • *Winter Phoenix: Testimonies in Verse* • USA

MÄRTA TIKKANEN • *The Love Story of the Century* • translated by Stina Katchadourian • SWEDEN

ROBERT TRAMMELL • *Jack Ruby & the Origins of the Avant-Garde in Dallas & Other Stories* • USA

BENJAMIN VILLEGAS • *ELPASO: A Punk Story* • translated by Jay Noden • SPAIN

S. YARBERRY • *A Boy in the City* • USA

SERHIY ZHADAN • *Voroshilovgrad* • translated by Reilly Costigan-Humes & Isaac Wheeler • UKRAINE

FORTHCOMING FROM DEEP VELLUM

FORTHCOMING FROM DEEP VELLUM